AUTHOR'S NOTE

The following is an updated and revised version of the story, A LITTLE SLICE OF HEAVEN, originally published by The Wild Rose Press in 2008.

THAT'S AMORÉ!

First edition. February 23, 2022.

Copyright © 2022 Gina Ardito.

ISBN: 978-1733655293

Written by Gina Ardito.

Chapter One

Wicked October wind propelled the rancid odor of rotting garbage into the crisp, late night air. Kyle Hayden crouched behind the rusted dumpster, buffeted from the cold, but helpless to conquer the godawful smell. Burying his nose in the grouping of yellow mums he held in his fists did no good, their perfume too fragile to overcome the noxious fumes.

"Ah-choo!"

Great. He was not only homeless, now he was coming down with something. Since he'd arrived in this Long Island resort town, he'd suffered untold indignities. How had he sunk so low so fast?

Cricka-cricka-cricka!

The dumpster's steel walls rattled on the howling gusts of a coming storm. Shivers racked him, and he yanked his thin jacket tighter to ward off the icy chill. He should have grabbed his shearling coat when he'd had the chance—and an umbrella. Fat lot of good either of them did sitting unused in a closet in Manhattan fifty miles away. Come to think of it, a pair of gloves would've been nice, too. Who knew autumn nights could be so damn cold when you didn't have the benefit of a roof over your head?

Closing his eyes, he envisioned where he'd be right now if things hadn't gone so horribly wrong. Before a crackling fire, a snifter of Napoleon brandy on the table beside him. Maybe a soft head lying in his lap. Not a woman—a retriever or spaniel, perhaps—someone loyal, someone who wouldn't run away the moment life got a little rocky. The way Lana had.

Lana. Bitterness dripped into his veins like burnt coffee when he recalled her betrayal. Kyle fisted his hands tight enough to choke the life out of the bedraggled mums, wishing he might choke his memories instead. Of course, Lana wasn't the only traitor. Well, he'd make them pay, *all* of them. First, though, he had to do something about the woman inside the restaurant. Once he'd accomplished this minor task, he could focus on his true agenda again: survival first, then... retribution.

Anger warmed his blood, and he straightened his posture again. Time to get his minor humiliation over with. Loosening his grip on the bouquet, he fluffed the spiky petals in an attempt to make them look perky, but failed. The wilted amber blooms looked as downtrodden as he'd become.

Near the pizzeria's back door, muted light streamed through a tiny window, golden fingers beckoning shelter. He considered knocking, but quickly dismissed the idea. No need to announce his arrival. Better to do what he had to do in secret and go before she could see him.

Over the last few evenings, the woman seemed to sense his need to maintain distance. Thus, every night, when she closed the restaurant, she'd leave the takeout meal on the bench at the edge of the parking lot, then hurry to her car before he crept out of hiding. To give him some dignity? Or because she feared him? He didn't know, but hoped it was the former.

He should move on. Staying here, subsisting on her charity, would do nothing to fulfill the terms of his agreement. He had to find a place to live, someplace other than the bridge he'd huddled under for the last nine nights. Harder still, he had to find a job. Not that he hadn't tried on both fronts.

Who'd have thought a man with his education, with his background and impeccable social standing, would be turned down for every job he'd applied for? Of course, Rory and David had insisted he couldn't use his connections to help him, making the task nigh on impossible. No one wanted to hire a man in his thirties with no references, no car, no phone, no residence. Still, he had to fight on. With all he'd already lost, he wasn't ready to give up Aurora, too.

The screen door squealed, and then clacked, and he scrambled to return to the relative anonymity of the rusty dumpster. Secure in his hiding place, he peered around the corner to watch her.

She stood near the door, as if trying to make up her mind where to go next. In her hands, she held the familiar aluminum foil dish. Her husky feminine voice hissed a series of what sounded like, "Pssst, pssst, pssst."

What the hell was she up to? Some demented game of hide and seek?

"I know you're here," she said in a sing-song tone. "Now, come on out." He shrank deeper into the shadows. "I'm not going to stand here all night waiting. If you want to come home with me, you'd better move your tail from behind that dumpster right now."

He stiffened. Move his tail? No one had ever dared speak to Kyle William Montgomery Hayden III in such an insolent manner. And falling on hard times was not a reason to permit rudeness now. Rising to his full six-foot-three-inch stance, he took two steps forward into the open. The woman shrieked loud enough to shame emergency sirens. The dish fell to the asphalt, spilling out what appeared to be anchovy filets, and she fled back into the pizzeria.

Stunned, Kyle could only seek the inherent vapor trail such an abrupt departure should have left. What the hell was that about?

GIANNA RANDAZZO LEANED against the locked door, palm against her chest while her heart swam in cold sweat.

"Whatsa matter for you?" Claudio demanded. "That mean black dog outside again?"

While his raisin eyes glared with I-told-you-so smugness, Gianna gulped huge buckets of air to regain some semblance of calm. "It-It's not a dog. Or the injured cat I've been trying to catch. There's a man out there."

"The bum you leave food for, eh?" Inching closer, he bounced a finger at her nose. "You should listen when I talk-a to you. I told you he no go away if you feed him."

"I always leave his food on the bench by the bridge after closing," she snapped. "I didn't expect him to be loitering in the parking lot tonight."

"I don't know why you're surprised," Claudio retorted. "All the strays eventually find their way to the door. This one... he no different. What'd you make him tonight? Maybe the smell so good, he couldn't wait."

"That dish was for Mr. Whiskers. You think I'd bring the poor man anchovy filets?" Gianna turned to peer out the window. Was the man still there? Yep. He stood beneath the grainy light of the street lamp, an oddly shaped item extended from his hands. "What's he holding?"

Claudio leaned over her shoulder. "You think he got a weapon? Here, wait." He ambled to the ovens and wielded one of the long-handled pizza paddles like a samurai sword. "You call the cops. I make sure he no leave 'til they show up."

"Stop it." She strained her eyes, watching as the man edged closer to her door. "I think..."

Could it be?

"I think..."

The bundle in his hands grew more defined, and a burst of color danced across the tops. Maybe they were... yellow blossoms?

"He's holding flowers."

As he stepped under the streetlight in the parking lot, halogen mist scattered over the bouquet. Yes, they were definitely flowers. And since he kept pointing to the blooms, and then to her, she surmised he intended them as some sort of gift.

Her heart slowed its drumbeat to a more normal rhythm, soft and steady, and she relaxed her fears. This man meant no harm, not with that pathetic little bouquet held out toward her.

What kind of misfortune had befallen him to place him in such a precarious position? Homeless, alone, destitute...

Gianna understood misfortune better than most. After all, if she hadn't been able to come home to Villa Mare, what would she have done when she quit Madison Elementary? Only her parents tipped the deck between her situation and whatever had happened to the man outside.

She had to help this poor soul. She and he were kindred spirits. Why didn't Claudio understand that?

"Quick. Lock the door," he ordered. "I'll have the cops pick him up. We can't have a bum hanging around outside. Bad for business. He's gonna scare away the good customers."

Gianna ignored his grumbles and pulled a round aluminum takeout plate from the shelf behind the counter, filled it with cooked penne, tomato sauce, ricotta and mozzarella cheeses. After she placed the pasta dish in the oven, she wiped her hands on a dishtowel hung near the display case.

Claudio's gnome-like face wrinkled in lines of disapproval. "What you doing now?"

With a wave of her hand, she gestured to the door. "Looks like I have an admirer. I'm making him a hearty meal. He deserves it."

He slapped a palm on his forehead. "What are you, *pazzo*? What he deserves is a ride to jail. Don't you go out there again." He handed her the paddle. "Here. You take this. I call the cops."

Without thinking, she accepted the makeshift weapon. But when he headed toward the phone, she woke up. "No, wait."

He turned, eyes narrowed. "What?"

She let the paddle's edge hit the floor and leaned the handle against her hip. "You can't call the police. He hasn't done anything. Besides, since I pretty much encouraged his presence by feeding him every night, I doubt we'll gain much sympathy from the county's finest."

"The police will listen to me," he said. "I no feed him. And I said you no should feed him, but since when do you listen to me, eh? You should show your godfather a little bit more respect, *cara*."

"I'll kiss your ring later, Claudio."

Tongue clucking, he shook his head. "No wonder your boyfriend is marrying somebody else. You too mean to keep a man happy."

The barb, meant as a jest, sliced her to ribbons. For Claudio, a man who'd known and loved her since infancy, to rub humiliation in her face was beyond cruel.

Tears stung her eyes, and she blinked them away with impatience. No more self-pity. Not when others had it worse than she did. She at least had a family, friends, people who loved her. Who did that poor wretch outside have? No one. No one except her. So be it.

With extra care, she lifted the hook off the latch and opened the door to peek outside.

Claudio's hand shot out, gripping her shoulder. "Where you think you going, eh?"

"To talk to someone who doesn't think I'm mean," she replied and shrugged out of his grasp. "Don't wait up."

"Go, then," he snapped, swinging the door wide. "I not only wait up. I stay here and watch. You get into trouble, holler. Maybe I help you." He cocked his head sideways, his lips twisted in a sneer. "Then again, maybe not."

"I'll take my chances."

Holding the paddle like a baseball bat, she strode outside and let the screen door slap closed behind her. The pathetic bouquet of dying chrysanthemums lay on the ground, roots straggling along the ends of the stem like mermaid's hair. Her softened heart melted to pudding, as she scanned the parking lot for movement.

While she and Claudio had argued inside, the man had disappeared. He must have rushed to hide behind the dumpster when she came out. Or... was he lying in wait to accost her when the time was right? Maybe at closing, when she'd be alone.

Dang, she'd done it again—leapt to action without considering the consequences.

Black clouds hovered overhead. The soft breeze from late afternoon had transformed into a blustery autumn wind. Rain would come soon. Even if she hadn't seen the forecast on the television above the sales counter, she would've smelled the moisture and sensed the turmoil in the air. Or did that chaotic feeling come from some other force of nature?

Maybe this was a mistake. Maybe she should return to the safety of the kitchen. But... no. Claudio was inside, waiting to say, "I told you so," again. She'd heard those four words enough over the last six months to last a lifetime. Mainly, whenever the topic turned to Frank or Rachel. No more. She'd cut those ties, almost entirely.

She lifted her chin, hefted her paddle, and stepped into the parking lot. "Sir?"

Tiny hairs danced on her sleeveless arms, and she fought the urge to shiver against the cold.

She tiptoed closer to his hiding place. "Would you come out please? I won't hurt you, I promise."

Unless, of course, you try to hurt me.

"If you've no plan to harm me, put down the oversized Louisville Slugger." His tone was cultured, each syllable succinct and tinged with a slight New England accent which made the prickly hairs on her arms do the cha-cha.

Their positions created an interesting impasse. If she put down the paddle, she had no guarantee he wouldn't attack her. But if she didn't put down the paddle, he probably wouldn't come out. At sunrise, they'd still be standing here: Gianna the Fearless Warrior, wielding her mighty pizza paddle while the White Knight cringed in the corner of the rear parking lot and the grumpy troll watched from the sidelines of the battlefield, rubbing his hands with malicious glee.

"Fine." Somehow she maintained an easy lilt to her voice, just as she would with a hyperactive child. "I'll lower the paddle. But I'm keeping my grip on it."

"Okay, Sheriff," he drawled. "I'm coming out with my hands up. Don't shoot. And don't swing for the fences, either."

As he strode from behind the dumpster, the streetlight's glow framed him in a golden aura. Gianna had expected someone heavily bearded, a toothless derelict with posture stooped from the burden of life's hardships. This man was fairly clean. In fact, he looked like no homeless man she'd ever seen. A mere shadow of a beard, sparse around the mouth, coated his chin. Above the beard, his cheeks were ruddy from the cold, but not hollow. Although she couldn't discern their color, his eyes were clear, with no alcohol- or drug-induced clouds. He stood tall and broad, hands upraised as promised. His teeth, even and white, flashed a smile born to make her knees knock together. Or had the bitter cold caused her tremors?

Say something, stupid.

"Wh-why did you bring me those flowers?"

Well, that was certainly something stupid...

"Because the doorman at Tiffany's refused me entrance, so I couldn't get you diamonds." He jerked his head, indicating his raised arms. "Can I put down my hands now?"

For a moment she hesitated, gauging the distance between them. What guarantee did she have he wouldn't pounce the moment she was unarmed?

Oh, stop it! You're being ridiculous.

"Yeah," she said at last. "Sure."

His posture relaxed when he lowered his arms. In response, she eased up on the paddle handle. The wind gusted, whipping brittle leaves across her scuffed white Keds.

She shivered, looked around at the naked trees, the ripples sweeping over the pond behind him. "It's pretty cold out here. Do you want to come inside? I've fixed you something to eat."

"No," he replied, clipped and curt. "Thanks anyway."

"Why not?"

He folded his arms over his chest. "I have my reasons. Why don't you go back to work? I'm grateful for what you've done, but I'm not in a sociable frame of mind right now."

Yeah, well neither was she these days. Still, she refused to give up. She'd dealt with stubborn children before.

Like the others, this stubborn child would eventually come round to her side, if she played the game right. "Okay. Have it your way."

With a nod, she headed for the restaurant's doorway where Claudio stood, watching, phone in hand, poised to dial 911.

"No hard feelings?" the man called after her.

"No hard feelings," she repeated and kept walking.

No way she'd let him disappear into a freezing, wet night without a fight, or at least, a hearty meal. She strode back to the restaurant, paused at the back step and scooped up the mums. No sense in letting them die. She'd have to bring them home with her and pot them. Once inside again, she hung the paddle on its hook near the oven door and took the mums to the sink. After rinsing out an empty can of plum tomatoes, she dropped the flowers inside and filled the makeshift vase with water. That would have to do until she got home tonight, she thought, and left the bouquet on the table of a booth by the front window.

Claudio grumbled, "You happy now?"

She ignored him and aimed her attention on the linen closet. There, she pulled out two large white tablecloths and two cloth napkins. A quick stop in the kitchen area garnered her a few pieces of silverware and two paper cups. Claudio still stood sentry by the door. She stalked past him, holding the assembled items against her chest.

In the parking lot, she spread the tablecloths on the ground. She then arranged the napkins, cups, and silverware into two place settings on her makeshift picnic blanket.

Without saying a word to him, she breezed inside to the counter and reached for a bottle of red wine. No. On second thought, what if her date was a recovering alcoholic? Smarter to stick with something less volatile. She returned the wine to the shelf and selected a one-liter bottle of ginger ale. The soft drink soon joined the linens at her makeshift picnic.

Claudio hovered like an overprotective Rottweiler when she returned to retrieve the casserole. "Why you doing this? Why you no leave this man alone?"

He'd never understand. And she could never explain why she felt a kinship with a homeless stranger.

Instead, she shrugged. "I honestly don't know. Something about his situation calls to me. I'm curious, I guess."

"Hmmph! Curiosity killed the *gato*."

"Which is why I have you here," she replied, pulling out the bubbling dish of pasta with cheese. "To protect me from my own foolishness, right?"

He mumbled something, something insulting no doubt, but Gianna let him rant. She grabbed her thick fisherman's cardigan from the hook near the door, and returned to the parking lot with two steaming plates.

Kneeling, she set one in front of her, the other on the opposite side, and then settled in to wait. "Your dinner's going to get cold if you don't eat it soon," she called in a tone normally reserved for a classroom full of rowdy kindergartners.

No reply.

Stubborn. Well, she'd show him what stubborn looked like. And since she had nowhere else to go tonight, she could wait as long as he could. Meanwhile, she'd eat while the meal was still hot.

Sitting cross-legged on the ground, she leaned forward to pick up her plate, and then dug into the casserole with her fork. She slid the food between her teeth and sucked in several breaths of air to cool the sauce and cheese burning her tongue.

"Mmmmmmmm." She exaggerated for his benefit. Kissing her fingertips, she exclaimed to the sky, "*Perfetto.*"

The wind howled and, as she'd hoped, blew the tantalizing smells in his direction. From the corner of her eye, she watched the stranger take a few steps toward her. Then, he stopped. Basically the same reaction she received from the stray cats she fed here. So she used the same response on the man. She ignored him and poured ginger ale into one of the cups.

As effervescent liquid bubbled and popped, she watched him over the rim. He inched forward slowly, wary gaze moving from side to side, alert to her every movement. He stood only a few feet from her now. She remained still as stone, waiting for him to make up his mind. Would he sit and eat with her? Or would he run away?

He took a long time to decide. But once he did, he moved so quickly she nearly missed the action when she blinked. One moment he stood over the tablecloths. The next, he sat across from her, the plate on his lap, silverware in his hand. With meticulous precision, his knife cut the penne into bite-sized pieces. He then speared a small bit of pasta, sauce, and cheese and slid it into his mouth. An expression of pure rapture, eyes closed, smile dreamy, lit up his features. Aha! She had him at last.

"I'm glad you decided to join me," she said, hiding a triumphant smile behind her soft drink.

Her gaze lowered to his fingers. Beneath smudges of dirt, remnants of clear polish remained on his nails. Did homeless men normally get manicures?

Once again, curiosity overrode common sense. "Can I ask you something?"

He pierced another forkful of pasta. "You want to know how I wound up in this situation, right?"

"Well, it's obvious you're not from around here. I mean, Setquott Beach is a small community and..." Heat rose in her cheeks, and she wondered if she'd overstepped some invisible boundary. Focusing on her fork, she toyed with the penne and cheese. Yikes, she was making a muck of this. "I'm sorry. Whatever happened to you is none of my business. It's just... well, you don't strike me as the typical homeless person."

"I'll take that as a compliment."

She looked up and caught a bemused smile twitching his lips. "You should. I mean, you're obviously not a drunk." She narrowed her eyes, studying his previously manicured fingers. "You don't look like a junkie. I guess I'm... well... nosy. You're not what I expected a homeless guy to look like."

"I've only been homeless for nine days." He spread his hands wide. "As you can see, I'm not very good at it."

"So what happened? How did you wind up homeless? And here?"

His expression muddled. "How does anyone wind up in this situation? A few bad decisions, a couple of miscalculations. One day, you're moving through life just as you always have. The next, *poof!*" He fanned his fingers like a magician at the end of an amazing sleight-of-hand. "Everything you've ever believed in is revealed to be a sham. And you're left out in the street with nowhere to turn, your foundations gone. No job, no income, no home, and no one but yourself to rely on."

She could certainly relate, especially about those disappearing foundations and losing a job. Hadn't she floundered when the dreams she'd built her hopes on turned into a nightmare? Deep in her scarred heart, a wave of pity converged with a tide of camaraderie. This man needed a friend. And come to think of it, so did she. Maybe they could help each other.

"Would you like to work for me?" The words flew out of her mouth before she considered the repercussions.

The fork fell from his hand and landed on the white tablecloth, leaving a bloody stain of sauce in its wake. "You don't even know me," he reminded her.

"I may not know your name, but I know you have a good heart. Your actions over the last week told me so, but the flowers tonight... well, they clinched my opinion."

"I stole them, you know. Which, hardly speaks volumes about my sterling character. "

She dipped her head, concentrated on the dish in her lap. He wouldn't like what she was about to say, but she needed to say it. Had to get the guilt out of her system, let him know where he stood from the get-go.

"I've been watching you," she confessed. Her throat dried to a pillar of sand, but she eked out the words. "After I leave at night, I park around the side of the building and hide behind the trees near the pond. I shouldn't have spied on you. I'm aware it's rude, not to mention a horrible invasion of your privacy. But I had to know something about you."

A shadow darkened his face, lending him a dangerous mien. "And what did you find out?"

Despite his expression, she kept her tone light. "Deep down, you're a good man. Because, no matter what I leave for you, you share your meal with Mr. Whiskers."

"Mr. Whiskers?"

"The cat with half a tail. I brought the anchovies out for him. I've been trying to catch him for two months now. He needs a vet's care. But he won't let me get close." She quirked a half-smile. "Any man who can gain a feral cat's trust is okay in my book."

He leaned forward and set his empty plate on the ground. "So because I share a meal or two with a beaten up old cat, who's as hungry as I am, you're willing to offer me a job?"

She clasped her hands, almost a sign of prayer. Maybe she was praying. For some reason she couldn't explain, a burning need to help him spurred her onward. "It's a win-win situation. I need another employee. You need a job and a place to stay. I won't lie to you. It's not the most exciting job in the world. You'll bus tables, help in the kitchen, that sort of stuff. But the offer does come with a one-bedroom apartment above the restaurant, currently unoccupied. You interested?"

His eyes widened, and she finally got a good look at them. Not green, not brown. Hazel, maybe. Nice eyes. Honest and clear.

"Do you always rescue people you find in the garbage?"

She laughed. "No, I rescue cats. You're my first human."

"I'm honored."

His teasing tone sent ripples of pleasure across her flesh. "Does that mean you accept?"

"I think it does."

"There's a catch, though."

Stiffening, he arched a brow. "What?"

"You have to tell me your name."

His posture relaxed, and the darkness fled. Eyes narrowed, he studied her when he said, "Kyle. Kyle Hayden."

Was she supposed to recognize his name? Had he been someone famous once? Well, she wouldn't dwell on used-to-be. She of all people knew used-to-be only mattered in memory.

"Kyle, I'm Gianna Randazzo," she said instead. "Welcome to Villa Mare. You can start your employment by bussing this table." With her chin, she gestured to the dirty dishes and silverware on the stained tablecloth.

He hugged the sleeves of what must have once been a very expensive jacket, now creased with greasy dirt. "Egads, what a frightening thought. I don't know if I can."

"Relax. I'll help you."

A quick look at the pizzeria door, however, sobered her instantly. One more discomforting task waited: convincing Claudio she hadn't lost her mind.

Chapter Two

When Gianna reentered the restaurant with Kyle, her grumpy godfather stood behind the counter, arms folded over his chest, that perpetual frown on his face. "Oh, so we going to do some work now, *cara*?"

She dropped the silverware into the stainless sink with a loud clank. "You mean you can't handle this place for five minutes without me?"

"Five-a minoots." He blew air out of his mouth with a rude noise, and then nodded at Kyle beside her. "Dis the bum?"

Way to make the poor man feel welcome, Claudio.

"This gentleman is our new employee. Kyle Hayden. He's graciously agreed to help us out for a while."

"He's a-gonna help *us*?" Claudio's sarcasm cut through her confident façade like a rusty saw.

Squelching a wince, she turned on the water and scrubbed the pile of dishes with vigor. "That's right."

She looked up in time to see Claudio focus all his displeasure on Kyle. "You ever work in a restaurant before?"

"Um, no," Kyle replied.

A stream of Italian curses flowed from the old man's sneering lips followed by the inevitable, "Your papa, he no gonna like this."

"My father will like this just fine." She slammed her scouring pad on the sink's edge, turned off the water, and then dried her hands. "By the time Mom and Dad return from Italy, Kyle will be an old hand at this business."

Claudio glared at Kyle, a rooster defying a grizzly bear. "So you're her latest wounded kitty, eh? You don't look like the others. You too big and strong to need a little girl to take care of you. You should be ashamed of yourself."

Gianna gasped. "Claudio!" If she couldn't rein in the old man's grouchy streak, Kyle would probably consider sleeping in the streets more comfortable than working here.

Kyle folded his arms over his chest. "Ten days ago, old man, I would've agreed. But having spent time outdoors, I'm willing to swallow my pride, if it gives me a chance to win back some of what I lost."

Gianna bit back a grin. A good answer, one Claudio couldn't argue with.

The old man must have sensed he'd score no points there so he leaned forward and took a long exaggerated sniff. "You may want to start with a shower. You stink."

Embarrassed on Kyle's behalf, Gianna stepped between the combatants before they started flinging tomato sauce, as well as insults. The last thing she needed while she was in charge was the appearance of blood on the walls. "Why don't I show you the apartment upstairs? You can get a good night's rest. Then you'll start work tomorrow."

"You letting him stay upstairs?" Claudio couldn't have sounded more surprised if she'd announced she planned to keep a gorilla in the apartment.

She arched a brow. "Problem?"

He shook his head. "It's your family's apartment. What can I say?"

"Nothing you haven't said before." She grabbed the key dangling from a red lanyard near the pantry wall. "Come on, Kyle."

Claudio's last rejoinder followed them into the hall. "You gonna tuck him in and read him a bedtime story, too?"

KYLE FOLLOWED HER UP the narrow staircase, doing his best not to stare at her swishing hips. Someone who had given him back his self-respect did not deserve to be ogled. No wonder that old man downstairs hated him on sight—or more likely, at first sniff.

Inside the close hallway, he got a good whiff of his own body odor and winced. Jeez, a hamper of used gym clothes had a more pleasant aroma than he did right now. He couldn't stand his own ripeness. Gianna must have Kryptonite fortitude to stand in this confined space with him.

"Don't let Claudio scare you," she said. "I know he's gruff and looks like a gargoyle, but he's an old softie at heart."

"Oh, yeah, I got that feeling the minute he spoke." He couldn't stifle his cynicism. "He called me a bum, and I got all gushy inside. I can tell we're going to be best friends in no time."

If she heard the scorn lacing his tone, she didn't address it. She simply fiddled with inserting the key into the doorknob.

"The apartment's a small one-bedroom," she said, craning her neck. "And I'm afraid there's a little bit of all of us stored here. We've had the place as long as we've owned the restaurant."

When she finally turned the knob, the wood creaked, but didn't budge. "When I was a kid, my grandparents lived in this apartment."

She threw her shoulder against the door. *Bam.* "Then my brother, Joey, moved in while he attended college in the area." *Bam.* "Now that he's in med school in California, it's unoccupied. We mostly use it when we have any kind of plans immediately after work. You know, to take a shower and change. Beats driving all the way home or showing up at a function stinking of garlic and tomatoes."

The door swung open too fast, and the sudden lack of resistance, sent her stumbling. She stayed on her feet, though without any grace. On a huff of air, she righted herself and gestured for him to join her inside.

She hadn't lied about the size. Good God, his sister's Yorkie, Chauncey, lived in more palatial quarters than this hovel. The kitchenette contained a two-burner stove, a refrigerator the size of a small man, and a wall oven, all in some molten gold shade. He sniffed and surreptitiously ran a finger across the sixties-style Formica countertop of teal and tan curlicues against a gold-spotted white background. Clean.

"You should have everything you'll need to be comfortable." With a sweeping hand, she encompassed the two front rooms.

Beige-striped wallpaper, filmy and faded, covered the living room, clashing with orange-cushioned rattan furnishings. Tired brown wall-to-wall carpeting completed the tacky décor. Still, it was warm. And dry. Sure as hell beat the places where he'd laid his head in the last few days.

"If you think you need something we don't have up here, let me know, and I can pick it up tomorrow before coming to work."

"Th-thank you," he managed, though his throat nearly choked on the words. Whether from lack of practice or out of awe for her beneficence, he didn't know. The sheer rockslide of her generosity crushed his ego.

With halting steps, he followed her to the bathroom.

When she flipped on the light, black and pink tiles assailed his sense of good taste. The shower curtain, filled with goofy starfish on a peach background, didn't come close to matching the other colors and seriously added to the suffering his poor eyes experienced. Once again, though, he focused on how clean the room was.

"My father's the fastidious sort," she said, as if she knew his thoughts. "Since we only use this place sporadically, he insists on keeping the toiletries well stocked and fresh." Sliding open the top drawer of the vanity, she pointed to the assorted travel-sized articles, all in original packaging. "Toothbrush, toothpaste, deodorant, razor, shaving cream. It's all here."

"Thank you. Again. I don't think I said it properly the first time." Even now the words tripped from his tongue, more foreign than ancient Greek.

She looked up from the drawer, a tremulous smile lighting her features. "You said it fine. Clean linens are on the top shelf of the bedroom closet. And until we can get you a few things of your own, my brother has some old clothes stored in the dresser in the bedroom, too. The shirts might be a little snug, but they'll do temporarily. No food in the kitchen, but I'll fix that by tomorrow morning."

On that note, she left the bathroom.

He extinguished the light and trailed behind until she turned to face him again. "Why don't you stay here and get your bearings? I'm sure you'll want to shower..."

A rosy hue infused her cheeks. Was she embarrassed for mentioning his current state of filth? Hell, it wasn't like he didn't know what he looked like, or smelled like, for that matter.

"Actually," he said, hoping to put her at ease, which was ridiculous considering she held all the cards here. "I'd love a shower. And maybe a shave, if it's all right with you."

Her eyes softened, and her smile returned, as bright as a toothpaste ad. "Take as long as you like. I want you to be comfortable here."

He had to bite back the caustic reply that sprang to his lips. Was she for real? She seemed to have no idea how much power she held right now. On a whim, she could banish him back to the streets, send him scurrying under a bridge for shelter from tonight's pending storm, yet she acted as if his approval meant the world to her. She certainly sparked an interesting quandary. Especially when he considered he'd spent the last thirty years of his life not giving a damn what anyone thought of him.

He knew the moment his scrutiny unnerved her. Her gaze fell to the floor, and her sneakered feet shuffled back and forth as if she'd stepped on hot coals.

"Um, I think I'll go downstairs and help Claudio," she murmured, never moving her attention from the threadbare carpet. "I'll leave the key on the counter on my way out."

Without another word, she exited the apartment, leaving him to wonder what made such a soft-hearted person tick. But he didn't wonder long.

The lure of a hot, steamy shower was too strong to ignore. His pores screamed to be clean again. A quick turn of the tap filled the bathroom with a noisy squeal, and then the heavenly sound of falling water. Not from the hellish rain he'd become accustomed to, but from the head of a spigot. And not icy cold, but comfortably hot. After removing his filthy clothing, he stepped into the tub and allowed the water to cleanse his mind and body.

Ah, God, was there any more perfect pleasure in life? Funny how a mere week and a half ago he would have taken such a luxury for granted. But by now, he'd gone without a shower for far too long. And he couldn't get clean enough. He reveled in the watery needles and fresh-scented soap.

By the time he finally left the bathroom, rain pelted the windows and lightning flashed in intermittent bursts. He couldn't believe his luck. If not for his decision to bring her those mums he'd swiped from the park tonight, he'd be huddled in some doorway or under an overpass, dodging raindrops, and sleeping on cement again. He supposed he should start earning his keep.

He found something decent to wear in the bedroom closet—a sweatshirt with some team logo emblazoned in bright purple and a pair of jeans—bounced downstairs, his mood vastly improved, only to find the restaurant was closed and locked for the night.

Gianna was gone. And with her departure, loneliness settled around him again, silent and suffocating.

"HAVE YOU HEARD ANYTHING from the bank yet?"

The curiosity in Joey's voice carried over three thousand miles of phone lines.

Resentment surged in Gianna, who sat on her bed, half a dozen throw pillows propped on the headboard. The bank. Another mountain she'd yet to scale, looming, ready to bury her in an avalanche of hopelessness.

"Is that why you called? To harangue me about the daycare center?"

Joey sucked in a breath.

Good. He realizes he's stepping on a live wire.

"No," he replied after a moment. "I called to chat with my big sister. Catch up on Setquott Beach news. So if the daycare center's off-limits, tell me what's up with the Wedding of the Century. Have you heard from Frank at all?"

At the mention of her ex, she plucked a stray nylon thread from her floral comforter, wrapping it around her index finger in rapid swirls, tighter and tighter, cutting deep lines into her skin. *Snap!* With a sharp sting, the thread popped off. She placed the injured digit against her lips and ran her tongue over the sore spot, but she refused to cry. She wouldn't start feeling sorry for herself again.

For the first few months after the school debacle, she'd shed enough water to fill the county's reservoir. Then one day, she'd decided she'd had enough. No more crying over someone completely unworthy of so much remorse. No more crying—period.

She stiffened her spine and resettled the phone against her ear. "I haven't heard from either of them since I mailed back the invitation."

Bitterness rose in her throat like smoke, choking her airway. Two days after she'd made her no-more-tears vow, the wedding invitation had arrived. In a moment's pique, she'd scrawled her intention to attend—with a guest—and dropped the offensive cardboard into the nearest mailbox.

"Besides, I don't want to hear from him." She stopped swirling her tongue around her injured fingertip as the throbbing eased. "He made his choice. I hope he's happy with Rachel."

"You keep telling yourself that," Joey replied. "Practice in front of a mirror. Eventually, you might sound convincing."

"Ha." The retort came out flat, humorless, like Gi herself.

"You have every right to feel hurt." Joey's bedside-manner-in-training mode prickled the fine hairs on her nape. "Rachel's a vindictive witch. The only reason she sent you that wedding invitation was to needle you some more. Like all the crap she put you through those last few months at school wasn't enough. God, she must really hate you for some reason to want to rub your nose in her and Frank's affair publicly. What better way to humiliate you than in front of two hundred guests?"

"I know." She sighed. Frank and Rachel's betrayal was just another huge mistake in an endless catalog of huge mistakes she'd made over the last year. "Which is why I think I'll just blow off attending. Maybe my best revenge is to stick them with the cost of two unused plates."

"Oh, no you don't." His impatience threw an invisible wall between them. "Who was it said, 'Looking good is the best revenge'?" he asked.

Oh, sure. 'Cuz she looked so hot these days.

"I don't know. Angelina Jolie?"

The wall crumbled beneath his deep laughter. "Doubtful. But it doesn't matter. Angelina's got nothing on you. Never did."

Despite the gushiness melting her bones, she snorted. "Yeah, right."

"Listen, Gi, you wanna move on with your life? Or do you wanna wind up a bitter old lady living alone in some dilapidated house with fifty cats for companions?"

Ouch.

Bristling, she sat up straight and set her feet on the floor. "That's hitting below the belt, Joey."

"All's fair in love and war."

When had her baby brother become this font of old adages? Next he'd be telling her every cloud had a silver lining.

"You're just chock full of clichés tonight, aren't you?"

"And you're angrier than a wet cat. So focus that anger on something useful. Go to the wedding with some super-stud on your arm. Both of you dressed to kill. Show Frank and Rachel that Randazzos always rise above the trash."

How long could she hedge about her dearth of dates? Better to come clean. Maybe he could help. Then again, maybe not.

"Which reminds me." Deep breath. "Do you know where I can rent a super-stud for the evening?"

"You mean you haven't found a date yet?" The surprise in his tone both warmed and depressed her.

"Not unless you count the ROMEOs. Every one of them volunteered for the task."

"Nice of them," Joey replied. "But a little too old, don't you think?"

"Definitely."

Thinking of the ROMEOs always brought a smile. Despite the fact that none of them were younger than sixty, the Retired Old Men Eating Out flirted their way through dinner at Villa Mare every week. Over time she'd learned to dodge the occasional pat to her bottom, ignore the winks, and deftly decline invitations to hockey games. The upcoming wedding, however, had added new fuel to their long-stoked amorous fires.

"Give me a day or two," Joey said. "I'll make a few phone calls."

"Forget it." She waved a hand as if brushing away a gnat. "Frank would recognize anyone you set me up with."

"Well, then, who do you know Frank wouldn't recognize? There's gotta be a customer or someone you could ask." Scanning her bureau, she glanced over framed photographs of close friends. No one suitable smiled back. She didn't exactly have a stable of men waiting. Except, of course, the ROMEOs. She shuddered. God, no. They were *not* an option.

Her mind clicked on the image of a man with wide-set hazel eyes and a clipped New England accent. No. Ridiculous. She barely knew him, for God's sake.

"Come on, Gi," Joey prompted. "Think."

"Maybe." She bit a ragged cuticle on her thumb. "I might know someone I could ask."

"Who?"

"Our newest employee at Villa Mare."

"You hired somebody?"

Ow! She bit too close to the nail and winced, but not at the pain. Joey would want details about Kyle now. And she didn't dare lie because Claudio would give her up for ten cents and a leaky bucket.

"I'll have to make sure he's available first," she said.

"Who is he?"

Stick to the basics. Maybe he won't ask the million dollar questions. "His name's Kyle. Kyle Hayden."

"Where'd you find him?"

Ding, ding, ding! No more calls, please. We have a winner.

"Umm..." Squeezing one of the throw pillows, she mumbled, "I found him in the parking lot."

"You what?" The fury in his voice compelled her to rush through an explanation.

She began with the details of her watching Kyle with the cat the last week or so, her unexpected offer, and his acceptance. At last, she finished with the fact she'd allowed him to use the family's apartment above the restaurant.

Done, she yanked the phone far from her ear while he ranted. Even so, she managed to catch a few familiar phrases.

"Have you lost your mind...? How could you be so naïve...? Of all the stupid things to do..."

After several minutes of recriminations, he paused for breath.

She resettled the phone. "What did you expect me to do? Ignore the poor guy?"

"That would've been the smart thing to do. Why couldn't you just stick to rescuing cats instead of graduating to bums?"

"He's not a bum." Kyle's hands, the clear polish on his nails, swam in her memory. "He's a nice man who's fallen on hard times."

"And you're a welcome mat, Gianna. You always have been. Mom would have a fit if she knew."

The age-old threat prickled her skin. Thirty-three years old on the outside, but when it came to Mom, Gianna was still a little girl. "Don't you dare tell, if she calls you."

"Oh, sure. I'm gonna tell her you're harboring a psycho—"

"He's not a psycho! I spoke to him for a long time. He's educated, cultured, polite..." None of which proved he wasn't a psycho. But she refused to admit any doubts about Kyle's character. "You'd like him. Even Claudio likes him."

"That's a lie," Joey snapped. "You and I both know it."

Of course he knew it. Claudio didn't like anyone. And California's sun hadn't baked her brother's brain in the slightest.

"Claudio *tolerates* him. How's that?"

"Definitely closer to the truth."

Silence filled the space between them, long and nerve-wracking, while Gianna tracked her breathing pattern. In, out, in, out, in, out...

Finally, he sighed. "All right. I'll let this go for now. But, Gi, promise me you'll be real careful around this one."

One heavy exhale. Out. "I promise I'll be *very* careful."

He clucked his tongue. "Couldn't let my grammatical transgression slip by unnoticed?"

For the first time since they'd begun their conversation, she smiled. "Once a teacher, always a teacher. Now, speaking of teachers, how are you doing? How's UCLA treating you?"

"Not bad. Professor Morgan's not big on praise, but he did say that my last two papers showed potential..."

With the subject drifting far from Kyle, the upcoming wedding, and the daycare center, Gianna settled against the pillows and allowed her brother's enthusiasm to carry her away.

Chapter Three

K yle woke up disoriented. Had he dreamt the whole thing? God, he hoped so. Then he focused on a large rust stain decorating the popcorn ceiling. Nope. This was no dream. He sat up in the lumpy, full-sized bed, smacking his lips and rubbing his eyes.

Jesus, what day was it? Sunday? Monday? Who could tell? What difference did it make anyway? He might not know the day of the week, but he knew today was Day Ten. Ten days since the moment his life had changed forever. And all because he was a fool.

Well, not anymore. He'd learned his lesson. A little late, but better late than never, right? Once this game was over, he'd go home and banish all the traitors from his life.

He'd start with the deceitful Lana who made promises of love forever, and then turned her back when he'd needed her most. Colette would be next. Colette, all sisterly devotion when he stood on his own two feet. But once he stumbled, the ideals of family fled faster than his Ferrari Berlinetta speeding on the Autobahn. He'd have nothing to do with women ever again. They were all poison.

An image of Gianna's face, her big Bambi eyes, popped into his head. Okay, so his lady of mercy from last night wasn't poison. If anything, she was the panacea for the ills he'd encountered. Such boundless generosity deserved something in return. More than a token of gratitude, something special.

What the hell. When he got home, he'd write her a check. Maybe she could use the money to hire a decent staff, rather than employing strangers she met in the parking lot.

What was in her pretty, naïve head, allowing a complete stranger to stay here? For all she knew, he could be a serial killer. Oh, he was grateful. And he still had fifty days before he could return home. So, he'd stay here, earning a living and proving to Rory and David he could rise above adversity. He was tougher than they thought—not necessarily smarter, but definitely tougher.

23

Tossing off the faded quilt, he rose from the bed and stretched the kinks out of his back. On his way to the bathroom, he spotted a photograph hanging on the wall. Taken at a beach somewhere, the picture showed a happy family frolicking in the surf together. Petite and dark-haired mom, tall and equally dark-haired dad, Gianna at the age of eight or so, holding hands with a diapered baby brother. All wore smiles of such familial joy he felt a pang of jealousy.

Bah! He had similar photos in his home. In better frames, of course. Snapshots sparked his brain, as if taken with old-fashioned flash bulbs. The Hayden family skiing in Biarritz, he and his sister standing in the garden on her wedding day, a photograph of his parents—happy and smiling for once—taken mere hours before his father's fatal heart attack.

Who knew if the images here weren't as much a sham as the ones he'd always believed in? Smiles could hide a multitude of ice and stone. Turning his back on the photographic vision of happiness, he entered the bathroom and closed the door. He cast the memories from his head by concentrating on the squeal of the tap when he turned on the faucet for another shower.

Later, when he descended to the restaurant, clanging pots echoed through the thin walls. He opened the door to the ripe aroma of garlic. As if by some inner radar, his gaze honed in on Gianna, who stood before an eight-burner stove. Based on his nostrils' opinion, she stirred what could only be a thousand gallons of tomato sauce. The pot was nearly as tall as she, and she stood on tiptoe to see the contents. Her thick hair was tied in a high ponytail, and a sheen of perspiration dampened her cheeks and forehead. Over a pale pink blouse and snug blue jeans she wore a stained white apron that did nothing to enhance her figure. But damn, if she wasn't the prettiest thing he'd seen in eons! Images of her standing in front of his stove in his Manhattan home, cooking just for him, brought a mixture of peace and regret to his subconscious.

Jeez, hadn't he learned anything from this experience? He pushed the mental pictures into the darkest corners of his mind. A lump the size of a baseball rose in his throat, and he cleared it away with a loud cough.

Gianna looked up, eyes wide and smile wider. "You're here. I'm so glad."

"Uh-huh," he managed.

Smooth, Kyle. Nothing charms a lady like the grunting of a Neanderthal. He couldn't help his sudden loss of verbal skills. She was prettier in daylight than he'd thought last night. And when she smiled, her entire face lit up.

"Before I show you the ropes, come into the storage room. I bought groceries earlier this morning. We'll bring them upstairs and put them away."

Wiping her hands on the apron, she led him into the storeroom where four filled mesh bags sat, waiting. She lifted two and, with a nod, indicated he do the same with the remaining two.

The weight of the bags took him by surprise. Expecting a few items, he didn't bother to put much muscle into the lift, and nearly fell on his backside for his troubles. "What the heck did you buy? Bricks?"

"I didn't know what you liked, so I picked up the basics," she said. "Mostly breakfast items. Milk, cereal, fruit, coffee, orange juice, bread, butter, and eggs. Usually, you'll be having lunch and dinner down here so..." She shrugged, hoisting the bags higher, and then headed into the hallway and upstairs.

Hefting his burden, he followed. "You really shouldn't have done this. You've done enough already." The more she did for him, the less he completed on his own.

How would that affect the rules with David and Rory? Honestly, he had no idea. But he'd hate to lose Aurora over a free loaf of bread.

"Nonsense." She stopped at the landing, waiting for him to join her. "You have the key."

After placing the bags on the floor outside the door, he fumbled in his hip pocket. The jeans were too snug, and he practically scraped the skin off his knuckles shoving his hand inside.

Luckily, two of his fingers pinched the thin lanyard, and he pulled the damn thing out, along with the pocket's interior lining. "Here."

He handed her the key, and then fussed with the white scrap of fabric sticking out from his hip like an elephant's ear.

Inside the apartment, they had their own assembly line. Kyle removed the items from the bags, and Gianna stored them on shelves in the cabinets and refrigerator.

Once they completed the task, she leaned against the counter. "There. All done. I hope I didn't forget anything. Maybe I should have picked up some cold cuts. Not everyone likes Italian food. There's a deli across the street. During lunch, I could take a walk over and—"

"Enough," Kyle interrupted. "Please. Stop."

His censure sent a fireball hurtling into her cheeks. Either she was the greatest actress who ever lived, or the worst. Every one of her moods communicated through her face. If her reactions were genuine, she wouldn't last a minute in his weekly poker game at the New York Legacy Club.

To ease his conscience and her embarrassment, he touched her hand. "You've done so much for me already. Please. Stop."

GIANNA BABBLED, AND she knew it. Obviously, he knew, too. But she couldn't stop her tongue from wagging. If she did, it would just loll out of her mouth like one of those Chinese dog statues at the antique shop down the road.

This morning, Kyle Hayden's appearance surprised her out of her wits. How could she not have seen how gorgeous this guy was? Okay, he'd washed up and shaved since she'd met him, but could dirt and stubble hide a man's finest qualities?

His hair, indiscernible last night, was a glossy golden brown with a hint of curl and a tad too long at the nape. Clean-shaven, his face resembled a Greek god's, with lots of angular lines and a cleft chin that brought to mind images of Hollywood's gorgeous screen legends. Of course, the first thing she'd noticed was his height, but now she realized that height carried a broad frame of sculpted sinew and muscle. He wore some of Joey's clothing, and she'd known the fit would be tight. But the extra-large shirt and size thirty-two jeans fit him like a second skin, accentuating every bulge and then some.

The change between the hesitant man of last evening and the confident stranger who stood in the apartment this morning pushed her off-balance. With shoulders thrown back and posture ramrod straight, he looked more like a captain of industry than a fledgling pizza man. In fact, only his eyes hadn't undergone a drastic change in the last twelve hours. They were still hazel and clear, framing an aquiline nose. Everything about him whispered of nobility and breeding.

She continued to stare, saying nothing, until his eyebrow arched. Oh, God! He probably thinks I'm staring.

You *are* staring, her brain reminded her.

Yeah, but I don't want him to know!

Well, then, stop.

Ha! Easier said than done.

Get a grip, Gi. He's just a man—a good-looking man, but a man nonetheless. And you know exactly what'll happen. If you give a good-looking man your heart, he'll trample all over it, then find someone else. Don't let that happen. Again.

With effort, she managed to tear her gaze away from his piercing eyes. Tracing an old knife cut in the countertop, she mumbled, "Um, I think we should get back downstairs. Claudio and Sal will be wondering what happened to us."

FOR TWO HOURS, KYLE worked alongside Claudio's son, a genial thirty-something named Sal. Hard to imagine the two DeNunzios shared any DNA. Where Claudio grumped all day, Sal wore a constant smile. Within ten minutes of meeting him, Kyle had seen photos of all four of Sal's kids and his lovely missus. Clearly, this guy was thrilled with the life of suburban husband and father. Kyle tamped down shivers of revulsion and feigned interest in Sal's boasts about his kids' soccer teams, dance recitals, and planned Halloween costumes.

"We no here to chat, Salvatore," Claudio interjected. Kyle shot him a look of undying gratitude. Claudio ignored him. "We here to work, yes?"

"Some of us can do both," Sal replied with a grin, and then whispered to Kyle, "Pop's giving you a hard time, huh?"

Kyle shrugged. "He's not too thrilled with my working here, especially since I have no experience."

"Nobody cares about your lack of experience," Sal replied with a chuckle. "After all, it's not like the world's most famous chefs are lining up to work out here in the sticks for pennies. The Randazzos generally hire temps, part-timers, or their own family members—most of whom have never been near a pizza oven or a food counter. Every year, in May, we go through a hazing period when we hire the college kids who come home for the summer. Inexperienced newbies are always dropping plates, losing silverware in the garbage, screwing up orders. If my father's not thrilled with you, it's not because you don't have experience."

"So what do you think it is?"

"Beats me. If you want to find out, you should ask him."

Kyle frowned. "No thanks. He doesn't seem the chatty type."

Apparently, though, Claudio had overheard enough of the conversation to grab the gist. He sidled over, eyes narrowed, dripping tomato sauce from the ladle in his hand. "I no like-a you because you take advantage of Gianna." He waved the long-handled ladle like a proctor's pointer, aiming at Kyle. "Big man." The ladle swung to where Gianna stood before a butcher-block table, slicing mushrooms at rapid speed. "Young woman. She no should take care of you like this. Real men take care of their own."

"Would it make you feel any better, old man, if I told you I'm taking care of her?"

Silence greeted his retort. The chopping stopped, and Gianna looked up, eyes wide with curiosity. "Taking care of me? What do you mean?"

"Yeah, Kyle." Sal winked, a needling communication of *Ooh, you're in trouble now*. "What *do* you mean?"

Swerving his gaze from one party to another, Kyle told her, "God knows, someone has to look out for you. Left to your own devices, you're inviting strangers into your life." He walked toward her, lowering his voice. "If I were not the man I am, I might have taken advantage of your generosity." Gaze solemn, he leaned over the butcher block. "If you know what I mean..."

Her gasp held enough outrage for a dozen divas, and her eyes blazed fire. "First of all, I haven't invited you into my life. I offered you a job. And if you were not the man you are, you'd still be huddled outside by the dumpster. Secondly, I can take care of myself."

He snorted.

Clunk! Gianna's cleaver came down like a guillotine on an unfortunate portobello, and Kyle jumped back in time to save his fingers.

"Contrary to your opinions," she said, taking out her anger on the mushroom. "I'm not a child. I don't need protection and I don't need 'taking care of.' Now if you three are finished playing Knights of the Round Table, we should get ready for the lunch crowd. Claudio, show Kyle how to make pizza. Sal, bring me some more sausage from the freezer." Finished murdering the poor vegetables, Gianna slapped the gleaming blade onto the butcher block.

Flashing a look that might have shot bullets from her eyeballs, she stalked past them and headed for the storage room.

"Has anyone ever told you you're beautiful when you're angry?" Sal called.

"Bite me," she retorted without looking back. "All of you."

When Sal snorted a laugh, Kyle's own amusement refused to stay bottled up. Chuckling, he peered around the doorway, watching her punish the linens while muttering about fools and men. Or was it foolish men? Regardless. Maybe he didn't have to protect her after all. Naive as she seemed on the outside, she had a ferocity he admired inside.

And she'd made her point. Hell, she'd literally fished him out of her garbage, given him a place to sleep, a job, and a second chance to win the game. What right did he have to berate her for her generosity? Yet by the same token, what right did she have to look so damn kissable while berating him right back?

FOR THE FIRST TIME in his life, Kyle suffered through hand-to-hand contact with grubby-faced kids, construction workers with dirt-encrusted fingernails, and other members of the unwashed masses. Shivers tickled his flesh.

Soon, avoiding prolonged exchanges became his top priority. At first, he planned to hide in the storage room. But when the lunch crowd arrived shortly after noon, Sal and Claudio began screaming his name, looking for help. He had no choice but to stand behind the counter and handle the clientele. Still, he didn't like getting close, and he maintained a civil distance.

Doctors, nurses, and professionals from the nearby hospital and office suites grabbed a slice and a soft drink before rushing off to other errands. Then the students appeared. Many came from the local high school, some from the state university in the next town. Having more time on their hands than their adult counterparts, they lounged in the orange booths, cell phones propped on tables and backpacks stored at their feet. High-pitched laughter and boisterous catcalls bounced off the painted mural of Venice before reverberating in Kyle's ears.

Good God, deliver me from teenagers! They lived in a world all their own, full of chaos and noise.

A shouted obscenity drew his attention to the booth in the corner where three teenage boys sat with a girl he might consider pretty if she hadn't dyed her hair purple. And the slender silver chain leading from her nose ring to her earlobe didn't do much for her looks, either.

One of the boys stood, anger sparking off him like a hot wire. "Take it back, Justin," he ordered. "Take it back right now."

"Aw, c'mon, Tommy," another boy whined. "I didn't mean nothing. She knew I was kidding."

"Yeah, well, I don't think what you said is funny. And if she's not gonna stand up for herself, I will."

In solidarity, four youths rose, taking places behind the furious Tommy and forming a solid wall of angst-ridden alliance.

Maybe these kids had redeeming qualities after all. Here they were about to come to fisticuffs over a bad joke. In Kyle's adult world of propriety and manners, no one had flown to his defense. What he wouldn't have given for a Tommy to come to his rescue a week and a half ago.

"All right, fellows, knock off the debate." Gianna stepped into the fray, clapping her hands. "Justin, apologize to Bethany."

"Sorry," the boy named Justin mumbled.

The purple-haired girl nodded her acceptance, and the wall of adolescent chivalry folded into their seats.

"That's better," Gianna said. "Now, you guys scat. Somehow, I doubt your parents think your curriculum includes sitting here all day."

"We got a half-day today, Gi." A bright smirk split Bethany's black-painted lips. "Faculty meetings."

"Nice try, but faculty meetings were last week. Now, out!" She waved her hands as if shooing flies. "All of you. Before I have someone escort you back to school."

Justin leaned close to Bethany. "Can she do that?"

He might have whispered, but Kyle heard him from across the room. So did everyone else, judging by the spate of snickers that erupted.

"Oh, she can definitely make a few phone calls," Gianna announced. "In fact, she's called several important people in the past. I can't make you go back to school, but I can throw you out of here. And I can contact some of your parents to let them know where you're spending your time instead of reporting to..." She glanced at the clock behind her. "...biology class right now, isn't it, Bethany?"

"Yeah." Bethany's sigh echoed with the disappointment of teenagers throughout time. "C'mon everybody. If Gianna wants us to go, we have to go."

They walked out the front door in one big wave, leaving a tide of paper plates, plastic cups, spilled beverages, and empty pizza pans in their wake.

Clucking her tongue, Gianna reached for the garbage on the first table when Claudio appeared out of nowhere. "The new guy and I take care of this," he said, jerking his head in Kyle's direction. "You and Salvatore run to the bank before they get busy."

With a nod, she pulled the apron over her head and disappeared into the back of the restaurant, leaving Kyle with the sullen Claudio for company.

Fabulous. No way he could hide in the linen closet now, not when there were just two of them left in the place. He was stuck trying to make small talk with the most taciturn man he'd ever met—which was quite a feat, considering he grew up under the aloof attention of Kyle Hayden II.

May as well start the torture-fest. "Gianna would make a good hostage negotiator, eh?" When he received nothing but a grunt for his comedic efforts, he tried again. "I assume those kids come here often."

"Every day there's school," Claudio grumbled. "Worse during exams. They use this place like a big revolving door. In and out, in and out, all day long. Makes Mr. Randazzo *pazzo*."

"*Pazzo*?" There was a term he hadn't heard since the summer after grad school.

He twirled a finger around his temple. "Crazy."

"So why does Gianna put up with them?"

Claudio wiped down the cleared table with a damp rag and shrugged. "She loves the *bambini*, always has. Why you think she grow up to be a teacher?"

Kyle paused, halfway to the garbage can. "She's a teacher?"

Growling, Claudio balled the rag in his fist and tossed it into the nearby dishpan of dirty silverware. "What you think? You think she spend her whole life in this place, eh? Think you're better than her? Bah! What do you know? Nothing, that's what. She came here last June, just at the end of the school term to help out, like she does every summer. And she's been here ever since, taking care of things 'til her mama and papa get back."

"Why? Where are her parents anyway?"

"Touring Italy for their anniversary. Before they leave, I tell Carlo, 'Gianna no should hide here. Best thing for her to go back to school and face those two.' He no listen. She no listen, either. No one ever listen to Claudio." He stopped, as if realizing Kyle probably wouldn't listen. "Maybe she go back after the wedding."

The paper plate in Kyle's hand wafted to the floor, smearing tomato sauce and cheese over the linoleum. "Wedding? What wedding?"

Was Gianna engaged? Why should he care? But he did. Hearing there might be a soon-to-be husband in Gianna's life chilled his skin, left him bereft and relieved at the same time.

"She got a wedding to attend next month," Claudio replied. "Needs a date. Too bad you a bum. You might have taken her."

Kyle's head spun, reckless with confusion. "Wait a second. Back up. What does some wedding have to do with Gianna returning to a teaching job?"

"You want to know about Gianna, you ask Gianna. I'm done talking to you." Claudio hefted the gray dishpan of dirty utensils and headed to the kitchen. Case closed.

Chapter Four

By three o'clock that afternoon, the crowds dwindled to an occasional customer. Gianna placed a steaming dish on an unoccupied table, and then gestured for Kyle to sit. "You should eat before we get busy again. I hope you like linguine with white clam sauce. After cooking and ladling tomato sauce all day long, I find the red stuff loses some charm."

"Linguine's fine." He pulled out the chair and sat. "But I would have made do with a slice of pineapple and ham pizza."

Sucking in a breath, she shuddered. "Yuck. Don't ask me how those kids can eat that stuff."

"You serve it, but don't eat it?" he teased.

"Unh-unh," she retorted. "Not for all the money in the world. I prefer pizza the old-fashioned way. With lots of sauce and mozzarella cheese, heavy on the garlic and oregano. On a good day, mushrooms and pepperoni as extra toppings. But the combinations people want nowadays make no sense to me. It's like some dumb chain restaurant came up with a gimmick, and now legitimate places like ours have to cater to a whim created by a Madison Avenue ad firm. I'm waiting for the day someone orders a pie topped with unicorn dust and fairy sprinkles."

He chuckled. "You sound like an Old World grandmother." Using his spoon, he spun the linguine onto his fork.

"And you eat pasta like an old Italian grandpa."

"Not surprising. I learned this trick in Rome." The bundled pasta slid into his mouth, waking his tastebuds to sheer joy.

Gianna stood over him, watching the fork move from his mouth to the plate, uncertainty plastered on her face. "Good?"

"Best I've ever tasted."

"Even better than Rome?"

"Better than Rome, Florence, and Sicily. Really." He kissed his fingertips. "*Questa pasta é perfetta.*"

She blinked. "You speak Italian?"

Rather than answer, he shrugged, then kicked at the empty chair opposite him. "Would you like to join me?"

"I ate already," she said, shaking her head. "While you and Claudio took care of that last group. We have to take shifts, in case it gets busy again."

Regret smarted, and he fought a wince. "Too bad. I've always believed a good meal tastes even better when accompanied by a beautiful companion."

Pretty pink color stained her cheeks, pleasing him immensely. Ages had passed since he'd seen a woman blush without simulated enhancement. Most of the ladies he met were painted and bedecked to reel in the richest wallet their artificial beauty could lure. But Gianna had a freshness he found charming, like discovering an innocent violet after spending years living in a greenhouse of lush, overly perfumed roses.

"Will you at least keep me company while I eat?"

Shrugging, she offered a half-smile. "Sorry, but I can't. A delivery truck just pulled in out back, and I have to take care of the provisions. Then we'll get ready for the dinner rush."

She didn't give him a chance to argue. One moment she stood before him while he savored the garlicky taste of the clam sauce on his lips and tongue. The next she'd disappeared into the back of the restaurant.

Over the course of the evening, Gianna seemed to hover everywhere. Kyle came upon her greeting the few regular customers who appeared in the dining room, cooking in the kitchen, working the front counter, clearing tables, and taking phone orders. Only once did he spot her sitting—for approximately three minutes with a group of wizened geezers who called themselves, of all things, the ROMEOs. Perhaps his angel was more goddess than human. Her constant activity would exhaust mere mortals.

At the end of the night, Kyle collapsed in the nearest chair in the dining room and slumped across the tablecloth. By God, when he returned to his old way of life, he knew one thing he'd do differently. He'd tip the help better. If they worked half as hard as he had tonight, they deserved a hell of a lot more than fifteen percent.

"This job isn't easy, is it?" Gianna's voice came from somewhere above him. No matter how tired he was, the sight of her still struck a chord deep in his ribcage.

With supreme effort, he picked his head up off the table, and even mustered a smile. "No, that's for sure. I don't remember when I've been this exhausted." He couldn't remember the last time he'd been on his feet so much of the day. Crazy as it seemed, he couldn't wait to get back upstairs to his little hovel overhead and just relax. "How do you keep going? You were here before me this morning, and you're still working." Worse, she was like a ball of electric energy, bouncing from room to room and back again.

"Oh, well, you forget, I grew up doing this. When my brother and I were kids, we'd come here straight from elementary school, and Dad would put us to work behind the counter."

As she reached across the table to remove the salad dressing cruet and Parmesan cheese shaker, her arm brushed the top of his head, and a jolt raced through him. Body pulsing, he pulled back his chair slightly.

"You..." Straightening, she juggled the bottles and jars into a cluster in her clasped hands before setting them on a round tray beside her. "You're just a rookie. Be grateful this is the off-season. In the summer when the tourists arrive, we need a staff of twelve."

"Twelve?" Hard to imagine this sleepy town ever bustled.

"Uh-huh. Three run the front counter, five handle the kitchen, and four wait tables. Trust me. If you're going to learn the business, autumn is the best time to do so. You'll see. The job gets easier the longer you work here."

He didn't intend to work here for long. The words, however, clogged his throat, refusing to exit into the air. So he said nothing while she sauntered off with the tray of seasonings. When she returned, he concentrated on pulling the linens off the table as if world peace depended on his success, hoping to avoid any further conversation.

After he had several tablecloths balled, she took them from his grasp, hugging them to her chest, almost like armor. "Would you mind a little friendly advice?"

Advice? Whatever she planned to say, he probably didn't care to hear. Still those Bambi eyes silently implored him to listen.

Taking her vulnerable pose into account, he offered a casual shrug. "No. I'm here to learn, right?"

A tremulous smile appeared. "Right. Umm..." She turned to place the linens on a cart. "The thing is... I know you're not used to this. I mean, back home you probably had servants who waited on you, you know?" Without waiting for a reply, she settled her attention on the nearest table, tracing circles in the dark wooden top with a fingertip. "But here, well, in this restaurant, the customer's our top priority. We get a lot of return business, even in the off-season like now, because we treat everyone like family. Do you think you can remember that?"

In other words, she'd noticed the way he'd cringed at handling the dirty dishes, his sighs when someone took forever to order, and his eye rolls, coinciding with a child's lisping command for "pisketti."

He would've loved to argue. Yet her censure came out with such sweetness, he had no choice but to nod.

After all, she'd taken him in, given him a chance to win back what he'd lost. So if he had to wear a humility suit for a month, he could manage the dent in his pride. The long-term prize far outweighed the short-term inconvenience. He managed a nod, but said nothing.

"Where are you from? Originally?"

At a cleared table, she sank into a chair and gestured for him to join her. Great. Now she wanted to talk. When he'd asked her to sit with him earlier, when he'd been alert, she was too busy. Naturally, the minute his guard failed due to exhaustion, she honed in for the kill. If he hadn't suspected she'd assume something suspicious in the action, he would've crossed his arms over his chest.

What magical powers did this dark-haired angel hide behind an ethereal face and an endless supply of patience? How did she manage to chip away at his barriers time and time again? Okay. He could handle her interrogation. Fisting his hands at his sides, he decided to pretend this was a spy movie. He'd provide nothing more than name, rank, and serial number.

"I grew up in Croton-on-the Hudson. And I have—had," he corrected quickly, "a place on Central Park West." *You'll get nothing from me. I'm closed up tighter than a biosphere.*

"How did you wind up here?" She pointed out the storefront window at the parking lot and beyond, toward the occasional car zipping down Main Street. "In the sticks of Setquott Beach, I mean."

He flashed an easy grin. "Do you know how expensive it is to be homeless in Manhattan these days?"

Her tinkling giggle reminded him of the wind chimes Lana hung on his balcony one summer. She'd claimed their soothing music would relax him, and it had, until the noise caused animosity with his neighbors. Then he'd removed them. Funny, he hadn't thought about those stupid chimes in ages. Lana, on the other hand, haunted him night and day. He always recalled the same vision of her. With hatred flashing like sharpened knives in her gray eyes when he'd confessed the severity of his misfortune. And the long curve of her back when she'd walked away a moment later.

"I'll take your word for it," Gianna said, snapping him into the here and now. "What did you do for a living?"

Uh-oh. Dangerous question. Yet one he felt compelled to answer. He owed her some sort of explanation. Maybe if he kept his background shadowy, she'd let the subject drop. "I handled investments. Stocks and bonds, estates and trusts." Mainly his own, but she didn't need to know that.

"And what happened?"

Unable to look her in the eye, he toyed with a pair of salt and pepper shakers. *Clink! Clink!* "I lost it all."

She placed a hand over his, effectively stopping the glass-on-glass noise. Then, she gave a reassuring squeeze. "I'm sure it wasn't your fault."

A flood of warmth enveloped him, but he shook away the coziness to stay on point. "Well, unfortunately, I have no one to blame but myself."

"You don't have family or friends who could have helped you?" Her voice was whisper soft, without demand or indignation. "At least until you got back on your feet?"

Given the opportunity, her doe eyes could easily melt the steel encasing his bones. "Nope." Righteous anger clipped his words, a clear warning she should back off.

"No one?" Rolling his eyes heavenward, Kyle sent a silent plea to the Almighty to call her off. "I mean," she said, pulling her hand from his. "Surely there must have been someone, a friend or client, willing to help."

Apparently, the Almighty held no more sway over Gianna than mortal men. Time to change the subject before she probed too deeply. "What about you? What's with this wedding Claudio told me about earlier?"

In an instant, her face paled to the color of milk. "Claudio told you about Frank's wedding?"

"He said you need a date. Don't tell me a pretty lady like you doesn't have a guy to accompany her."

This time, she backed her chair from the table. "It's a long story." She rose and turned away. Interesting. He'd obviously touched on a sore point. Nonetheless, he didn't push for more information. He didn't dare. After all, wasn't he being cagey about his background? Those who knew him might call him many insulting names, but "hypocrite" was never among them.

No matter. Eventually he'd find out her secrets. And then, perhaps, she wouldn't enchant him. He'd discover she was like all the others, sweet and loving when he pleased them, cold and harsh when he didn't.

After a long moment of silence, Gianna must have decided their conversation had run its course. "Why don't you go upstairs?" she suggested. "Claudio and I can finish here."

In other words, take a hike. You've encroached on my privacy enough for one evening.

Without waiting for a reply, she bustled off to the kitchen to help the old gnome with the dishes. Alone in the silence, Kyle swore he heard his heart beating in his ears when he thought about the wounded look on her face when she talked about this wedding Claudio had mentioned. He wasn't a hundred percent sure, but something about the upcoming nuptials upset her. The thought someone might have hurt her evoked a simmering rage inside him, and his hands curled into fists.

Before he could register surprise over that change in his mindset, though, Gianna returned. "Kyle, go on. You've done enough for one day. I'll see you tomorrow."

He could've argued, could have demanded answers to his questions right then and there, but his aching muscles secretly rejoiced at the lure of a hot shower and a soft bed. Kyle rose and, bidding her goodnight, strode out the side door to the hallway leading to his temporary quarters upstairs. Time enough to figure out the puzzle that made up his boss.

STILL RATTLED FROM her conversation with Kyle, Gianna walked back to the kitchen without the tablecloths she'd gone for. Claudio stood up to his elbows in soapsuds, washing dishes. If he noticed her distraction, he didn't remark on it and went straight for his personal annoyance instead.

"Why you let Kyle go?" He jerked his head toward the closed door. "I thought he was gonna be the new busboy."

Arms folded over her chest, she leaned one hip against the counter. "Have you seen his hands? That man has never done any physical labor in his life. Why shame him with it now?"

"So we hired him to look pretty, *cara*?"

"No, but we didn't hire him to escort me to social occasions, either."

Claudio shrugged off her anger as he would a jacket four sizes too big. "If he no gonna work, the least he can do is look good on your arm for a night. Besides, if not him, who will you ask to go with you? You can't go alone."

She dropped a handful of silverware into the water with a plop. A balloon of suds splashed up and smacked him between the eyes. "*Chiuda in su*, Claudio."

"What? You don't agree so you tell me to shut up?" He wagged a gloved finger. "If your papa were here, he'd turn you over his knee for speaking so rudely to poor Claudio."

"'Poor Claudio' gives as good as he gets. And Dad would probably say, '*Brava, cara*,' for the way I'm handling things in his absence. Including you and all your nonsense."

Claudio cocked a silver eyebrow. "You think so, eh? You think he be thrilled to know you still cry yourself to sleep?"

She whirled from the steel table behind him, her hands full of dirty ceramic casserole dishes. "I do not!"

His finger waved again. "You no lie to Claudio. You still pine for that no-good heartbreaker. How can such a smart girl be so dumb? Go home, Gianna. I finish cleaning here and I lock up when I'm through."

And let him have the last word? Fat chance.

Besides, she'd bet every last dime in her diminishing bank account the second she pulled out of the parking lot, he'd be dragging Kyle out of the apartment to return down here to scrub the tile floor with a toothbrush.

"I'm going to try to grab Mr. Whiskers again. We're supposed to get another thunderstorm tonight. I don't know how much longer he can go without seeing a vet."

"You need a box," Claudio said. "I been seeing on the internets. All cats love boxes. Even jungle cats."

The internets. Gianna bit back an indulgent smile. Claudio had received a tablet for his last birthday from his grandkids and now believed himself an expert on thousands of topics, from politics to medical concerns to, apparently, animal behavior. "Think a pizza box would work?"

He missed her joke and shook his head. "Too flat. It needs sides. Like a shoebox, maybe."

She tried needling him again. "We're a pizzeria. We don't have shoeboxes."

"You could probably find one upstairs." He shot his gaze at the ceiling and gave her a mischievous wink.

Gianna put her foot down—literally. "I am not going to bother Kyle for a box. I just sent him up there for the night. Quite frankly, I think he's had enough people interaction for one day."

Claudio made exaggerated clucking noises. "Buck, buck, buck-aw!"

"Please," Gianna said with a huff. "Calling me a chicken hasn't worked since I was eight."

"So, then what you gonna do?"

She thought for a moment, then headed into the storeroom in the back. After studying the racks of canned tomatoes, plastic jars of spices, and other assorted pizza ingredients, she set her attention to the paper goods. As she catalogued the napkins, toilet tissue, waxed paper and aluminum foil, she silently chastised herself.

This is stupid. Why am I listening to Claudio's advice anyway?

Because you're wasting time to avoid going home to an empty house. At least, if you have the cat, you'll have something to focus on.

"Pathetic to lose an argument with yourself," she muttered.

She turned around to return to the kitchen when an idea struck. Of course! Why hadn't she remembered the Chinese takeout place at the end of the strip? They had tons of boxes. With a quick call of, "Be right back!" she raced out the back door and into the rear parking lot.

Fifteen minutes later, she had Mr. Whiskers safely transferred from a cardboard box to the pet carrier.

"Told you," Claudio said with a superior air. "You should listen to me more often. I know what I say. Tomorrow, you ask the bum to be your date for that other bum's wedding. You'll see. I'm right about that, too."

Chapter Five

Gianna leaned back in the chair in her best friend's kitchen. Sipping decaf coffee, she inhaled the subtle hint of cinnamon and stroked Bomber's dense multi-colored fur. The big cat purred and dug her claws into Gianna's thigh, only to retract them again and again. Bomber had been one of her first rescues, a three-week old kitten she'd discovered dumped in the woods behind Villa Mare. Look at him now, she marveled. Sleek and sweet and fat and spoiled rotten by Nicole. Someday soon, Mr. Whiskers would have the same opportunities. Of course, he needed treatment for his feline rhino-pneumonitis first, but Dr. Crane had assured her plenty of cats lived long happy lives after diagnosis, with proper care and treatment.

"So, how soon will you hear about the loan?" Nicole asked, jolting Gianna away from her concerns for Mr. Whiskers.

Again with the loan. Didn't anyone have anything else to talk about? Why did her problems take up so much interest with her family and friends? First Joey, now Nicole. Even the ROMEOs had harped on the status of the daycare center last night—until she'd promised to let them know the moment she had her approvals in hand. Didn't they all realize if she had her approvals, they wouldn't have to wait for her to tell them? They'd hear her hooting and shrieking for miles around their little town.

While her best friend deserved more information than the old men, Gianna still had no compulsion to divulge too many details for fear of jinxing the deal. Hiding her frown, she nuzzled the cat. "Not for another week."

"Have you looked into the permits yet?"

"Why bother?" She shrugged. "I don't have the money yet."

Nicole's blue eyes opened wide in surprise. "Do you have any idea how long it takes to get building permits? To find a decent contractor to do the renovations? And you haven't filed for anything except the bank loan?" She clucked her tongue. "What about that lawyer referral? Did you follow up with him, at least?"

With every question Nicole hammered, Gianna sank a little deeper into her chair. "No."

"Have you gone to Town Hall to see about rezoning the property?"

"I don't own the property. How can I apply for rezoning without a deed?"

"Gi, it takes weeks just to find the department head who'll tell you it takes months to get the approval for a rezoning."

She refused to look at Nicole, concentrating on the cat on her lap. "So?"

"So?" Nicole parroted. "You need a workable business plan to get the loan from the bank. Do you know how much money it'll cost to bring that site up to code? Even if you get the loan, you need a whole bunch of stuff to obtain the state approval. Just to apply for the license for a daycare facility requires..." Hands splayed, she counted on her fingers. "...a list of employees with background checks and references, detailed plans and procedures for the day to day operations, your financial obligations. What are you waiting for?"

"I don't know," she admitted, self-consciously running a hand through her hair. "I just can't think straight right now—"

Nicole slammed her palms on the table, bringing Gianna's head up with a snap. "Because of that stupid wedding invitation."

The crushing weight of failure slouched her until she was almost part of the chair's upholstery. "Let it go, Nicole."

"No, I won't let it go. But you should. Frank was a snake, and Rachel was Medusa. But that part of your life is over. Don't let them continue to ruin your future, especially since neither one of them is worth it." Her lips pursed in a moue of thoughtfulness. "Did you find a date yet?"

Oh, goody. Let's move on to the next juicy tidbit. When had her life become the stuff of soap operas? And when would the temporary amnesia set in so she could escape for a while? She frowned. "Yes and no. I made the mistake of confiding in Claudio, and he mentioned the idea to Kyle."

"Kyle? The dumpster guy?"

"He's not a 'dumpster guy.' He's actually very nice, and not bad-looking."

"Define 'not bad-looking.'"

"Tall." She lifted a hand above her head. "Dark curly hair, hazel eyes, cleft chin, broad shoulders..."

"Yum." Nicole smacked her lips. "Sounds like the perfect specimen. Of course, if you decide to take Mr. Yummy, you'll have to get him something to wear. Knowing your brother, I doubt his closet's chock-full of formal attire."

"I know." She sighed. "And even if there was a tux hanging in there, the fit would be positively indecent on Kyle."

"Really?" Piqued interest flowed into Nicole's tone with the force of an oil derrick atop a gusher. "Gee, maybe I should start hanging around dumpsters to meet men. Sounds like you found a real prize in yours."

"I didn't say that," she replied a little too quickly. "And anyway, you're blowing Kyle's looks way out of proportion."

"Oh?" A golden eyebrow arched, and then fell. "My mistake. Here I thought you were telling me this guy's a bigger hunk than your brother, which, in the grand scheme of hunkdom, puts him pretty high on the desirable list. So, what's your Kyle like?"

"He's not *my* Kyle, Nicole."

"Uh-huh, sure."

When had Nicole turned up the thermostat? The air had become unbearably warm. Perhaps steam from her coffee cup bathed her face. Or maybe Bomber's excessive weight added to her body temperature. Either way, she resisted the urge to fan herself. No doubt, Nicole would take such a gesture the wrong way. And she wasn't in the mood for another round of Nicole's favorite game: *Could This Be Mr. Right?*

Focused on her breathing, she waited until the fever flooding her face and hands cooled. "What I meant was Joey's clothes are too snug."

"And I repeat. 'Yum.' So when do I get to meet this Adonis in bum's clothing?"

"Anytime you like. I'm not hiding him."

"Maybe you should."

Puzzlement furrowed Gianna's brow, embedding imprints on her brain. "Why? There's nothing between us, Nicole. I'm his boss—"

"As well as his landlady."

Shaking her head, she snorted. "Only in the loosest definition. We're becoming friends. That's all there is to our relationship."

"Uh-huh." Nicole tossed a curl of hair over one shoulder with that flirtatious grace Gianna envied so much. "Don't you think it's about time you considered a new guy for more than friendship? For heaven's sake, you and Frank broke up six months ago. Why are you waiting so long to replace him?"

"Maybe because I have scruples." A little testy, but between the hair flip and the smart-ass attitude, Nicole deserved a little testy.

"Or maybe you still haven't gotten over him. But, hey. All the more reason to have a fling with your dumpster hunk."

"I don't think—"

"Ooh, ooh." Nicole waved her hands like a contestant on a game show. "Take Kyle to the wedding. We'll do it the way you planned. You all dolled up with a new dress, new hairstyle, a whole Cinderella-makeover kinda thing. Frank'll take one look at you and wonder what made him choose the runner-up instead of the real prize. Even better, he won't be able to do a thing about it, 'cuz the yummy Kyle will be draped around your shoulders like a cheap cape."

"I didn't say I was taking Kyle, remember?"

"You're running out of time, sweet cheeks. Besides, Claudio already put the idea in his head, right?"

"Well, he didn't say he'd go," she murmured.

All trace of humor gone, Nicole leaned on her elbows. "Maybe because you haven't asked him yet. So what are you waiting for?"

The heat in the room increased to the interior of an active volcano. Gianna scanned the grapes and apples decorating Nicole's wallpaper, the oaken tabletop, the mug of coffee, and Bomber's swishing tail. She had no one to blame but herself. All she wanted was the opportunity to shine, to show Frank and his backstabbing bride she'd survived how they'd lied to her, made a fool of her, tried to humiliate her in front of the other teachers—in front of her kids.

At the time, the plan seemed so simple. But in the last thirty days, she'd only discovered one viable candidate to play the gorgeous man on her arm for the evening, and he was a homeless stranger she'd found lurking around the restaurant's dumpster. God, wouldn't Frank and Rachel *love* hearing that? Talk about embarrassing.

Humiliation scorched her cheeks, and she fought the urge to hide her face. Then, a little voice inside her head whispered, "Frank and Rachel don't have to know how you met him, or who he really is."

True. The bride and groom would be playing host to two hundred guests. If she and Kyle got through the receiving line with a minute or two of idle chitchat, Frank and Rachel wouldn't have time to find out who Kyle was or where she'd met him. He'd just be the nameless Greek god on her arm.

Maybe this was doable after all.

WHEN KYLE PLACED THE pineapple and avocado pizza with extra cheese in front of the gaggle of teenagers, Bethany, the purple-haired girl, fixed him with a solid stare. At least today she'd ditched the nasal chain.

"You're new here, aren't you?"

"Yes."

She leaned forward to inhale the scent of the pizza in one loud sniff. Sliding her black-rimmed granny glasses down her naked nose, she inspected him from brow to chin. "What's your name?"

He didn't reply to the teenage interrogation. This Gothic librarian would soon learn he didn't play adolescent games.

"You dating Gianna?" she persisted.

"No."

"Why not?" Her voice increased an octave and a decibel. "You prefer guys?"

In a curling wave of interest, a dozen teenagers stopped all conversation, slamming textbooks closed, to pay devoted attention to his reply. "No," he managed on an exasperated breath.

"No one would care if you're gay," she answered. "I mean, it's not like when you were in school. People nowadays are more... what would you call it? *Hip.*"

"Great," he replied through gritted teeth.

"Can you speak in more than one syllable?" Tommy interjected from the far corner of the booth.

"When the mood strikes me."

Their amused snorts followed him to the counter where Gianna stood.

Curiosity reflected in her unwavering stare, but he shook off her silent questions. Dating Gianna. What a ridiculous supposition. Oh, she was pretty enough. And in an unspoiled way, not like the debutantes and social climbers with whom he normally came in contact.

Still, she and he had nothing in common. He was a product of breeding and Fifth Avenue. His family could trace their roots back to the Mayflower. She was a product of the suburbs. No doubt her roots were steeped in extra virgin olive oil.

Unaware of what he hid behind his furrowed brow, she smiled. Molten heat simmered in the pit of his belly, and then spread through his limbs like hot coffee, enervating and energizing him at the same time. With the same strength Atlas must have used to carry the world on his shoulders, Kyle tore his gaze away from her intoxicating mouth and frowned. Gianna evoked the strangest emotions in his psyche. While he couldn't wait until this episode in his life came to an end, a part of him knew he'd miss her smile, the powdery scent of her skin, the thick river of black hair cascading to the middle of her back, the melodious song of her voice...

"Don't let Tommy scare you off, Jeeves," Bethany called, breaking the mystical spell Gianna cast. "We're just having a little fun."

At first he thought to ignore the name, but the snickers grew so loud they burned his ears.

"Yeah, c'mon, Jeeves. Can't you take a joke?"

"Hey, Jeeves, what happened to your sense of humor?"

He whirled from the counter, his gaze boring into the leader of the brat pack.

"Uh-oh, Beth. I think you got Jeeves mad now," Tommy announced in a mock whisper.

"My name is Kyle," he finally said through clenched teeth.

"Too late." Bethany waved off his angry stare with a flutter of silver-ringed fingers. "You had your chance to tell us your name, but you didn't answer. So we made one up. From now on, you'll be known as Jeeves."

"Bethany," Gianna chided gently. "Don't tease Kyle."

"His name is Jeeves, Gi," Bethany insisted.

"My name is Kyle!" By God, how many insults would he be forced to take from these hooligans?

Gianna leaned over the counter and placed a hand on his wrist. Amazing how, with such a simple gesture, she instilled peace to his frazzled nerves. "Remember what I told you about treating everyone as if they were family?"

Yes, but for every rule there was an exception. "To quote Rodney Dangerfield," he replied, jerking his head toward the teenage ambush squad. "'Now I know why tigers eat their young.'"

She giggled, and then lowered her voice. "If they see they've got you rattled, they'll keep harassing you. Don't give them the satisfaction. And if it makes you feel better, when they first met me they gave me the name Mama Celeste."

Despite a fight for self-control, a snicker escaped his clamped lips. Her eyebrows shot up in a questioning glare. "Sorry."

"Don't be." She held a finger before his nose. "But if you tell anyone what they used to call me, you'll go through the rest of your days here as Jeeves."

"Fair enough," he agreed. Just then, Claudio shuffled by, dragging a wet mop across the floor. Kyle nodded in his direction. "What'd they call him?"

"What they still call him... Mumbles."

He tossed his head and laughed. "Perfect!"

"So you'll put up with Jeeves for a little while?"

"For a very little while. How'd you get them to stop calling you Mama Celeste?"

"I made up names for them." She shrugged. "I guess they didn't like my choices because they mutually agreed to go back to our given names."

"How long before they changed their minds?"

"Three months."

Three months. He'd be long gone by then, thank God. This place with all its loony residents would fade into distant memory, like a nightmare brought on by watching a horror movie after eating bad Thai food. He'd go home and forget all about Villa Mare, Claudio, Bethany and Tommy, and Gianna.

So why did that knowledge make his heartbeat slow? Why did he have an inexplicable urge to stop time? Why did his gut twist at the thought of never again seeing Gianna? Where did the stabbing pain beneath his ribs and between his temples come from?

Heartburn. This sudden sickness had to be heartburn from all the heavy garlicky food he'd consumed in the last few days. Not that he wasn't grateful for Gianna's meals. Dining here beat trying to ignore the pangs of hunger biting his belly like a nest of vipers.

Still, he couldn't wait to return to his regular diet and normal routines. All he had to do was put up with the Bethanys in this place for a little while longer.

But deep down he knew Bethany wouldn't cause him trouble. Gianna was the one who could turn his whole world upside-down.

KYLE AVOIDED ANY ISSUES with Gianna for almost thirty-six hours. Then she cornered him, and he forgot all about his vow to keep her from getting under his skin. His only excuse was she caught him at the end of another grueling shift, and exhaustion had stolen his willpower. Who knew she could be so devious? Once the last patrons had exited the restaurant and the doors were locked, she approached him, a porcelain cup of cappuccino and a cannoli in her hands.

"Ah," he said, eagerly reaching for the treat. "You've already learned my weakness. Not good."

She sat across from him, eyes glistening with what he thought was concern. "How's everything going? Are you comfortable upstairs? Do you need anything?"

In hindsight, he should have realized the interrogation was a set-up. Blissful in his idiocy, he simply bit into the confection, savoring the mini chocolate chips and sweet cream surrounded by a crisp shell.

Swallowing, he replied, "Everything's fine. I appreciate all you've done for me."

As always, the foreign words tripped his tongue, yet she smiled as if he'd presented her with a rope of perfect pearls. "Do you appreciate me enough to return the favor?"

Caught. By a cannoli. He took another bite for sustenance. "I suppose. Why? What did you have in mind?"

"You know that wedding Claudio told you about?" She traced curlicues into the tablecloth beside his untouched cappuccino. "It's a week from next Saturday, and I still need a date. Think you might be interested?"

"Maybe." Last bite. Could he stall until the dessert euphoria passed? "What's the big deal about this shindig?"

"No big deal. Just a wedding." A hint of anger laced her words, but he let her speak without drawing attention to her mood shift. "I used to work with Rachel. From what I've heard, this is going to be a big, splashy affair—two hundred guests at a catering hall called The Crystal Palace. Of course, no one needs to know how we met and we work together or anything. We'll rent you a nice tux—"

"God, no." Jeez, the idea of a rental tux made his flesh crawl, and the cannoli threatened to do an about-face in his stomach. "What I mean is, I can get my hands on a tux."

She cocked her head. "Really? Where?"

"From a friend."

"Wait a minute."

Beneath the stained glass lamp, her eyes narrowed slightly. Only an excellent gambler would have caught the subtle change, the expression used before calling someone's bluff. Lucky Kyle was an expert gambler.

"You know someone who'll give you a tuxedo for nothing, but this person wouldn't help when you needed a place to stay?"

He shrugged. "What can I say? I need a better caliber of friends."

"That's an understatement." She propped her chin on her hand. A tendril of black hair fell from its ponytail confines to settle between her eyes, and she blew the hair atop her head.

Kyle stared at the small O her lips formed. By God, what he wouldn't give to feel those lush red beauties on his own lips. They looked as velvety as rose petals, and he'd bet they tasted better than the Napoleon brandy he'd longed for on the night he first met her.

Unaware of where his fantasies led, she leaned to take the plate. Hesitating, she pointed at the coffee cup. "Are you going to drink that?"

Doubtful. Too much heat already infused his insides. "No," he said. "Thanks, anyway."

As she drew near, his fingers itched to release her hair, to pull that black cloud free and feel the silky softness against his skin. Then he'd kiss her until the world stopped revolving. Given the chance, he'd begin his onslaught at the nape of her long, delectable neck. He'd plant slow, moist kisses, gentle as morning mist, along her sweet flesh. While easing his way from the bottom of her ear to the curved juncture where her shoulder met her throat, he'd pay particular attention to the pulse throbbing beneath that creamy column—

"Hey, that's my goddaughter you're ogling." Claudio's gruff voice jerked him from the sensual vision and tossed him into cerebral reality.

Gianna had already left the dining room. Odd, he'd never noticed. "I wasn't ogling her, old man."

His heart wasn't in the lie, and Claudio obviously knew. The old man's face creased into thousands of disapproving wrinkles. "You hurt her," he warned in a whisper deadlier than a rattler, "you answer to me. *Capisci?*"

"Yeah, I *capisci*." Kyle shook his head to clear any vestiges of the daydream from his mind.

How long since a woman had affected him so deeply? Too long.

Even before he'd wound up here, Lana had built a frigid wall of ice between them—a private, personal igloo for two in their bedroom on Central Park West. Which was one of the reasons he'd started this whole mess, to learn the truth. But despite what anyone said, the truth did not set him free. Not in the manner he'd expected. Damn him for the fool he was! And damn Rory and David for knowing all along how this game would turn out.

Chapter Six

D ay Twenty-two. At the end of another exhausting night, Gianna slapped a long white envelope into Kyle's hands.

"What's this?" he asked, turning it over to see his name printed along the outside.

"Your paycheck." Apparently she didn't realize what a momentous occasion she'd engendered because she returned to the kitchen area without waiting for the grand opening.

"My...?" He ripped the envelope's flap and pulled out the green strip of paper inside. His eager brain barely registered his name and a dollar amount printed across the top, Gianna's signature gracing the bottom.

"It's not very much, but you haven't been working for us a full two weeks yet so next time around, it'll be a little bit more."

Kyle paid no attention to Gianna's promises. *My very first paycheck.* Now what? The only vision that came to mind was the doleful expression on good ol' Rory's face when the stiff-backed accountant found a photocopy of this little gem in his office mail. And David! David's Norse looks would turn a new shade of purple.

By God, he'd won a battle! Things might not have gone the way he'd anticipated when he started, but the end result proved more satisfying than he'd ever dreamed.

Even better, Rory and David would owe him something in return for this triumph. He stared at Gianna's pixie princess face as she piled dozens of dishes onto a tray for transport to the kitchen sink. *And I know exactly what to ask for.*

"Which reminds me," she said, hefting the tray onto her slender shoulder with well-practiced ease. "How'd you like to go shopping tomorrow morning? You need some decent clothing. You can't keep wearing my brother's hand-me-downs. We could go to the mall before work."

"The mall?" He'd never been to a mall in his life. The idea of enclosing himself with the unwashed masses held little appeal. Still, if he could pick up some jeans that fit better, he might feel more comfortable around here.

"Mmm-hmm. Brookland Mall is only three miles from here."

Brookland Mall. Well, if nothing else, the excursion should prove interesting. He wouldn't hope for more. "Sure, why not?"

"Great. The bank there will cash your check so long as you have ID. You have a driver's license, don't you?"

"Of course. I'm homeless, not helpless."

"Sorry," she said, the familiar pretty blush creeping into her cheeks. "What a stupid thing to say."

"No harm done."

He watched her retreating back, and that pang of regret echoed in his chest. He rubbed the area with an absent air and stared at the slip of paper until the characters blurred into dancing dots of black ink.

Not yet, anyway...

THE NEXT MORNING, GIANNA approached the apartment door that had once housed her brother and now sheltered her...

What should she call him? When she introduced him at the wedding, what would she say? "I'd like you to meet Kyle, my..."

What? Her employee? God, no! She'd die of embarrassment if Frank found out she'd brought the hired help.

Her escort? No. That sounded like she'd called up some service and ordered him from an online catalog.

Her friend? Well, she supposed, friend worked better than any of the other terms she could say.

Still, the description wasn't a perfect fit. Rather like the clothing he wore these days, the word was too small for the individual.

Temporarily shrugging off thoughts of how to identify him, she knocked twice on the door and waited.

"Just a sec." Kyle's voice filtered through the barrier, sounding deeper and sexier, if that were possible.

Following the noisy click of the double locks, the door opened, and Gianna sucked in her breath. A sculpted chest, like hewn golden oak, filled her view. Kyle wore no shirt, just a pair of faded black jeans. They hugged his hips in a manner suitable for the male models on billboards towering fifty feet high in Times Square. Water droplets trickled from his neck, nesting inside the tight curls of dark hair upon the broad expanse of flesh. Beneath the bare bulb serving as a light in the foyer, the slighter curls on his head, still wet from his morning shower, glistened.

"Hi." Amazing she got that one syllable out. Her tongue, dry and woolen as an old ski sweater, had swelled to ten times its normal size.

"Good morning," he greeted her with a lazy grin. "Come on in. I'll be ready to go in a minute."

While she watched his back muscles ripple, he quickly strode down the hall toward the bedroom. Lord, he had more hypnotic motion in his upper body than the tide rolling in to shore. Hugging herself to ward off the shivers, she stepped inside the apartment.

A wave of unfamiliarity flooded her veins. Odd, since she knew this place as wholly as she knew her own home. This apartment came with the original lease for the restaurant twenty-five years ago. How many times had she strolled over these carpets, stood in this kitchen? Thousands. First, when her grandparents lived here, and then when her brother, Joey, had moved in. She'd hosted slumber parties in this living room as a child. Some of her happiest memories lived in these walls, and hours of laughter echoed in the air.

Since Kyle's arrival, however, the same old place took on an originality she didn't recognize, as if conforming to the new occupant. Photos of her family still hung where they always had. But now they looked out of place, encroachers on someone else's private domain.

"You don't happen to have a scanner downstairs, do you?" His voice halted her hand just as she'd reached to straighten a vacation photo hanging slightly askance. While she'd been studying the atmosphere, he'd reentered the living room. The hunter green shadow-stripe shirt he'd donned enhanced the shade of his eyes and complemented his broad shoulders.

God, those shoulders belonged on a superhero. Part of her wanted to play Lois Lane to his Superman, to wrap her arms about his waist and let him carry her away. Somehow, she knew his physique would shelter her from all the troubles in her world. Not just today, but every day of her life.

"Gianna?" He snapped his fingers near her eyes, and she snapped to reality.

"Oh, umm, sorry. A scanner. Like a photo scanner? We've got the printer in the back of the restaurant—in the office. I think it has a scan feature. Why?"

He waved the long green check like a banner. "I want to make a copy of this before we cash it."

Her heart filled with compassion. How sweet! The paycheck obviously meant so much he wanted a copy for posterity. "I think that's a wonderful idea. We can stop downstairs to make your copy first, and then head over to the bank."

He glanced at the clock. "Are you sure we'll have time?"

"Mmm-hmm. Claudio and Sal will open today, so we can take a little longer. Most of the stores at the mall open at nine-thirty, but all of them are open by ten. As long as we're at Villa Mare by eleven-thirty or so, we should be fine. So that gives us a good two hours."

"Great. Then let's get going." He followed her, stopping to lock the apartment door, and then allowed her to lead the way downstairs. She led him into the office, which was little more than a corner of the storeroom with a battered old desk full of office supplies and a wooden chair. "Here you go." She lifted the lid of the printer, then held out her hand for the check.

He kept his grip on the slip of paper. "Why don't you walk me through how to do it?"

"Oh, sure." She stepped out of the way to give him access. "Not much to walk through, really. Put the check face-down on the glass, close the lid, and follow the prompts on the screen. When it says 'okay to scan,' hit the green button."

He did as she'd advised and while the machine performed its magic, Kyle pointed to the phone attachment. "It faxes, too?"

"Well, yeah, it's a multi-machine. We don't do much with it. My mother is the one who handles any of the tech stuff for the restaurant. She took classes at the local library. I guess you're more used to big, separate equipment and a bunch of staff members who do nothing but copies or faxes all day in a corporate office."

"How does it work?" He picked up the receiver. "The fax, I mean." She glanced at him with curiosity. "I haven't seen one in over a decade."

"Simple." She took the receiver from him, showed him how to place a document in the feeder and dial the recipient's number.

"Ha. It's pretty much like the old ones from the nineties. Who uses these anymore?"

She shrugged. "I guess it seems like a dinosaur for someone like you. But a few of our regular customers still fax their lunch orders to us. Then they can send one employee to pick up for a whole department or group of workers. This is probably as modern tech as my parents will ever get. It took Mom ages to master her smart phone when she upgraded last year. If she had her way, she'd still have her old flip phone. And Dad...? We lost him when cordless phones became the norm. Now they both refuse to have to learn anything else the digital world develops. This is where they drew the line." She pulled his photocopy out of the tray and handed it over while he took the original off the glass. "Are we ready now?"

At his nod, she led him outside to the rear parking lot where her car waited. A light mist fell this gray October morning, and she tilted her chin to catch the moisture on her face. Early autumn was her favorite time of year. A sharp chill suffused the crisp air. Red, yellow, and orange leaves scattered over the blacktop like paints on an artist's palette. Gianna reached into her purse and fumbled with her key ring until she found the button to unlock the car's doors. The moment the click echoed in the empty lot, a firm hand clamped down on her wrist, sending a ribbon of tingles up her arm.

"If you don't mind," Kyle said, "I'd like to drive."

She dropped the keys into his outstretched palm. Wow, she hadn't expected the he-man attitude. First with the copy machine and now her car? Why did all men have an aversion to watching a woman handle machinery with proficiency? Bad enough he had to take over a simple copy task, but now he insisted on driving her car?

Her teacher mind easily came up with a reasonable explanation. Maybe his need to be behind the wheel had something to do with regaining control. After all he'd lost in the last month, maybe he thought driving would give him a chance to feel more like his old self. In that case, she could be flexible.

Okay, fine. So long as he didn't drive like a maniac, she'd let him have his power moment.

Inside the car, he started the engine with a quick turn of the key, and then fiddled with her radio stations, scanning through bits of noise and talk with rapid-fire flicks of his wrist. Through his machinations, she said nothing. Even when he finally settled on some kind of monotonous chamber music to fill the silence.

No doubt, sitting in the driver's seat and making simple decisions restored some masculine pride. And Kyle's pride had taken an awful beating lately. First he'd lost all his money. Then he wound up homeless until he gained employment as a busboy. His humiliation only culminated with the nickname Bethany had bestowed upon him.

Jeeves. Gianna wouldn't admit the thought aloud, knowing the idea would anger him, but she liked the name. Somehow, Jeeves fit the man who walked with long-legged strides, shoulders thrown back, and head held high. As if he'd been born a prince and only played the role of pauper as a temporary measure.

Yes, she liked the name a lot. Almost as much as she liked the man, she thought as she gently rubbed a circle around her wrist where he'd clutched her a moment ago.

BROOKLAND MALL SPRAWLED over an acre of prime real estate at the intersection of two major highways. If the location didn't impress Kyle, the sheer genius of the interior awed his business acumen. Dozens of stores surrounded him, each selling shoddily made, overpriced versions of high-quality merchandise. Ghastly track lighting beamed down on the wares, lending them an artificial glisten meant to last only long enough to purchase and package the items. With Halloween just around the corner, holiday-related paraphernalia—costumes, smoking cauldrons, mummies in coffins, eerie music, orange and black streamers—decorated windows and festooned entrances. A few stores even had costumed employees. As he peeked through the windows of one establishment, he spotted King Kong ringing up a lady's purchase while a vampire folded sweaters on a counter. And the crowds! Every size, shape, age, and background wandered through the atrium, expressions wearing the same vacant stare. He remembered his cousin, Lucinda, once referred to these shoppers as "mall zombies." Now, he knew what she meant.

Even at nine a.m., the smell of old grease permeated the air. A kiosk selling mass-produced hot cinnamon buns twenty yards away enhanced the oily aroma with cloying sweetness. The mingled fumes made Kyle's stomach dip. To keep his breakfast from rising into his throat, he clutched his abdomen.

On the other hand, Gianna appeared unaffected by the nauseating odor when she gestured with a quick head jerk. "Come on. The bank's at the end of this corridor."

"Miss Randazzo!"

The high-pitched voices provided the only warning before a swarm of youngsters encircled a startled Gianna. Kyle found himself on the outside of a midget mob.

"Hello, my cherubs!" Arms thrown wide, Gianna knelt to give each of the four pint-sized rabble-rousers a hug. "What are you doing here? Where are your parents?"

"My mom's in there with Ashley's mom." A gap-toothed little girl jerked her pigtailed head toward the racks of greeting cards near the entrance of Ha-Cha-Cha Cards and Gifts. "We're looking for a card for Miss Donahue. She's getting married soon."

A pained look crossed Gianna's features. By the time Kyle's gaze traveled from her to the towheads and back again, her furrowed brow had relaxed. She smiled, translating her anxiety into a façade of serenity. "Yes, I know. I've been invited to her wedding."

"You have?" another little girl asked. "Is that why you're here? Are you looking for a present for Miss Donahue too?"

"No, Ashley. I'm here with a friend." She glanced at Kyle. "Ladies, this is Mr. Hayden."

"Hello, Mr. Hayden," the four singsong voices chorused.

Ashley, the curious one and most likely the leader of the quartet, tilted her head like a quizzical parakeet. "Are you Miss Randazzo's boyfriend?"

"No," he told her. "We're just friends."

"How old are you?" the child asked.

He glared at the little girl, and she leveled a steely stare right back. This kid was going to grow up to be a hard-hitting investigative journalist.

"How old are *you*?"

"I turned six in September," Ashley replied with all the maturity her age required.

"Well, I turned six a long time ago." Apparently his answer satisfied the inquisitive Ashley, who returned her attention to her friends.

"When are you coming back to school?" the smallest of the girls asked.

Sadness floated over Gianna's face, and she shook her head. "I'm not coming back to school, Megan."

"Never?"

"I might come by to visit now and then. But I won't be teaching there anymore."

"But I promised my little brother you'd be his teacher," Ashley said. "He starts kindergarten next year."

As if in pain, Gianna grimaced. "I-I'm s-sorry, Ashley. But I work somewhere else now."

The child's lower lip protruded and puckered. Then she snuffled. While the drama unfolded, Kyle didn't know with whom he sympathized more. Ashley was crestfallen, but Gianna's eyes threatened to overflow. Neither female maintained full emotional control.

"Gianna?" He moved one step closer, and his action must have alerted her to her tenuous state.

Rising again, she quickly wiped the back of her hand across her eyes. "You girls should go back to your parents before they begin to worry."

Instantly, four heads dropped to stare at the floor.

"O-kay," Ashley said, scuffing her pink sneakers across the white-tiled floor. "Promise you'll come visit soon."

"I promise. Now, go." She waved them off.

The girls scampered away, but not without one last aria. "Goodbye, Miss Randazzo and Mr. Hayden."

"So long." He turned to Gianna, who leaned against a pillar as if her legs lacked the strength to keep her upright. "You okay?"

Brushing off some imaginary lint, she ran her hands down the front of her jeans. "Oh, sure. I'm great. Why wouldn't I be?"

If the unshed tears didn't give her away, her pallor spoke volumes. Nevertheless, he shrugged. "No reason."

"Come on." A ghost of a smile flickered between them. "Let's go cash that check and spend some of it."

Linking her arm through his, she led him past the perfume kiosk and a noisy place where, apparently, children could create their own stuffed animals while shrieking at the top of their lungs. He noticed how Gianna purposely avoided the store where those other little girls clamored around two harried-looking women, but he said nothing and followed her.

Keeping with the atmosphere around them, the bank in the mall more closely resembled a department store than the staid branches he normally visited in Manhattan. Pale blue walls, blue-and-gold patterned carpet, and tellers dressed in bright colors contrasted with the austere white-gray-and-black ensembles Wall Street offices wore like uniforms. Velvet ropes penned customers in a serpentine procession. Impatience etched a permanent residence in every tightened mouth, every wrinkled forehead, every knitted pair of eyebrows, and every sigh.

"You go there." Gianna pointed to the end of the line, somewhere in Albuquerque. "I have some personal business to attend to. I'll join you in a few minutes."

While Gianna walked toward the row of desks to the right, he headed to the end of the line on the left. His attention, however, remained fixed on her. He watched as a woman in an ill-fitting burgundy pinstriped suit and pink blouse came forward, one hand outstretched in greeting. After shaking the offered hand, Gianna followed the woman to one of the desks and sat. The usual pleasantries followed—a smile, a few nods, and a nervous giggle he knew came from Gianna when the sound rippled from the nape of his neck to the base of his spine.

He shook his head. Useless to force a lighthearted air to disguise her anxiety. Anyone who knew her moods would see right through her deliberate attempt. Did Ms. Knock-Off Pinstripe sense Gianna's nervousness? Dumb question. Did a shark sense wounded prey in bloodied waters?

A moment later, Gianna placed her hands on the edge of the desk to pull her chair closer. Tension snapped in the air like fireworks of doom. Meanwhile, the woman on the desk's other side lost all pretense of friendliness. Her expression froze into a business demeanor he recognized from images in his mirror at home. The downcast mouth and narrowed eyes communicated the firm, unequivocal, no-holds-barred message, "No."

But "no" to what? He hadn't a clue. A poke in his right shoulder prompted him to look forward. While he'd pondered the interaction between Gianna and the cheap suit lady, the line had moved. To prevent another finger stab from the beefy woman behind him, he shuffled up the three footsteps and closed the gap. By the time he returned his gaze to the desk area, Gianna had risen, nodding solemnly. The misery on her face had the force of a prizefighter's punch to his stomach. Jeez, her world had crumbled. Disaster flashed like a neon sign. The misty eyes, slumped shoulders, and shaky smile all added up to bad news.

"Next!" His head snapped to the row of tellers in front of him, and more specifically, to the woman at the end beckoning with an impatient finger.

When he reached the counter, Gianna met him, her crestfallen face failing to hide her sorrow. "What was that all about?"

"Nothing important." Every impulse crackling between them assured him she lied.

DENIED.

Gianna sank deeper into the hot water and citrus-scented bubbles, wishing to drown her troubles. The bank had turned down her loan application, citing her lack of business experience and suitable collateral as reasons for destroying every dream she'd harbored for the last ten years.

"Perhaps if you had a co-signer?" Ms. Manning had suggested with a haughty sneer. "If your parents would be willing to—"

No! Not in a million years. Somehow, she'd raise the money, but she refused to ask her parents. She wasn't nineteen, for God's sake—she was ten years older. Ten years older, and not much wiser, still floundering for a future. Without the bank loan, she'd never get enough financing for her daycare center. A state grant would only take her so far. And since this was an election year for local representatives, every penny of state funds would be carefully monitored before filling public coffers.

A pity she didn't have a rich and powerful lobbyist backing her. Then, she'd have no trouble getting her congressman to approve the funds. But a woman of moderate means doing something important for the underprivileged didn't stand a chance of receiving the monies supposedly earmarked for just that cause. How ironic.

Her cell's musical wail interrupted her melancholy, but she sank lower in the water, immersing up to her earlobes, and ignored the nagging tune. She didn't want to talk to anyone right now. The noise stopped when her voicemail clicked on, but no accompanying ding followed, meaning the caller left no message. Good thing she hadn't bothered to climb out to answer. Probably Nicole on the other end, anyway. And the last thing she wanted was an "I told you so" lecture from a woman who couldn't balance her checkbook without an army of CPAs standing by.

What did Nicole know about finance anyway? Sure she knew local real estate, but that didn't make her much of an expert, not as long as she remained living in that old beach house like a squatter, refusing to let her mother sell it out from under her.

God, what a pair they were! She and Nicole were both too ruled by their sentimentality to succeed in their lives. No wonder they were best friends. Fifty years from now, they'd both still be toddling around Setquott Beach, unmarried, probably living together in the apartment above Villa Mare with a hundred cats. Meanwhile, the Kyles and Bethanys of the world, stronger and more goal-oriented, would be ruling the world. She and Nicole would point to them on television as somebodies they used to know a long time ago.

Wow, she really had to dig out of this hole. Maybe that pint of ice cream in the freezer would help get her through the night.

Oh, eventually, she'd have to tell her best friend. But not now. Definitely not now. Right now, she couldn't bear the thought of Nicole rubbing her nose in her own stupid mess. She'd had a hard enough time getting through a full day's work, especially after the fruitless excursion to the mall. Usually, a little retail therapy would cheer her up by distracting her with useless stuff and shiny objects. Who knew Kyle would turn into such a pain in the butt during a routine shopping trip?

For a man wearing filthy rags a week and a half ago, he sure was particular about his clothing. Two wasted hours spent roaming the mall—minus the twenty minutes lost at the bank—and what did the man finally buy? A pair of socks! No shirts, no pants, no shoes. Just socks.

In between his berating the unfortunate salespeople, he hammered her with questions. "Are you sure you're all right?"

"Yes, Kyle, I'm fine."

"Are you sure?"

"Yes, I'm sure." At his dubious look, she added, "Really."

"Why don't you tell me what's wrong? Maybe I can help you."

Yeah, right! As if he'd suddenly transformed from a down-on-his-luck homeless man to a fairy godfather. She could just picture that conversation.

Well, Kyle, it's like this. I need a hundred thousand dollars to open a daycare center for low-income families.

Is that all? Wait here, Gianna. I'll get my checkbook...

She raised a trembling hand out of the water for the glass of chilled Chardonnay beside the tub. God, what a day! Even now, she didn't know how she'd kept from bursting into tears when Ashley mentioned her baby brother attending kindergarten next year. Then to suffer through the debacle at the bank!

Once she'd left Ms. Manning's desk, all she wanted was to pick up a few items for Kyle and get out of there. Get out of the mall, far from the innocent questions of starry-eyed six-year olds, far from Federal Credit Union of Long Island and its sanctimonious loan officer, far from Kyle's incessant curiosity. Get to the restaurant where she'd immerse herself in the day-to-day ennui of pizza and pasta.

But when she arrived at Villa Mare, Claudio took over where Kyle left off. "Whassamatter for you? You walk around all day with a puss on. Somebody die or someding?"

Not somebody, Claudio. Something. My future. All my dreams.

Life had taken on a gray pallor she'd never be able to escape.

She took a sip of the buttery white wine and let the cool liquid slide down her parched throat. The sweetness lingered on her tongue, but couldn't soothe the sour memories of the events of fourteen hours ago. Nothing could. With a deep sigh, she placed the wineglass on the floor and, using her big toe, pushed the trap down on the tub. As the water drained away, she wished she could flush her troubles so easily.

Ice cream time.

Chapter Seven

"**I** finally got the listing for Dr. Weber's old office."

At the flatness in Nicole's tone, Gianna stared into the black void inside her coffee cup. She still hadn't told anyone about not getting the loan. Now, she'd have no choice. Hoping to buy time, she looked up. "And...?"

"I think you can forget that place. Even if I waive my commission, you can't afford the rent. Not unless you raise tuition rates by about a hundred bucks a month per child. Or you could budget a year's worth of rent into the loan to get you by for a while, but then you'd have nothing left to pay for the renovations."

With her usual *blow-blow-slurp* routine, Nicole sipped her coffee. "I hate to say it, but that office needs a lot of changes for what you want to do. If you were dealing with older kids, you might be able to get away with some stuff, but little ones require all kinds of safety guidelines, from plastic caps on all the electrical outlets to nibble-friendly plants in the landscaping."

The news went from bad to worse. Beneath the weight of today's headlines, Gianna's posture became as stiff as overcooked pasta. "I told you the place was a long shot."

"Yeah, well, don't give up hope. Something's gotta break for you soon."

Time to come clean. "Not soon enough. I stopped at the bank the other day while Kyle cashed his paycheck. I didn't get the loan."

Nicole's coffee cup slammed onto the table, sloshing tan liquid all over the cuff of her blouse. "Dammit! You're kidding!"

Gianna grabbed a wad of napkins, blotted them on the stain. "Nope."

"What'd they say?"

"Everything you warned me they'd say," she admitted.

"So now what?" Gianna shrugged. "You mean you're just gonna give up?"

Sometimes, Nicole could be so dense. Living rent-free in her mother's beach house, she had no idea how other people juggled their finances for big-ticket items like cars or daycare centers or safety protocols for toddlers.

"What choice do I have?" Gianna demanded.

"Well, there has to be another option."

"Yeah, sure. I could marry a wealthy man and have him buy the school for me."

Nicole rolled her eyes with all the impatience of a teenager. "Can the sarcasm, okay, Gi? I'm only trying to help."

"If you really wanna help, drop the subject."

"Fine." She lifted the napkins to check the spreading stain and frowned at the results. "How'd the shopping trip go?"

Gianna sighed. "Honest to God, you'd think he'd never seen the inside of a mall before."

"Well, maybe he hasn't." Her index finger bobbed toward Gianna's nose. "You said yourself Kyle's probably never really worked a day in his life. And trust me. A man who has enough money to afford a place on Central Park West does not buy his clothes off the rack at a department store in the Brookland Mall."

"I guess you're right." Again, Gianna sought answers in her coffee cup. She found none. Instead, she noticed the brew ate away the waxy interior and left translucent curls atop the black surface. Her stomach flip-flopped. Gross. She'd have to check with their distributor about getting hot cups without that icky lining in their next order. Luckily, they didn't sell hot coffee to go. These cups were used for family and staff. Still, she hated to think about anyone swallowing those wax curls with their caffeine jolt.

"What about you?" Nicole asked. "Did you find something to wear to the wedding?"

Her head jerked up, nearly snapping her neck. "Who had time? Appeasing Kyle and his, 'these cuffs are too wide,' 'this stitching is deplorable,' 'where on earth did you get such shoddy fabric?' mentality ate up ninety minutes of good shopping time. And in the end, do you know what he bought?"

Nicole's grin grew wider than the shoreline at low tide. "A pair of socks?"

Gianna's jaw dropped. Oh my God.

"How did you know?"

Had she followed them?

"What?" Nicole shrugged. "You think your Kyle's different than any other man?"

"He's not *my* Kyle—"

"Yeah, yeah. Listen, kiddo. When the topic is shopping, there are two kinds of men." Leaning back, she studied her French manicure as if reading her future in the pink polish. "The first kind hates to shop and will buy anything in order to get in and out of the store as quickly as possible. Those are the ones you see at restaurants wearing plaid pants, floral shirts, and striped ties." With a hiss of inhaled breath, she shivered. "Hideous."

Shaking her head, Gianna grinned. No doubt Nicole referred to her coworker at the real estate office. Ryan McKnight was a nice enough guy but he always looked like he dressed in the dark.

"Now, the second kind claims he hates to shop," Nicole continued, "then spends hours looking for the right garment. If the buttons on a dress shirt are spaced an eighth of an inch too far apart, he'll complain to the salesman. The salesman will convince him to try the shirt on anyway. He'll walk around the store in it for three-quarters of an hour, asking you every five minutes what you think. And regardless of what you say, he won't buy the damned shirt because of the abominable spacing of the buttons. Your Kyle sounds like the second kind of male shopper."

Theories aired, Nicole relaxed and folded her arms over her chest. *Your Honor, I rest my case.*

"Did I hear my name?"

Gianna whirled to see Kyle standing in the doorway. Fire consumed her neck and cheeks. How long had he been there? Had he overheard their conversation? No, a ridiculous thought. Nicole would have said something earlier. She whipped around again to take note of any guilt in her best friend's face. Judging by the sparkle in Nicole's eyes, he'd only appeared in the doorway a moment ago.

"Good morning," Nicole purred in a smoky, come-hither voice Gianna didn't recognize.

Great. A good-looking man walks into the restaurant and suddenly I'm sitting with Scarlett Johansson.

"You must be Kyle." The new voice floated through the air, wafting like heavy perfume on a spring breeze. In one fluid motion, Nicole rose and extended a hand. "I'm Nicole. Nicole Fleming."

"Kyle Hayden," he replied, shaking her hand.

Still burning with humiliation, Gianna felt a new emotion tighten her face: envy. With her peaches and cream complexion, thick honey blond hair, baby blue eyes, and luscious curves—all packaged in a five-foot-three-inch frame—Nicole had a way with men. Everything about her suggested she was a helpless female in dire need of a big, strong, handsome man to carry her off to a faraway kingdom and make love to her for hours on end. Nicole was a human candy box, for God's sake. When near her, Gianna always felt like a clumsy stork. Too tall for most men, long-legged and gangly, hair usually unkempt, blotchy skin with a smattering of freckles over her nose.

Nicole flashed a wink. "This one's perfect for the wedding, Gi. You couldn't have obtained a better specimen if you'd sent a detailed description to Santa Claus."

Ears buzzing with the full impact of Nicole's remark, Gianna dropped her head to the table to hide her face in the crook of her arm. If only she could bury herself deep in the earth, far from Nicole's smirk and Kyle's curious stare.

Over the noisy bees in her head, she heard Kyle ask, "What's the deal with this wedding anyway?"

"You mean she hasn't told you?"

Nicole's gaze bored into her neck with the power of a speed drill, and she lifted her head to form some kind of explanation. Too late.

"Frank was cheating on poor Gianna with this woman, Rachel," Nicole provided. "Poor Gianna found out about it when he proposed to Rachel in front of the whole school. Then, he booked the most expensive catering hall in the county for the wedding. Now to add insult to injury, Rachel had the audacity to invite poor Gianna to this shindig to show her up! Like the fact they were sneaking around behind her back wasn't humiliating enough."

"Nicole, you call me 'poor Gianna' once more, I'm gonna—"

"Shut up and drink your coffee." Nicole softened the blow by giving Gianna's hand a quick squeeze, then fluttered an index finger at Kyle. "Now, you are the perfect weapon for poor Gianna's revenge. I only wish I could see Frank's face. Next to you, he'll resemble a weasel. A weasel who's the costar of the grand show, but a weasel, nonetheless."

"Nicole," Gianna murmured. "Could we please change the subject?"

Nicole's tongue cluck dismissed her. "You'll have to play the role of smitten suitor. Really cozy up to poor Gi, lots of slow dances." She paused. "Oh, crap. I didn't even ask. You can dance, can't you?"

"I've had a few lessons," Kyle replied, leaning one hand on the edge of the booth near Gianna's shoulder.

God, he smelled good. Like sun and citrus. Clean. Sweet. Not like garlic and onions and sweat, the way she did.

"Mmm," Nicole said, fingers dancing across her chin. "I figured as much. Society waltzes and such, right? In the good old days?" Panic flashed in her baby blues. "Oh, but Frank mustn't find out you work here. Cripes, that would ruin everything. Gianna said you were a stockbroker or something before you met her. Right?"

"Or something." His words held a trace of laughter, as if he only humored Nicole until a more interesting topic stole his attention.

"Okay, that'll work. You're still a stockbroker. Now, where did you two meet? You can't tell people you met in the garbage." She held up a hand. "Don't get me wrong. It's a cute story for your grandkids someday, but totally inappropriate for this crowd."

Grandkids? Gianna's coffee erupted in her throat, and she coughed. Who'd said anything about grandkids? Or kid-kids, for that matter? This was supposed to be a one-night date, nothing more.

"How about if I say I saw her across a crowded room? I swept her off her feet, and then we flew to the moon on gossamer wings of love."

Nicole didn't recognize the sarcasm lacing Kyle's suggestion, but Gianna did. Flinching, she reached for Nicole's wrist to stop her, but Nicole was on a roll. And no one stopped a rolling Nicole.

"Ooh, I like that! Love at first sight. Just don't go *too* overboard with the romance schmaltz. Keep it credible but *in*credible at the same time. You met at a party among mutual friends and discovered an instant attraction you couldn't deny. It would help if you were able to list all Gi's good qualities. I can help with that, if you need me." She rested her chin on her fist, her expression sparkling. "We've been besties for ages! The guests will eat up your devotion to each other with a spoon."

"All except Frank and Rachel, of course," he added.

Can't she tell he's toying with her?

"Of course. That's the point, right? To get Frank to realize he lost a treasure when he dumped poor Gi?"

Poor Gi's temper flared.

Nicole shimmied in the booth. "We want the buzz to be about you two instead of the bridal couple. That'll really tick off the newly Mister and Missus Cheater." She sobered. "But you're gonna have to dress the part of successful New York businessman. And not in little Joey's hand-me-downs." Heated eyes scanned him from the top of his head to his midsection. "As much as they do for your physique and my heart rate, you'll need something more devastating for this crowd. We want Frank to think poor Gianna came out on top in their sorry little episode. Plus, the wedding's a formal affair. God, I hate the idea of putting someone as scrumptious as you into a rented tux!"

"Don't worry. I already told Gianna I know where to get my hands on a decent tuxedo for the occasion."

"Well, that may take care of you, but poor Gianna still needs a decent dress." Nicole's calculating gaze moved from Kyle to Gianna, giving off vibes of day-old fish lying on a bed of cracked ice. "Maybe you could borrow the little green number in my closet."

To break eye contact, Gianna waved her off. "Forget it, Nicole. It would be way too short on me."

"You're probably right. That dress is a petite, after all. But we'll have to find something..."

"Why don't you let me worry about the details? I'll find something to wear."

"Like what?"

"I don't know." Gianna placed her hands palm up on the table. "I'll find something. Will you drop the subject already?"

"I can't drop the subject. You have to look purrrrrrrrfect for this event." One finger under her chin, she tilted her head, first to the right, and then the left. "You know what you need?"

Borrowing a phrase from Kyle, Gianna replied, "A better caliber of friends?"

Nicole's lips twisted in a frown. "I'll ignore that. You need a fairy godmother. Someone who can give you a Cinderella-style head-to-toe makeover before you see that no-good, cheating rat again. Like so." She raised a hand and pretended to wave an invisible magic wand. "*Bibbidy-bobbidy-boo*!" Then she studied Gianna with a critical eye. "Hmmm... no change."

No surprise. "Why don't we hire an actress to play my part for the day?"

"I'd love to, but Frank and Rachel both know what you look like," Nicole said with a wide grin. "I'm not trying to hurt your feelings, sweetie. But think. When a woman is in love, she gets this glow."

"I thought pregnancy made a woman glow."

"That's a different glow. Love has a glow all its own. When you're in love, you look like you, but happier. Everything's wonderful in your world. Right now, you look like your world's been flushed down the toilet. We need to artificially create an in-love glow."

To keep from slapping Nicole silly, Gianna sat on her hands. "Gee, is it too late to call Hollywood to hire a special effects team?" Kyle and Nicole both stared as if she were a new specimen in the science lab, and she prayed lightning would strike her dead on the spot. No such luck. She'd have to make her own escape from this situation. "Don't you have to go to work, Nicole? And Kyle, I bet Claudio could use some help in the kitchen."

"Actually," Kyle replied, "I just realized I forgot something upstairs. I'll be back in a flash."

KYLE TURNED TO LEAVE the dining room, but still caught Nicole's next remark. "Damn, I wish I'd been invited to this wedding! I'd give anything to see Rachel's face when you walk in on Kyle's arm. She may have stolen Frank from you, but you definitely got the best man."

Gianna sighed, mournful as a phantom moaning in a graveyard. "Nicole, let the wedding go. *Please.*"

Her patience was obviously stretched to the breaking point. No wonder, with a friend like Nicole. God, the woman exhausted him within five minutes of their meeting. And what gave her the right to tell a complete stranger about Gianna's troubles?

When he closed the door, he lost the conversation, but didn't care. His mind still whirled around the subject they'd discussed when he first walked into the restaurant. What had he overheard? Something about Gianna getting turned down for a loan? Well, that explained what happened at the bank the other day. At least to some degree. He still had no idea why she needed a loan.

For such a transparent woman, Gianna certainly kept a lot of secrets—big secrets. No matter. He'd found out the secret behind the wedding, hadn't he? He'd learn all about the loan, as well. Five more minutes in Nicole's company should be enough. Which was fine, because five minutes was about all he could stand of Nicole's company. Right now, though, he had a phone call to make.

With an itchy trigger finger, he punched in the number, began to pace and got tangled in the serpentine cord. God, hadn't they heard of cordless phones in this town time forgot? Then he remembered Gianna babbling about her mother trying to learn to use her new smart phone. Right. He pictured a little old lady in a housecoat with a crocheted shawl draped on her shoulders and her cat eyeglasses sliding down her nose while she tried to figure out how she could make phone calls without being connected to a cord.

While he waited for the secretary to pick up, the rings buzzed like angry mosquitoes in his brain. When she finally answered, he got right to the point. "Rory Abernathy," he barked.

"Just a moment, Mr. Hayden," her slightly nasal voice replied. "He's expecting your call. I'll put you right through."

Good old Doreen, the epitome of efficiency. Even with everything that had gone wrong, some things never changed. A second later, he heard a click.

Then a booming male voice came on the line. "Kyle? Is that you?"

He didn't bother to confirm his identity. If the secretary could recognize him, Rory should as well. "Did you get my fax?" He'd had to go through a helluva lot of subterfuge to send it, from pretending fascination with that stupid multi-machine in the Randazzo's makeshift office to slipping in while Gianna oversaw a morning delivery outside and the dishwasher ran through its first cycle so no one heard the recognizable static and squeal of the transmission.

"It was on my desk first thing this morning." Rory's tone filled with open admiration. "I don't know how you managed, but I guess congratulations are in order."

Yeah, right. Like he didn't picture Aurora slipping farther and farther out of reach as he stared at the papers Kyle had sent. "Stuff the congratulations. I'm only calling to make sure you hold to your end of our deal."

"What are you doing for this Villa Mare place? Consulting work? Per diem, I assume, based on the low dollar amount. But hey! It's a start, right?"

Since he had no intention of telling Rory about his life as a busboy, he deftly set the conversation on course. "According to the rules, I'm entitled to two favors for my little success."

"Okay, so what do you want?"

"First, I want a set of formalwear. My Dior tux will do. And not just the tux. The whole outfit. From the skin out." He paced the kitchen as far as the coiled phone cord would allow. "Underwear, shirt, socks, and dress shoes, too. Lana knows where everything is."

"Yeah, well, about Lana..." Rory's tone changed from the exuberance of admiration to condescending pity.

No need for a brick to fall on his head. "She's gone, isn't she?"

"Moved back to Boston two days after you left Manhattan."

All motion stopped. Not that Lana's swift departure surprised him. After all, they'd said their goodbyes when he told her of the sudden change in his finances. What surprised him, though, was how the news made him feel. Numb. No sadness or sense of mourning, no bitterness or thoughts of betrayal. Her loss affected him with the same ambivalence he'd feel for a clipped toenail.

His eyes focused on the photograph of Gianna standing with her brother during his graduation. Gianna would never abandon the man she loved. Hell, Gianna wouldn't abandon a stranger fallen on hard times. He'd known her two weeks and already understood that should tragedy befall someone close to her, she'd sell her soul to buy that someone a new start in life. Long past time someone bought something special for Gianna in return.

"I'm sorry," Rory said. "If you want to go back on our agreement, I'll understand."

"Oh, sure. You just want to get your hands on Aurora." His pacing resumed, this time quicker. "Thanks anyway, but I'll stick to the original deal. I've got twenty-eight days left, and I can do that standing on my head if I have to. Now, about the tux—"

"I'll get the tux. What else?"

His attention returned to the photograph, and he smiled. "Call my cousin, Lucinda. She's a marketing exec at Gardener's." With the terse moderated tone of a drill sergeant, he barked out a list of what he expected Rory to do and how

Lucinda should handle her role. "Have her cook up some kind of sweepstakes or free gift or something. You got all this?"

"Yes. But one question. What's all this for? I mean, Gianna Randazzo. Isn't she the one who signed the paycheck you sent me?"

"Yes. So?"

"Well, now," Rory said slowly. "I'm going to have to run this past David—"

He nearly laughed, but kept his emotions in check between gritted teeth. "Go ahead. Run everything past David. I want our legal eagle to see his dire predictions didn't come true. Show him I'm doing fine."

"That's not what worries me, Kyle. This could be considered a conflict of interest and therefore, inadmissible under the rules of the agreement."

"Why the hell would you think that?"

"Well, it could be some kind of quid pro quo you cooked up between you and her. I mean, how can David and I be certain Gianna Randazzo didn't sign a phony check on your behalf, so we'll assume you're succeeding when you're not? Particularly if she's receiving something from you in return."

Was he kidding? The blood in Kyle's veins chilled to ice water. "Call the bank and verify I cashed the damned thing."

"Still wouldn't be enough. David and I will have to talk about this and get back to you. You have a number where I can reach you?" He read the blurry numbers from the tiny strip in the center of the old world phone. "Okay," Rory replied. "I'll call you as soon as David and I come up with a solution."

A solution for what? If Rory planned to stall in the hope Kyle would stumble, he obviously underestimated Gianna, who'd pick him up before he hit the ground. All the more reason to make this dream come true. "I want this to happen within the next twenty-four hours," he insisted.

Without waiting for a response, he slammed the phone back on the cradle for effect. Why hadn't he ever noticed before now that his best friend was a pencil-pushing idiot?

THAT TUESDAY EVENING, the ROMEOs arrived at precisely seven o'clock. Well accustomed to their routine, Gianna had kept their traditional corner table set and waiting. Within minutes, the five men sat in their usual seats, placing their usual orders. Naturally, the usual banter rang around them.

"How's my favorite schoolteacher doing?" bald, heavyset Angelo DiNunzio, former electrician, asked.

"I'm fine," Gianna replied. "What's up with you guys?"

"Same old," tall, slender Mike said, raking a hand through his snow white hair. "Did you see the Islander game last night?"

"You guys were at the game?" Gianna asked.

Angelo jerked his head toward the man on his right. "Curt knows a guy who works for the arena's food distributor. Got us some great seats."

"You ever wanna attend anything there: concert, game, ice show, let me know, Gi," the third member, Curtis Washington, retired postal worker, chimed in. "Depending upon the demand, my pal Don can usually finagle a coupla chairs on the floor. Sometimes he gets box seats."

"You shoulda been there last night," Angelo exclaimed. "The score was tied with less than two minutes left in the third period. Then, Ebba makes this shot." In imitation of a hockey puck gliding over the ice, he slid his hand over the tablecloth. "Beautiful. Just beautiful. You oughta go with us sometime, Gianna. We even got Nicole over her 'all Yankees, all the time' fixation to attend once. She had a blast."

Yeah, Nicole had gone into great detail about that trip, bringing Gianna to belly-aching laughter with her descriptions of a night with the ROMEOs. Before they left Setquott Beach, Angelo stopped at the supermarket to buy a five pound bag of unshelled peanuts. Once at the arena, he insisted she stuff the nuts in her purse to get them past security. After they found their seats, the five men polished off the entire bag, letting peanut shells fall on their laps and the floor because, "that's what the cleaning crew gets paid for." Cups of beer flowed like water from Niagara Falls, and when the nuts finally ran out, the men turned their appetites to hot dogs.

During the game, they cheered every punch thrown by the players, booed every call the ref made against the home team, and got to their feet to argue with another fan about a questionable penalty charge. At the end of the night, before taking Nicole home, they made a run to the nearest drug store for antacids and Tylenol.

Throughout the evening, poor Nicole wound up acting like a den mother at a Cub Scout jamboree. She broke up arguments, mopped spilled beer from shirtfronts, and then chipped in for gas for the ride home.

Thanks, Gianna thought, but no thanks.

"Can we get some of those little flat breads, Gi?" Curtis asked, bringing her back to the here and now.

"You bet." Gianna headed for the kitchen.

Curtis grabbed her hand. "And a house salad? With dressing on the side? Balsamic vinegar and olive oil, if you've got it."

"Are you on a diet, Curt?" Number four, retired police officer Patrick O'Mara, asked.

"Yep." Curtis circled his round belly with the flat of his hand. "I forgot how much walking I used to do on my route. Sitting around all day has made me paunchy. I need to lose a few pounds. I even started working out at the gym. I get a discount on my health insurance for going."

George Fuchs, the last of the red-hot ROMEOs, chortled. "Sounds like Curt's got a new lady friend."

All five of them were unattached, widowed or divorced. After all, Angelo always said, "What wife would allow her husband to go out without her three times a week?" Not to mention the many golf excursions, pilgrimages to every major sporting event from baseball to wrestling, and other field trips the ROMEOs took on a regular basis.

"Nah." Still holding Gianna's wrist, Curt lifted her hand to his lips. "This lady here's the only girl for me. What's the date of that wedding again, Gianna? I'll make sure my best suit's cleaned and pressed for the occasion."

With a gentle tug, Gianna pulled her hand away. "Umm..."

"You?" Angelo scoffed, puffing out his barrel chest. "Why would she take you when she could go with me?"

A quick hand wave and George sneered, "Please. Neither of you can dance worth a damn. I, on the other hand, used to teach at Arthur Murray."

"Yeah," Mike added with a snort. "In the seventies. Trust me, George, dancing's changed a lot in the last fifty years."

Sensing a crisis brewing in this United Nations, Gianna attempted to halt the speculation before fists flew. "Actually, I've—"

Too late. Curtis plucked ice from his water glass and tossed a cube at Mike's nose. In retaliation, Mike balled his napkin and pitched the white paper, missing Curtis and hitting ten-year-old Gabriella Tullo's head.

With a shocked gasp, Gabbie whirled. "Hey!"

The men broke into guffaws of laughter while Mike effused red-faced apologies to the entire Tullo family. When Mr. Tullo continued to glare daggers, Mike announced, "Their dinner's on me, Gi," which calmed the brewing kerfuffle before it got off the ground.

"I'll tell Kyle," she said. "That's his table."

As if summoned by her mention, Kyle strode past her then, a gray dishpan filled with dirty plates and plastic soda tumblers gripped in his hands.

Before she could mention the Tullos' check, however, Angelo chimed in. "So, who's it gonna be, sweetheart? Which of the ROMEOs gets to take you to the social event of the century?"

"Actually," she said again, "Kyle has agreed to take me."

"Kyle?" Mike's voice boomed off the walls, and several diners turned to stare.

"Who's Kyle?"

"I am."

When Kyle spoke, his breath brushed her ear. How had he slipped up behind her so quietly? While the old men had distracted her, Kyle had somehow managed to drop off his burden and pop up inches from her side.

Curtis slid his thick bifocals down his nose and peered over them. "You? Who are you?"

At the same time, George asked, "Can you dance?"

"I'm Kyle Hayden. And yes, I can dance."

George harrumphed. "Prove it. Take Gi here for a whirl."

The room spun. As if she held a life preserver, she gripped her order pad and clung. "Now?" she croaked through a tight throat. "Here?"

"Yes, here and yes, now," George insisted, getting to his feet. "I proclaim a dance-off. Best partner wins! You up for the competition, Kyle Hayden?"

Kyle shot his cuffs and smiled. "Bring it, old man."

A flurry of applause erupted from the ROMEOs and the other patrons.

Hold up. This was getting ridiculous. "Come on, guys," Gianna said. "Knock it off. I'm not playing this game."

George looked past her. "Sal?"

She whirled to see Claudio's son leaning in the doorway near the kitchen, arms folded over his chest, an indulgent grin lighting up his face.

He offered a mock salute. "I'm on it."

When she flashed him a look meant to send him scurrying, he did just that. Seconds later, the sounds of Tony Bennett singing, "The Very Thought of You" filled the room.

Arms open, Kyle waited. "Shall we?" No panic reflected on his features.

What drugs had he taken, and where could she get some? The idea of slow dancing in the middle of this dining room for an audience made her feet leaden. Muscles constricted. Taking a step required more effort than a team of workhorses could muster.

He must have sensed her immobility because he came near and folded her into his embrace. One hand clasped hers, secure but not suffocating. When he bowed forward, she automatically tipped back.

"Relax," he murmured in her ear. "I've got this."

The music took control, or Kyle did. Either way, she no longer directed her movements. Some invisible puppeteer pulled her strings, making each step, each glide across the floor, like dancing on a cloud.

Tony's voice crooned words echoed in her heart. *I'm living in a kind of daydream...*

That much was true. Kyle led her with effortless grace. Beneath the colorful glow of the stained glass lamps, his eyes took on a rainbow of hues, warm and comforting, hot and intoxicating. She found it impossible to tear her gaze away from his. The walls and tables faded away, the customers and staff disappeared. Nothing else existed. Only the music mattered, the music and the man.

The first song ended, and after a brief pause, Tony broke into the slightly up-tempo, "Rags to Riches." Without missing a beat, Kyle swept her around the room, never brushing against a chair, a knee, or a tablecloth. Boneless, Gianna depended on him for everything but the air she breathed.

The next song, "Steppin' Out" sped their pace, but Kyle never faltered. When the third song ended, Kyle slowed, and then stopped. Dropping his arms to his sides, he offered her a slight bow and returned to the Tullos' table without a word. The moment he turned, Gianna left her celestial playground, crashing to earth on the applause of the entire population of Villa Mare.

"I'd say that's a big yes for Kyle." Mike's awed tone filtered through her cloudy brain.

Quick, she told herself. Do something.

"Umm," she managed, "I'll get your salad."

Somehow, she managed to walk sedately to the kitchen where she headed straight for the Sub-Zero. Swinging the door of the giant freezer wide, she ducked her head inside to inhale frigid air and cool the fire crackling over her skin.

Chapter Eight

A s he'd done for endless days and nights since his arrival at Villa Mare, Kyle pounded another ball of dough into a thin, round crust and ladled tomato sauce atop. While his gloved fingers gathered shredded mozzarella from the nearby stainless steel tray, his eyes watched Gianna. Nothing in her demeanor had changed over the last several days, and his impatience grew as the minutes ticked by.

Dough, sauce, cheese. Pop in the oven. Dough, sauce, cheese. Pop in the oven.

Damn Rory! He should have straightened out this mess by now. When the telephone rang for the millionth time since his conversation with his accountant, he nearly jumped out of his skin. Again.

"Thank you for calling Villa Mare," Claudio mumbled into the receiver. After a pause he continued, "Large-a pie, extra cheese. Anything else? No? Phone number?" Another pause as he scribbled the information on an order pad. "Ten-a minoots."

Nope, not Lucinda. Just another damn pizza order. Before Claudio hung up the phone and ripped the paper off the pad, Kyle had opened the refrigerator door beneath the counter and pulled out another ball of dough.

"You got that, Jeeves?" Claudio waved the order. "One large-a pie with extra cheese."

"Got it, Mumbles."

Lord, he was sick of making pizzas. At least the dining room was closed on Wednesday nights, which meant less work than usual. Take-out orders consisted of the mundane—large pies, occasionally with toppings, a few heroes, several calzones, and the rare baked ziti or ravioli parm for a late working employee from the hospital or university. Only a few weeks working here and he already looked forward to Wednesdays.

Despite the lighter workload, though, on this particular Wednesday, Gianna wore the same expression of thoughtful misery she'd donned since the other day with Nicole. Occasionally, she winced or sucked in a sharp breath, as if Nicole's backhanded compliments and evil step-sisterly advice bounced around inside her brain with the force of a racquetball in eternal play. But she wouldn't confide in him.

He glared, willing the phone to ring with the power of his eyes. *Come on already, Rory. What kind of fairy godmother are you? How much time do you need to make a wish come true?*

The bell over the front door jangled, and he jumped. Shoot. Just another customer, this one a tired-looking woman in her mid-thirties with three boisterous, dark-haired toddlers in tow.

"Mrs. Melendez," Gianna greeted her. "I haven't seen you here in weeks. How's the job hunt going?"

"Eh." With an exhausted sigh, the woman sank into the booth nearest the window. "I have an interview with a new computer company off the Expressway. You know the one, CompTech?"

Order pad in hand, Gianna strode to the booth. "That's wonderful!"

"Not so wonderful. The interview's tomorrow at eleven, and I don't have anyone to watch the little ones."

Oh, God, no. Kyle knew exactly where this conversation would lead. Though the idea repulsed him, he could more easily stop a runaway train than keep Gianna from offering help to someone in need.

"Bring them here," Gianna suggested.

Kyle cringed. Bethany and her gaggle of teenagers were bad enough, but these kids were no older than four years of age. And he'd be damned if he'd spend tomorrow changing diapers and potty-training someone else's snot-nosed brats. No matter what agreements he'd made in the past, there were some lows to which a Hayden did not sink.

"Oh, no, Gianna." Mrs. Melendez's eyes widened. "I couldn't!"

"Of course you could. I'll be here by ten o'clock for the first delivery anyway. Drop the children off here before ten-thirty, and you should have plenty of time to shoot down the Expressway for your interview."

The little girl tugged on her mother's jacket sleeve. "Can we, Mama? Please?"

Mrs. Melendez's glance swerved from Gianna to the child and back again. "I don't know. What if they want to hire me? I still don't have a regular babysitter."

Smiling, Gianna tousled the girl's curls. "My parents come home Friday morning. We'll be closed for the day so I can pick them up at the airport. By Saturday, Dad will rule the roost again. And Mom will start insisting I look out for my own interests."

Wonderful. As if he could erase the scene, Kyle scrubbed the counter with a damp rag. One great, big, happy family reunion.

"Even if CompTech wants you," Gianna continued, "I doubt they'll ask you to start before Monday. And if you can't find anyone to watch them on a regular basis between now and then, I'll be happy to care for them. I'll no longer work here, so I can come to your house. This way the children will be in familiar surroundings and feel more comfortable."

Wait a minute! Once her parents returned, she didn't plan to work here anymore? He'd be stuck with grumpy Claudio, Sal the devoted family man, *pazzo* Mr. Randazzo, and a little old lady who no doubt kowtowed to her husband's despotic whims to keep the peace? Terrific.

"I'm not sure," the woman said. "I doubt I'd be able to pay enough to make the job worthwhile for you."

"I don't look after children to become wealthy," was Gianna's reply. "I'm sure we can work out something to benefit each of us when the time comes."

"You're an angel, Gianna." Mrs. Melendez grabbed her hands and kissed them. "God bless you."

Quickly, Gianna pulled away. A familiar pink blush rose in her cheeks, warming Kyle's frigid exterior. "It's nothing, Mrs. Melendez. I only wish I could do more."

"You've had no luck then?"

"Not so far." On a sigh, she shrugged. "But Nicole keeps telling me something will break soon."

The woman fingered the thick gold cross around her neck. "And something will. The good Lord doesn't ever give us more than we can handle."

Blinking rapid-fire, Gianna nodded with little enthusiasm. "The usual? Large pie, one diet cola, and three chocolate milks?"

"Yes, please," Mrs. Melendez replied.

"You got it."

When she turned away from the booth, Kyle noted fear, similar to a trapped animal, shining behind her thick lashes. How could someone who sympathized with the plight of Everyman be so uncomfortable receiving that same sympathy for herself?

Hoping to break the sudden tension in the air, he flashed another look at the black phone hanging on the wall.

Dammit, Rory! Have Lucinda make the call already...

VILLA MARE'S TELEPHONE rang the following morning shortly after Mrs. Melendez had dropped off the children.

Gianna left the three-year-old twins and their older brother occupied with coloring books and crayons, tousling their bent heads as she walked away from the booth. "Thank you for calling Villa Mare. May I help you?"

"Good afternoon," a clipped New England-accented twang intoned. "May I speak with Miss Gianna Randazzo, please?"

"Speaking."

"Miss Randazzo, my name is Lucinda Barrows and I have wonderful news! You've won a five thousand dollar shopping spree at Gardener LeClair and a day of beauty at our very own Spalon de Soleil."

She snorted like a pig into the receiver. "Ha-ha, Nicole, very funny."

"Miss Randazzo, I assure you this is not a joke," the woman on the other end replied. "You have truly won this fabulous grand prize. All you need do is provide a date that will be convenient for you to come to our Fifth Avenue store."

A thrill tickled her spine, but Gianna refused to be taken in by a sick joke. With effort, she kept her voice flat and moderated. "Uh-huh."

"I shall meet you outside the front entrance of Gardener's at nine a.m. sharp on the day of your choice," Ms. Barrows continued. "We'll allow you three hours to peruse our aisles while I personally assist you in finding the right clothing to suit your needs, style, and figure."

I'm not falling for this, Nicole. Or whoever you are.

"O-kay..."

"Then you're off to the fabulous Spalon de Soleil. After a wonderful infusion lunch in their dining area, you will receive a full body massage, facial, manicure, and pedicure, all with the finest members of the Spalon's staff. And the pièce de résistance? You'll be treated to a hair and makeup consultation with none other than the world famous Jean de Viv, himself."

Even Nicole wouldn't go to this much trouble in the name of a joke. Would she? Excitement tingled in her blood. Was this what people called "synchronicity?" Then again, the timing sounded too good. Could this offer possibly be legitimate? No way. She'd never won a contest in her life and hadn't entered anything in ages. So, if Nicole hadn't dreamed this up as a great gag, someone signed her up for a promotional come-on of some sort.

Tamping her enthusiastic skitters with deep, calming breaths, she shifted the receiver on her shoulder. "What's the catch?"

"I'm afraid I don't understand. Catch? What catch?"

"That's my question. What's the catch? What do I have to do to claim my prize? Spend four hours listening to a sales pitch for a new timeshare condominium in Oingo-Boingo? Sacrifice my first born male child on the altar of high fashion?"

"You have a very strange sense of humor, Miss Randazzo." A brief pause followed, and then a nasal giggle broke the silence. "I like that."

"Thank you. I think." Unless this is one colossal joke. "May I ask you something, please? Do you know how I won this contest? I certainly don't remember entering any raffles or sweepstakes. And I'd remember such a great first prize if I had."

"Oh, this wasn't your typical sweepstakes. Your name, along with nine others, was chosen from a computerized list of eligible ladies in the tri-state area. This free gift is to celebrate Gardener LeClair's one hundredth anniversary. For a century, our store has provided our clientele with the best of fashion, furniture, and décor. What better way to celebrate than with a special promotion?"

Gianna gripped the phone receiver tight enough to crack it. "I see..."

But she didn't. Not really. This just seemed to go to be true. And Gianna might be naïve sometimes, but she wasn't a sucker.

How could she possibly believe this woman's spiel was legit? She turned to note if anyone listened to her conversation with more than idle curiosity. Nearby, Claudio, mumbling as usual, dragged a mop across the floor. Sal emptied the commercial dishwasher. The children giggled and scribbled their crayons across ecru pages, paying no attention. Her gaze locked on Kyle's.

Curiosity glimmered in his bright eyes, but he smiled and turned away to cover the tables with fresh linens.

Kyle. Could he have had something to do with this? Sometimes, when she caught him staring at her, she had visions of the iceberg from Titanic, the visible tip appearing harmless and negotiable while the danger hid beneath the surface. But she shook off the frigid water of suspicion sliding down her backbone in rivulets. Silly.

"I'll tell you what." Her fingers clutched for the pen behind her ear, painfully yanking a stray tress of hair. "How about I take your number and get back to you?"

"Very well," the woman replied. She rattled off a phone number, which Gianna scribbled onto an order sheet. Then, she ripped the paper from the pad. "Thank you. I'll call you as soon as I have a date in mind."

"Well, don't wait too long, my dear. This offer expires two weeks from today."

"All right. Fine. Thank you." While considering the expiration time, she hung up the receiver.

A calendar hung above the butcher-block, and she flipped to November. Thirteen days from today put her at a very specific date: Frank and Rachel's wedding day. A perfect day for a makeover. The more she thought about this fabulous grand prize, the more her radar beeped. Something didn't sit right. Nicole suggested she needed a

Cinderella makeover, and *Bibbidy-bobbidy-boo*, she won one. This was no coincidence.

The suspicion froze her bones, like a sudden chill in an overheated room. Someone planned this, someone who knew her current predicament and sought to repair the exterior damage for appearance's sake. So who wanted her to look her absolute best for this upcoming affair?

Claudio? No way. He loved her, but didn't have the panache for this kind of subterfuge. Upon learning about the wedding invitation, he'd suggested she break into Frank's house the night before and paint "Loser" on the soles of his dress shoes. "Dis-a way, every time that worm kneels, everyone in the church will have a good laugh eh?"

No, this definitely was not Claudio's style. And since the apple never fell far from the tree, she discounted Sal for the same lack of imagination.

Who else? Her parents were in Italy and didn't know what she'd decided to do about the wedding invitation, which ruled them out.

The ROMEOs? Not a chance. Unless the Islanders hosted home games at Gardener's. She'd never told them *why* she needed a date for the wedding, only that she had no escort. And she hadn't even told them that much, come to think of it. She had Claudio to thank for spilling those beans.

After several minutes of cataloging, she came to an inevitable conclusion. Only one of two people might have had a hand in this unexpected windfall: Nicole or Kyle. Leaning an elbow on the counter, she chewed the pen cap.

Kyle was out of the question. The man depended on her for everything he had, from the roof over his head to the food in his mouth and the contents of his wallet. She knew he didn't have that kind of money. After all, she signed his paycheck. So unless he'd won the lottery in the last few days, he couldn't be the culprit.

Which left Nicole. But where would Nicole get such an exorbitant sum? Even if she'd recently sold the Taj Mahal and made a killer commission, why would she spend her money on such a frivolous thing as a shopping spree at Gardener's? And a day of pampering at the tony Spalon de Soleil?

True, Nicole had always despised Frank, even before his marriage proposal to Rachel. She'd always insisted something about him got her back up. But wasn't a pricey gift like this going too far in the name of friendship—or revenge? After all, Frank hadn't broken *her* heart.

Like a rubber band, Gianna's brain stretched and flexed, first in one direction, and then another. Still, she came up with no answers. Only one thing to do. She had to confront the most likely suspect and hope for a full confession. And not tonight, when Nicole had time to think up a reasonable explanation. No, this couldn't wait. If she wanted straight answers, she had to shoot from the hip.

In one smooth arc, she pulled the apron over her head and slapped it atop the counter.

"Kyle? I'm going out for a few minutes. Would you keep an eye on the children for me?" An exaggerated moue, eyebrows drawn together in a tight line, told her the idea disgusted him. "They're children, Kyle, not cockroaches."

"I think I'd rather have cockroaches underfoot," he grumbled. "At least I can squash them."

Frustration coursed through her veins, and she slammed her palms on the countertop. An empty pizza pan went crashing to the floor. *Clang!*

"Dammit, that isn't funny! How could you say such a thing?" She thrust her arm toward the booth where the Melendez children sat, wide-eyed in alarm. "Look at them! Can't you see the promise in their eyes, the innocence in their faces?" Her voice shook with fury, but she couldn't stop. Angry words poured from her lips, poisoning the air. "You make me sick! You and all your wealthy friends on Central Park West are the reason parents like Mrs. Melendez are stuck without proper daycare for their children. Oh, there's always enough money for an evening out on the town or to buy the new hot stock your broker's pushing, but never enough to fund a childcare center geared to molding the minds that will shape this country's future. Do you realize the monthly rent on the apartment you lived in would probably be enough to pay for an entire year's care for one of these children? You should be ashamed of yourself."

He held up his hands in surrender. "Hey, take it easy. I was just kidding."

"You're not funny." Tears welled, and she squeezed her lids closed to keep them in check. When drops trickled down her cheeks despite her efforts, she headed for the front door. She needed to get outside before the trickle became a flood. Her sudden tantrum had frightened the children. She wouldn't make the situation worse by breaking into tears. On a deep inhale, she ordered in a softer, more level tone, "Just watch the little ones. I'll be back in ten minutes."

As she strode away, the trembling descended into her legs. But she didn't stop. If she fell to her knees, she'd crawl out of here, away from the children and away from Kyle's snide comments. With all the force she'd stored in her fist, she shoved open the door.

Bright sunlight streamed into her eyes, causing the tears to flow harder. *Just get to the beach. Then you can cry to your heart's content without anyone else knowing.* The tears fell in twin rivers, but she no longer cared. Dammit, she hurt!

The last few months, hiding her true feelings, keeping everything walled up behind a façade of nonchalance, smiling until her cheeks felt like they'd crack. The strain had squeezed her like a python's grip. Well, she couldn't take the pressure anymore. She needed some kind of relief—even if it meant sitting in the cold on a rock on the empty beach for ten minutes to have a good old-fashioned, feeling-sorry-for-herself weep-fest.

She'd only reached the sidewalk when Kyle's voice halted her. "Gianna? Wait. Please?"

"What?" She turned, glaring daggers through her wet eyes. "What do you want?"

He stood outside the door, arms open in surrender. "I'm sorry, okay?"

Swallowed tears choked her, but she managed to rasp, "No, not okay. You've touched on a very sore subject with me."

"I can see that. I can also see you're shaking. Which means you're either upset or cold. Or both." He stepped closer. "Come here."

Without hesitation, she took a dozen steps toward him. He opened his arms wider, and she walked into his embrace. The moment he folded her against his hard chest, the talons of tension raking her spine melted and flowed into the pavement. His citrusy aftershave enveloped her in orange and sunshine, evoking images of a tropical paradise: warm, bright, and carefree. Safe within his protective grasp, she pressed her face into the crook of his neck. The tears still fell, but their descent slowed to a crawl while he crooned in a voice rich and deep.

"Ssshh, easy, sweetheart. You've had a rough time lately. You take too much upon yourself. Do you know that? You should trust someone to help you every once in a while."

Instantly, her eyes dried. His advice stung, and she pulled away. "Trust someone? Do you really believe that? You, who couldn't find a helping hand at the lowest point in your life? You're going to lecture me about trusting someone?"

A fingertip whisked across her cheekbone to dry the last teardrop. "We're not talking about my situation, Gianna." His hand slipped to her nape. Fingers pressed against the base of her skull, massaging the stress from her brain, and he pressed his lips to her forehead. "Besides," he added. "I asked for help and didn't receive it. You never asked."

"What makes you say that? You don't know anything about me. You don't even know why I'm so upset. I'll bet you think—"

Without warning, his lips came down on hers, cutting off her argument and sending logic fluttering like a feather in a windstorm. His breath jetted warm air into her mouth as his tongue swept inside. To her surprise, she welcomed this invasion, winding her arms around his neck to pull him closer.

Her tongue fenced with his, delighting in the flavors of his mouth. He tasted sweet and heady, like a sip of dessert wine after a big meal.

Her bones melted, leaving her completely dependent upon her hold around his neck to keep from sinking to the ground in a pool of liquid. Thunder roared in her ears, and her heartbeat galloped against his. Nothing existed but the melding of their lips, their breaths, their souls. His hands moved to her shoulders. With a hint of pressure, he broke contact.

"Wh-why did you do that?" Her voice sounded breathless and a little shaky in her buzzing ears.

"Beats me," he said with a lazy grin and an even lazier shrug. "But I think I'd like to try again."

She inhaled deeply and closed her eyes, waiting for the tentative connection to bring her to the brink again.

"Gianna?" A child's voice shattered the hazy dream around her.

As if she'd stuck a fork into an electrical outlet, she snapped to reality. One of the Melendez children, four-year-old Riel, stood beside them, waving a paper. Good Lord, where had her common sense gone?

"Look what I made you," Riel said. Shaky hearts and flowers covered the paper in a riot of pink, blue, and green.

"Oh, Riel, how beautiful! What do you say we go inside? I'll tape this on the wall for everyone to see." Ignoring Kyle, she took the child's hand and guided him into the restaurant.

Don't allow anyone to see the way your hands shake or how your heartbeat echoes in your throat. Feign indifference. Cool as a cucumber. It was just a kiss after all.

Nothing to get weak in the knees about. Just a simple little kiss.

Chapter Nine

Kyle followed Gianna and the little boy inside. Mentally, he retraced his steps. Where had he gone wrong? Then again, his outrageous action had made her forget her errand. So maybe the end justified the means. Even if the means weren't what he'd originally planned.

Based on what he'd overheard, he knew that last phone call came from Lucinda. And when Gianna left the children in his care for a few minutes, his instincts screamed she intended to confront Nicole about her possible involvement in the makeover. In hindsight, maybe having this mock sweepstakes happen within a mere week of their fairy godmother conversation hadn't been his best idea. So he'd followed her out of the restaurant to buy time, to distract her. And if she'd given him no other choice, had insisted on confronting Nicole, he would have used his minute knowledge of Gianna's best friend to persuade her that, even if Nicole were responsible, she'd never admit to the subterfuge.

When he saw her crying, however, thoughts of Nicole and Lucinda fled his mind with the speed of a hungry lion chasing a herd of gazelles. Still, kissing Gianna went far beyond common sense. In one instant, she'd looked so vulnerable, yet so alluring. Logic took a vacation. Because she stepped into his embrace so willingly, he couldn't stop from kissing her any more than he could stop the sun from rising.

And Lord, she was the sweetest ambrosia he'd sipped in ages! Soft and honeyed, even finer than Napoleon brandy. Now, having tasted her once, he longed to do so again. His heart knew another kiss would be a huge mistake. In all their time together, Gianna had given freely of herself. How could he possibly repay her generosity, her openness, by beginning a relationship with her that could only be temporary? Such an action would make him no better than that unfeeling clod, Frank.

If he were honest with himself, he'd admit he liked Gianna far too much to treat her badly. In another time and place, he might have tried for some sort of semi-permanent connection to her. He'd spent enough sleepless nights envisioning having her curvaceous figure in his home, in his arms. But New York society would welcome Gianna Randazzo with the same enthusiasm offered to a cockroach in a pantry.

No doubt, his co-op board would have a field day deriding her lack of pedigree, her working class background, and her less than stellar social skills. At every important function, she'd face the snubs and insults the matrons regularly inflicted on outsiders. Someone as tenderhearted as Gianna simply wasn't strong enough to handle that abuse.

Oh, sure, she could play nonchalance for short spurts of time. Her handling of Bethany and the rest of the teen army of hooligans told him that much. But how long could she pretend the barbs didn't hurt when her method of defusing them, turning their snide comments back on them, only made their insults and snubs more painful? He'd seen first-hand how the cream of society could be a cruel, isolating world when your status didn't fit their expectations.

Then again, since Gianna currently seemed intent upon ignoring him, his opinion hardly mattered. Perhaps she hadn't been as affected by their kiss as he. Or perhaps his little faux pas had affected her more than she let on. Probably for the best, since he had no way to explain any of his concerns to her without revealing his own secrets.

Whatever went through her mind, she sat in the booth across from the Melendez children writing something with a purple crayon, her attention completely focused on this new task. Curious, he leaned over her shoulder to see a large A drawn in the shape of an arrow.

"Who can tell me what this letter is?" She pointed with the tip of the crayon.

"I know," the girl screeched. "A. A for arrow."

"Very good, Crystal. That's correct." She clapped, and then quickly sketched a new picture, a butterfly containing a B.

"Christopher, do you know what letter this is?"

"Hey, Jeeves." Claudio drew Kyle's attention from the little boy's answer. "You working today?"

He jerked away from the table. "Of course."

"Then how about you drag your sorry behind over here and gimme and Salvatore a little help, eh?"

With a tired sigh, he left Gianna instructing the children in their letters and took his place behind the counter to create so many more pizzas. While his hands busied themselves with dough, sauce, and cheese, his eyes watched Gianna.

For over an hour, she sat at the booth with the children, drawing pictures, singing songs, and telling stories. Strangely, the more time Gianna spent with them, the more animated and child-like she herself became. Her eyes grew wider and rounder, her smile broader, her motions and gestures less controlled. In a nutshell, she changed from a subdued adult to a wild child.

Kyle found the transformation so utterly charming, he almost wished he could be five years old again and join the fun. She created hand puppets out of plastic gloves and drums from washed out cans of tomato puree. After crafting hats from sheets of aluminum foil, she led the children in a parade around the dining room, using a pepper grinder as a baton.

With a sparkle in her eyes, laughter filling the pizzeria, and her poise while she sat on the floor, he could easily see her gift for teaching. So why the hell wasn't she pursuing the profession she obviously loved with her whole heart? What would make someone relinquish a calling so strong in favor of stirring tomato sauce and serving pizzas in her family's restaurant? Why wasn't this talented and generous woman teaching lucky students on a daily basis?

His mind itched to find answers, but nothing came to mind, no matter how he mentally scratched his brain. The arrival of the lunch crowd distracted him from pursuing the subject more seriously.

A squat man, tools dangling from a heavy belt around his waist, flashed puppy dog eyes at Gianna. "How's it going, Gi?"

Cross-legged on the floor, Gianna looked up, straightening her foil hat before it slid off her head. "Good, Tony. How 'bout with you? How's AJ doing?"

"Gained three pounds already," Tony replied with a proud grin. "You'd never know he was sick a month ago."

Smiling, she rose. "That's great. I'm so glad his condition wasn't serious."

"You ain't kidding. He gave us some scare, eh?" He gestured to the Melendez children with a head jerk. "What's with the rugrats? You taking in kids here until you get your permits?"

"No, I'm just helping out a friend."

He nodded. "Uh-huh. Have you heard anything from the state yet?"

"Not yet." Gianna's lips disappeared in a tight line.

"You'll be sure to let me know the minute you get the approvals? I still owe you for what you did when AJ was sick."

Once again, Gianna dismissed the man's gratitude with an easy hand wave. "You don't owe me anything, Tony."

"Like hell. Rosa considers you her guardian angel. If you hadn't taken care of our daughters while I was working, Rosa wouldn't have been able to stay with AJ at the hospital." He thumped his chest. "You did for us, now we do for you. I told you then, 'Whatever you need in the line of construction work, you let me know. Done deal. No charge.'"

"Tony, I couldn't possibly accept—"

"Tony," Sal called from behind the counter, a brown bag dangling from his hand. "Your veal parm hero's up."

When he turned to grab the bag, his heavy tool belt hit the Formica's edge with loud clanks. "I gotta get back to work, but be sure to call me the minute you hear from the state, okay?"

"We'll see."

The bell jangled behind Tony as he left the restaurant.

While Gianna started the children singing, "The Wheels on the Bus," Kyle turned to Sal. "Who was that?"

"Tony Garibaldi," Sal said. "Owns G&D Construction. His son had a medical scare last month. Poor little guy's only five months old."

"What happened?"

"AJ started running a pretty high fever one night," Sal replied. "They rushed him to the hospital. Doctors thought he might have spinal meningitis. They quarantined him in the hospital for five days while they waited for the results of a spinal tap. In the end, the fever came from some mild virus."

"What does he have to do with Gianna?"

Sal jerked his head in Gianna's direction. "Tony and Rosa have two little girls at home, too. Marissa is eight, and Dina is eleven. Gianna volunteered to watch them so Rosa could stay at her son's bedside at the hospital."

Gianna pulled off the foil hat and dropped it on Sal's head. "I picked up the girls at school in the afternoon and stayed with them until their dad got home.

That's all. Tony and Rosa make a huge fuss over no big deal. I didn't exactly give AJ a kidney."

Surely, she didn't intend to minimize her generosity again. The woman had a heart as wide as the ocean. He had no doubt that if the kid had needed an organ, Gianna would've been first in line to donate.

"Kidney or not," Kyle said, "Tony seems to think your staying with the kids was a big deal."

"Parents always think it's a big deal when they have to find childcare for their little ones," Sal remarked. "Whether it's for an emergency or just day-to-day."

"You got that right." Gianna returned her attention to the little ones currently seated in the pizzeria. "'The people on the bus go up and down...'"

The three children chorused, "'Up and down, up and down.'"

Quirking his mouth, Sal sucked air into his cheek. "She's something, isn't she?"

More than something. In a picture of nonchalance, Kyle folded his arms over his chest and leaned against the orange Formica counter. "You could say that."

"I just did," Sal retorted. "I swear, if I weren't married to the love of my life, I'd have run off with Gianna years ago."

"Bah!" Claudio popped out of the storage closet. "You not good enough for Gianna. I should know, eh? I'm-a your pop." He leveled a predatory eye on Kyle. "You not good enough either, so fuhgeddaboudit. Now get back to work. Both of you. Lazy bums..."

For the next hour and a half, Kyle slid slices into the oven and pulled them out, filled paper cups with ice and soft drinks, and made idle chitchat with Sal and the locals. Once the crowds eased, he leaned against the counter to catch some breathing room.

The little girl—Crystal?— yanked on his shirt sleeve. When he looked down, she presented him with a piece of construction paper on which she'd drawn a long line with a big circle on top. The circle held a half-moon in the lower part and two dashes above. Eyes and a smiling mouth, he surmised. A lopsided pink heart surrounded the stick figure.

"That's you, Kyle," she lisped, pointing to the circle. "I'm sorry I don't draw good. You're prettier in real life."

The image looked more like a lollipop than a person, pretty or otherwise, but he knelt to accept the drawing with a smile. "I think you drew me very well. And besides, you're the prettiest person in this whole town."

Crystal's big brown eyes grew wider. Long, thick lashes batted against peachy cheeks. "Really?"

"Really." Catching her somber expression, he added, "Except maybe Claudio."

Laughter exploded from Sal. Even Crystal gave in to a fit of giggles. But she took her approval one step further and flung her skinny arms around his neck. "I love you, Kyle. When I grow up, will you marry me?"

"I'll be waiting," he assured her, gathering her close in a bear hug.

What a little sweetheart! If he thought his own daughter would turn out this charming, he'd have married and had dozens of children by now. Above the tiny head, his gaze locked onto Gianna's. Her mute approval charged the air with static electricity. God, he wanted to kiss her again more than he wanted breath to fill his lungs.

But no, he'd walk this tightrope without losing his balance. He'd made a decision. Gianna was off-limits. He settled for placing his lips against the top of Crystal's hair, breathing in the watermelon scent of her shampoo.

WHEN MRS. MELENDEZ returned to take her children home, they wrapped their arms around Gianna, buried their faces against her stomach and clung.

"No, Mommy, no!" Riel exclaimed. "We want to stay here."

With an apologetic smile, Gianna looked up from the three dark heads burrowed in her waist. "How did the interview go?"

Mrs. Melendez nodded. "Good, I think. I'm sorry I'm late. I met with the personnel director and the head of the department. They said they'd get back to me by Friday afternoon."

"Well, that sounds encouraging."

"I thought so, too. But now I have to find a babysitter." She crossed her fingers. "Just in case."

"I told you I'd watch them."

The children, listening with big ears to the adults' conversation, immediately pleaded with their mother. "Please, Mommy, can Gianna watch us? Pretty please?"

"And Kyle, too!" Crystal chimed in. "Kyle can watch us, too."

Mrs. Melendez's dark eyes studied Gianna's face. "Why do you suppose she wants Kyle there?"

"I can't imagine."

"We're going to get married someday," Crystal replied. She turned to Kyle, standing behind the counter. "Right?"

"You bet, sweetheart," he said, winking at the child.

"But only if Gianna doesn't marry him first. She kissed him outside in the parking lot. On the lips!"

A dozen heads swerved between Kyle and Gianna, each more curious than the other. Gianna's cheeks burst into an inferno, and she stared at the parking lot until the fire cooled.

"Well, well," Mrs. Melendez remarked, folding her arms over her ample bosom. "Out of the mouths of babes."

"I gotta admit." Bethany pointed from her usual seat in her usual booth. "The kid makes sense. You two make a great couple. I don't know how I missed the signs until now. I'm going to be a psych major, after all. You and Jeeves are perfect for each other, in that whole 'opposites attract' way. He's stiff and way too serious. Poor guy can't take a joke. Good-looking but prickly, downright harsh sometimes. You're fun and pretty, but way too soft. Think about it. You're a doormat, and he's a pair of kick-ass black leather boots."

The fine hairs on her nape danced with indignation, and she fisted her hands at her sides. "I am *not* a doormat."

"Sure you are. But I mean it in a good way."

Gianna quirked a brow. "There's a good way to call me a doormat?"

"Yeah. You've got 'Welcome' written all over you. You don't turn anyone away, no matter what they need or want from you. You're open, twenty-four/seven. Now, Jeeves, on the other hand, well, he doesn't take crap from anyone. Not even from me. He's got brass ones." She chuckled and leaned back, swinging her legs onto the bench. "Face it. You guys balance each other out. You're a match made in heaven."

Gianna's feet wanted to run, but with hands fisted at her sides, she held her ground, glaring at Bethany. *Et tu, Brute?*

Now what should she do? Any denial she made would add fuel to the fire. And Kyle's rounded eyes said he was as surprised by this turn of events as she. Try as she might, no clever quip or sarcastic reply came to mind. And all those eyes...

Why did everyone stare at her? What did they care if anything happened between her and Kyle anyway? It wasn't anybody's business if she wanted to kiss him—or anybody else, for that matter. Her personal life wasn't up for their discussion.

"Don't you have a class now, Bethany?"

"Nope." She flashed a grin, black lipstick ghoulish against white teeth as she sipped soda through a straw. "I'm all done today. So I'm gonna stay here 'til Tommy gets out of football practice at five-thirty."

"Lucky us," Gianna muttered.

"Well," Mrs. Melendez cut in as she tousled her twins' heads, "I'm going to take my guys home. Gianna, if you're serious about watching them, you'd really put my mind at ease."

"Of course I'm serious." With the subject now off her and Kyle, she could relax and resume normal conversation. "Call me the minute CompTech offers you the job. We'll go over all the particulars then. You want me at your house, I'll be there. I promise."

"Kyle, too?" Crystal repeated.

Gianna's focus flipped to Kyle who stood near the oven, a charming smile softening his features. For all his protests to the contrary, he obviously had a weakness for children. Then again, maybe only pretty girls managed to break through his cool façade. Like every other man she knew, did Kyle only warm up to an angelic face and adoring eyes beneath fluttering lashes?

Well, one thing was certain. Unlike every other man she knew, Kyle packed a kiss that still burned her mouth hours afterward. Okay, so she hadn't kissed every man she knew, but of the men she had kissed, none of them—

"Mommy, is Kyle coming, too?" Crystal's insistent whine broke Gianna's musings and cooled her burning lips more efficiently than lip balm with aloe.

"I don't see how he can, sweetheart," Mrs. Melendez replied. "He works here."

In direct imitation of her mother, Crystal folded her arms over her chest. "So does Gianna, but she's coming."

"Yes, but, Gianna was helping out while her mom and dad were away. This is Kyle's job, sweetie. He's a pizza man. He can't leave for the day because you wish him to play with you."

Mrs. Melendez's description of Kyle as a "pizza man" struck a tremendous blow to his pride.

Gianna saw him wince and hurried to ease the unintentional insult. "Actually, Kyle's only working here to help out as well. He's really a stockbroker in Manhattan."

"Oh, yeah?" Piqued interest radiated from Bethany's black-rimmed eyes. "Stockbrokers make a truckload of money, don't they? Why would you give that up to work here?"

"Because I needed him," Gianna said firmly. "And he was nice enough to come through for me in a pinch."

"Sweet." Bethany folded her arms behind her head. "See what I mean? He's perfect for you, Gi."

Oh, no. She was not about to traipse down that path again!

"What makes you think any man is perfect for me?"

"You like girls?"

"Um..." Mrs. Melendez hastily gathered her children. "I think we'll be going now. Thank you so much for your help, Gianna. I'll call you as soon as I hear something."

"Bye-bye, Kyle," Crystal shouted as her mother pulled her out the door. "See you soon! Don't forget your promise."

While the family headed out, Gianna spotted Kyle studying his shoes. Poor guy apparently suffered the same discomfort she felt. Hoping to break the tension, she cleared her throat.

Her ploy must have worked since he leaned close enough to whisper, "Thanks for coming to my defense."

His hot breath filled her ear, rousing memories of when he'd kissed her. Her lips tingled, and she clamped her teeth to stop from swooping in for a landing. The heat of his eyes trapped her as neatly as a fly caught in a spider's web. Without thinking, she stepped forward, one finger stretched toward the cleft in his chin. She burned to touch his jaw line, to feel the rough texture of his skin against her cheek, to fold into his embrace and let the tension recede from her bones in one long flood...

"Yup," Bethany interjected. "A match made in heaven."

Chapter Ten

On Friday, Kyle's plan to sleep until noon disintegrated when, at ten, the telephone seared his consciousness. Initially, he thought to ignore the incessant ringing. Today was his day off, and he intended to loll around all day. He couldn't remember when his daily activities left him so damn bone-tired. Funny. He and his friends always thought their weekly squash game was exhausting. None of them had any clue what real hard work entailed.

After ten rings, blissful silence reigned, and he burrowed under the covers. Thank God. He could still go back to sleep. Thirty seconds later, the noise began again. Muttering about the rudeness of suburbanites, he tossed aside the blankets and padded into the kitchen, nearly yanking the phone off the wall.

"What?" he barked into the receiver.

"Kyle?" A male voice, low and urgent, asked.

"Yeah?"

"It's me. Rory."

Sleep still clouded his brain, and Kyle came awake slowly. Rory? Oh, right. Rory, the accountant with an agenda.

"You okay?" Rory asked.

He scratched his scalp, and his senses tingled to life. "Of course, I'm all right. Why?"

"You have a television where you are now?"

The tingle grew into pins and needles across his skin. "Rory, what the—"

"Turn on NNC, if you get it out there," Rory demanded.

"Hold on a sec." Fully awake now, he placed the receiver on the countertop and strode into the living room. Picking up the remote control, he switched on the television and flipped around for a moment until he found the National News Channel.

A familiar face filled the thirteen-inch screen. What the...?

He recognized her immediately, if not her surroundings. The perfectly-coifed hair, the creamy pearls around her alabaster throat, and that stupid Yorkie, Chaucer, sitting on her lap in a matching red-plaid vest and bow tie all dragged him back to another time, another world. They'd posed her in front of some stone fireplace hearth, fake flames dancing behind her and the damn dog. Green screen, no doubt. Colette would never allow the public into her true home.

Adding to his morning surprise, an inset in the lower corner of the screen held a snapshot of him taken six months ago at a dinner party at the Legacy Club.

Now, standing in this shabby room in an apartment the size of the club's men's room, he cringed at the arrogance the half-smirk on his face displayed. God, had he ever really looked so smug, so self-possessed?

Forcing his eyes away from the unflattering photograph, he listened to the well-known voice filling the living room with liquid charm.

"...missing now for over a month," Colette said into the camera, "and my family is desperately worried about him. We want to be certain he's all right..."

"Son of a—" Heart thudding in triple time, Kyle raced into the kitchen again and fumbled for the receiver. "Why is my sister speaking to the press?"

"She's looking for you."

Gee, no kidding.

"I can see that. But why?" His legs shook so badly, he had to sit. But he wanted to hear what else his sister might reveal. Extending one bare foot, he pulled a chair near. This way, he could still see the television while anchored to the phone.

"...he couldn't bear the shame of filing for bankruptcy..." Her words slithered into the kitchen, and the blood froze in his veins.

As she dangled his closet skeletons before whirring cameras on national television, the realization of how this would affect his future chilled him.

Shut up, his mind screamed at the screen. *For God's sake, Colette, shut up! You'll ruin me.*

"Jeez, Rory, couldn't you stop her?" No answer, which only confirmed the suspicions bouncing around Kyle's head. "You set this up, didn't you? You and David. You couldn't stand the fact I was winning. You convinced Colette to go public so I'd have no choice but to back down and return home with my tail tucked between my legs. How low can you get?"

"That's not true, Kyle." Rory's speech pattern grew staccato. "David and I didn't know Colette was planning this. I swear. You have to believe me."

"Terrific." He scrubbed a hand over his unshaven cheek. "What am I supposed to do now?"

"You want to call off the bet?"

"You did set this up!" The shouted accusation made his head throb, and he softened his tone to a fatal hush. "By God, you'll do anything for Aurora. I should have known—"

"To hell with Aurora, Kyle! Let's just call this whole thing off. Get your ass back here before the situation gets any worse."

His sister's cultured, precise words beckoned from the living room, pouring salt into his open wounds. "Kyle, if you can hear me, please return to the loving arms of your family. We'll work out solutions for all your problems *together*. I promise..."

Loving arms, ha! Where were those loving arms when he first told her about his misfortune? As he recalled, Colette had sniffed in disdain, told him she hoped he didn't expect her to bail him out, and then slammed her mahogany door in his face as if he were already the homeless man he soon became. Now, she showed up on television, begging him to return to her loving arms? What audacity!

"This performance just might net her an Academy Award."

"Look, Kyle, she may be acting, but she's right. Give up and come home. David and I proved our point. We'll confess the whole thing to everyone, have a big laugh, and go back to the way things were before this mess ever started."

"You and David proved your point? What point would that be?"

Just when he'd adjusted to God's great practical joke, he awakened to a new nightmare. Hadn't he been punished enough for his stupidity? Would his private hell never end?

"You're taking my words out of context—"

"And you seem to be taking lessons from David now. Quit practicing for the bar exam, and think about this." Panic gripped his gut and twisted. "We're not in prep school anymore, for God's sake. Do you think those stuffed shirts in the Legacy Club will take kindly to what we did? Especially when they realize the public might learn they threw me out on my butt the moment I told them about my financial downturns? Their motto of 'With malice toward none, with charity for all' would take a tremendous beating underneath the media spotlight. Do you think they'll suddenly welcome me with open arms because I'm not as broke as they thought?"

"Dammit, Kyle, what do you want me to say? I'm sorry, okay? None of us expected this."

He ran his fingernails through his hair again, tingling his brain into desperate damage control. "Whether we expected her to pull this maneuver or not, we have to do some major mea culpas before this gets even farther out of hand. Privately. And right now."

"So, what? What do you want me to do?"

Ideas whirled at lightning speed. Most of his thoughts, however, were destructive and useless. Finally, he stood and, as if the change in stance shifted something loose, his logical side grasped the obvious. "Call Colette, tell her you've heard from me, and that I'm all right. If she insists on details, tell her what we did and where I am. I honestly don't care how you get her to agree. Just get her to stop talking to the damn press!"

"O-okay." Rory's shaky breath whistled through the receiver. "Are we going to call off the wager then? Are you coming home?"

"Hell, no. A deal's a deal. I'm gonna do my time."

Before Rory could continue the argument, Kyle slammed the phone on the receiver. With trembling hands, he filled the ancient coffeemaker and waited with one hip against the counter until he could fill a mug. He returned to the living room with his coffee, grateful to see the news anchors had moved on to discussing the weather forecast. His knees buckled when they hit the couch, and he sank into the lumpy cushion and stared at the television screen until the image blurred into a mélange of colors. Thanks to a high-pitched buzz in his ears, he didn't hear another word.

Only the ringing of the damn phone broke through his subconscious. Once again, he forced himself up and into the kitchen to pick up the receiver. "Hello?"

"Kyle? It's me, Gianna. Did I wake you?"

"No." This could prove to be a long day. He sank into the kitchen chair.

Her long exhale whooshed through the receiver. "Good. I have wonderful news. Your sister is looking for you. I saw her on TV this morning. She wants you to go home. All you have to do is call her, and she'll come get you."

If this was such wonderful news, why did Gianna sound like she'd announced the death of a loved one?

"I've already called to tell her I'm fine," he lied.

"You have? So I guess you'll be leaving us."

Poor Gianna. She couldn't hide her feelings, even when she tried. Everything reflected in her voice, her soft eyes, her sweet lips...

"No," he said to stop the images.

"No? I don't understand—"

"There's nothing to understand. Colette and I have never been close." Just the thought of his sister's performance made his fingers curl into a tight fist. "And we're certainly not going to become close now."

"Oh, Kyle, all families fight," she exclaimed. "My parents and I have had some real beauties in the past. Trust me."

"Really?" Hard to imagine her parents faced any more difficult task than protecting Gianna from her own naïveté. "What nefarious activities did you get into in your sordid past?"

"Never mind." He could hear her indulgent smile framing the words, belying any frustration. "The point is, when push comes to shove, your family will always stand by you, no matter what."

Yeah, right. "Maybe your family's always been supportive, Gianna, but when I needed help, my sister turned her back on me."

"Well, she obviously wants to make amends now."

"I don't think that's possible." In his opinion, Colette's gesture was way too little, way too late.

"Reconciliation is always possible," she retorted. "She's your sister, for heaven's sake."

"She ceased to be my sister when she slammed her front door in my face a month ago." The memory still left a bitter taste, and he smacked his lips to dispel the acid. "I owe her nothing. All I have at this moment, I owe to one person and one person only. *You* took me in. *You* gave me a place to stay and a job. *You* stood by me. And now, I owe you something in return."

"No, really. You don't owe me anything."

Lord, he could almost hear the blush rising in her cheeks. "Yes, I do. I promised to be your date for the wedding next week. Remember?"

"Oh. Right. The wedding..." Her voice trailed off for a moment, and then returned with forced cheer. "Listen, just think about what I said about the importance of family, all right? You should go home. You belong there."

"Right now, I belong here." Not that she could see him, but he stood, pointing to the floor, confirming his resolve.

"Well, right now, I have my own family to deal with. My parents' plane lands in about two hours, and I'm picking them up at the airport. Enjoy your day off, and I'll see you at the restaurant tomorrow at eleven."

Enjoy his day off? Impossible. His sister's stupidity had blown the day to bits. The moment he said goodbye to Gianna and placed the phone on the hook, the ringing began again. Jeez, he hadn't had this many telephone calls since the financial downturn of 2007.

"Hello?"

"Kyle? I hope I didn't wake you. Do you know who this is?"

The name struck his brain with laser precision. Nicole. Good God, even Nicole saw his sister's public appeal? Didn't anyone listen to the radio in the morning? Then again, with his luck, Colette probably purchased airtime on every station on both AM and FM dials, as well as satellite. "You didn't wake me. I had to get up to answer the phone anyway."

She giggled a little too hard. "I'm sorry. I should have realized—"

"What do you want, Nicole?" The last thing he wanted was another lecture on the importance of family. And from of all people, definitely not Nicole. Since she knew so little about him, what could she say?

"Sorry," she repeated. "Um, well, um, I just thought since the restaurant was closed today, and Gianna would be spending the day with her family, um..."

Spit it out already! He rolled his eyes toward the fluorescent lights in the ceiling.

As if she'd heard his unspoken demand, she blurted, "Would you like to have lunch with me today?"

"Lunch?"

"My treat," she added hastily. "I'll show you photos of houses available in the area, you'll say they're not what you're looking for, and I'll write the afternoon off as a business expense. This isn't a date, just two people using a timely opportunity to get better acquainted. Okay?"

"O-kay," he drawled, his mind scrambling to figure out her ulterior motive.

"I mean it, Kyle. I've got no hidden agenda. Gianna's my best friend and I—"

"And you always ask your best friend's employees to lunch, right?"

"You know what?" Solid steel laced her words. "Forget it. Forget I called. Go back to sleep. Enjoy your day off."

He laughed. Who knew he could push her buttons so easily? "Oh, no you don't. You made the offer. I'm accepting."

A complete reversal of his first reaction to her invitation, but why not? If he stayed inside these walls with the phone ringing every thirty seconds, he'd go insane. Even spending the afternoon with Nicole held more appeal than sitting here trying to figure out how to dig out of the muck Colette's little performance had poured on him.

"Well," she grumbled, "if you're going to be a butthead, forget I offered you anything."

A butthead? No one had ever called him that before. At least, not to his face. Oddly, he didn't take offense. Hard to argue with the truth. He was acting like a butthead.

"I'm sorry, Nicole. I woke up to a crazy morning, and I took it out on you. Lunch would be great. Thanks for the offer."

"That's better," she said. "And you're welcome. I'll pick you up at twelve-thirty. We'll go to the Inn on the Sound. They've got great food and even better water views. Okay?"

"Fine. I'll see you then." Shaking his head, he hung up. Never in his wildest dreams could he have predicted he'd have a lunch date with Nicole Fleming. What in God's name did she want from him?

Chapter Eleven

"**I** saw your sister on the news this morning."

Wow. The waiter had barely left the table after taking their orders when Nicole moved in for the kill.

"No warm-up question or introduction of the contestants? We go straight to the lightning round?" he retorted. "Let's get to the goods then. You want to know about my sister and me?"

"No." She sipped her cosmopolitan, her expression void of interest. "Not particularly."

His jaw dropped. "You don't?"

"Kyle, I haven't spoken to my mother in three years, except through lawyers. Do you care?"

"No," he parroted, right down to sipping his vodka martini. "Not particularly."

She smiled. "There. See how easy this is going to be? We already agree on stuff. As for your sister and my mother…" She waved her hand. "That's nobody's business but ours. I only care about Gianna. I want to know what's going on between you two."

The waiter appeared and placed a basket of warm rolls in the center of the table. The yeasty smell floated straight through Kyle's nostrils and into his empty stomach, eliciting a loud, rude rumble.

After one sharp look in his direction, Nicole thanked the waiter, paused until he was out of earshot, and then spoke in a hushed tone. "More importantly, I want to know about the whole bit with Gardener's and the Spalon de Soleil."

Uh-oh. He forced a confused expression. "What would I know about Gardener's and some spa?"

"Don't play innocent." She tipped her martini glass toward him. "You're not that good an actor. I know you had something to do with the sweepstakes. I want to know why."

Smooth iced vodka became drain cleaner, scraping his gut. "What makes you think I had something to do with it?"

Her grin turned mirthless as she traced the outline of her glass with a fingertip. "Because I had a reporter friend call Gardener's Public Relations Department. They know nothing about a shopping spree and makeover prize, but they confirmed this year is their one hundredth anniversary. Nice touch, made the sweepstakes concept more believable. Your idea?"

Okay, time to come clean. "The anniversary part? No."

Nicole's piercing blue eyes fixed on his face like a deer fixes on headlights. "I didn't think so. This Lucinda Barrows came up with that one, didn't she?"

What happened to the woman who hemmed and hawed her way through the invitation to lunch? In her place sat a barracuda with a keen sense of purpose, razor sharp teeth, and a finely honed tongue. And the barracuda wanted an answer. Now.

"Yes."

"So?" Folding her arms on the table, she shifted forward. "How'd you pull off this scam and why?"

"A friend owed me a favor, and I called it in."

Like a chess player pondering her next move, she stroked her chin. "Hmmm. A friend and a favor. Sounds familiar. This wouldn't be the same friend who owed you a tuxedo, would it?"

He could have sworn he heard the Jaws theme as Nicole honed in on her target. But he brushed off the weirdness as if a goldfish swam by. "What if he is?"

"Nothing." The intense focus of her gaze relaxed, and she actually smiled. "But I'd like to meet him if an opportunity arises. Must be nice to have a friend who pays his debts with tuxedos and shopping sprees."

"Look, Nicole, this really is none of your business—"

One manicured claw shot up, bracelets tinkling. "Wrong-o, reindeer. If something has to do with Gianna, it's my business. She's more than my best friend. We're like sisters. I've known her since we were five years old. Where were you when Frank told her their relationship was over by getting down on one knee in front of Gianna and her entire kindergarten class to propose to her assistant? On the golf course somewhere? In some big budget meeting?"

The shock sucked the air from his lungs. "Jesus! You mean she really didn't know 'til that moment?"

"She never suspected a thing. In fact, she anticipated he'd be proposing to her on the last day of school, in front of all 'her kids.'" Lifting her martini glass by the stem, she swirled the contents. "To say the truth came as a blow is an understatement."

"No wonder she left teaching."

Nicole slammed the glass down, clinking it against her bread plate. "She didn't leave teaching. She quit working in that school. Do you blame her? I can't imagine how she bore the humiliation until the end of June. The pitiful looks she endured every single day, the whispers behind her back, and that damn pear-shaped diamond flashing under her nose hour after hour after hour. But she refused to leave those kids before the school term ended." With forked talons, she grabbed a warm roll, shredding bits of bread with ferocity. When she spoke again, her voice was murder-soft. "So, I'll ask you again. Why did you make up this sweepstakes thing?"

Kyle imagined Frank's head sat in her hands. A massacre of crumbs littered the forest green tablecloth. Picturing his own head among the mess, he looked out the wall of windows. Directly below them sat the rocky beach, and in the far distance, sailboats scattered over the shimmering Long Island Sound. To the right, a family of swans waltzed over the water's surface, peaceful and placid. He kept his gaze on the swans until his blood pressure calmed. Then he faced an expectant Nicole.

"Well?" she prompted.

Checkmate.

"I wanted to do something nice for her. After all she did for me, I believed getting her a new look for this wedding was the least I could do."

"The least you could do," she murmured. "Okay, I can see that. I'm still not a hundred percent sure how you pulled the whole thing off, but I'll let you keep that secret for now."

Thank God. Who knew Nicole would prove such an intriguing adversary? "Good. Are we done with the interrogation now?"

"Not quite. I want to get a few things straight between us first." With the flat of her hand, she brushed crumbs into a neat sawdust pile. "You don't like me, do you?"

After all she'd dragged him through since this meal began, he had no desire to pull his punches now. She wanted honesty, he'd give her honesty. "Not particularly."

To his surprise, she laughed. "Well, guess what, pal? I like you. And Gianna likes you, too, which makes me your new best friend. So I'm going to give you a little warning."

Now, he held up a hand. "Save the speech. I've already heard Claudio's. If I hurt Gianna, he'll make me suffer. I don't need another of her protectors on the warpath."

The waiter returned with their salads, and Nicole stabbed a plump cherry tomato with her fork. Again, Kyle's imagination veered to Frank, but this time, the casualty of Nicole's anger transformed into the worm's heart.

"Gianna doesn't need protection from anyone." She swallowed the heart—er, tomato—in one gulp. "That's where the warning comes in. Everyone thinks she's a doormat because she's so generous and giving. But the exact opposite is true. Gianna Randazzo is the toughest woman I know."

Despite his intention to remain impassive, a snort of disbelief escaped his lips.

"Scoff all you want, Kyle, but I'm telling the truth. She's had a rough time the last six months. Turns out she'd built her castle on a mound of sand. But by God, she never gave anyone the satisfaction of seeing her pain." Her fingers toyed with the breadcrumbs, providing an image of sand running through an hourglass. "Think about what she had to put up with. How much guts she had, to stay in her classroom for eleven and a half weeks while Rachel prattled on and on about plans for her wedding. Do you know anyone else who would have the courage to stand up to the gossipmongers in the teacher's lounge? Would you be able to paste a smile on your face and pretend nothing was wrong if someone who claimed to love you betrayed you like that? In public?"

"Probably not—"

"I couldn't, either. But Gianna did. That's why I'm warning you. If you're not in this for the long haul, you should stay far away from her."

"Well, that's a little difficult if you expect me to play the attentive suitor at this worm's wedding, isn't it?"

"Not at all," she replied, spearing a curly lettuce leaf. "So long as you and Gianna agree your act is for appearance's sake, there'll be no problem. But this..." She paused a moment, eyes scanning the ceiling as if seeking the proper word from among the recessed brass lighting fixtures. "...This gift of yours goes beyond the realm of appearances."

"So are you going to tell her not to take advantage?"

"Hell, no! Matter of fact, since you can't tell her the truth, I'll take credit for the gesture. If she asks, I'll say I finally unloaded that two point five million dollar house on the bluffs and used the commission to buy the spa package. That is, if you don't mind."

As if he had the power to stop her. "Go right ahead. As long as she goes and Lucinda takes care of the details, I don't care what you say or do about this."

"Good. Because I'm going to make sure she doesn't chicken out." She stirred the cosmo, and then ran her tongue across the swizzle stick. "But I don't want you thinking because you threw around some influence, you'll be able to take advantage of Gianna's Texas-sized heart. That day at Madison Elementary, if her precious cherubs hadn't been there, she would have kicked Frank's and Rachel's butts all over the schoolyard. In fact, I'd bet Frank proposed to Rachel in the classroom because he knew Gianna would kill him if she could. The next guy who tries to hurt her won't be as lucky."

The more she spoke, the more Kyle found himself enjoying this side of Nicole Fleming. The thorny and righteous side. "Why do I get the feeling you never liked Frank?"

"Because I didn't," she replied with a grimace.

"Yet you like me?"

In one long gulp, she drained the last of her drink. Like a child seeking parental approval, Kyle waited, gaze never leaving her face, searching for some clue in her expression.

"I like you fine so far. But there's one other thing you should do if you want to stay in my good graces."

"Oh?" To control his trembling hands, he reached for a roll and split it open. Why did her approval matter so much? He couldn't explain the why, but accepted that he suddenly craved her good graces as if she offered water to his parched life. "What's that?"

"Call your sister and let her know you're all right."

With a pat of butter hovering in mid-air, he paused to grin. This was the nosiest town he'd ever visited. And yet, he was beginning to enjoy life in the suburbs. Sure beat the backstabbers he'd always considered his friends. Here, each person was judged on his own merits. Not on his bank account or address. Which brought him full-circle to Colette. Maybe he did owe her a phone call—not because he believed the act she'd put on for the masses this morning. No, he wanted a chance to tell her off, to point out to her that, as his only living family, she should've been first in line to help him when he needed her most.

"I'll call my sister on one condition." He didn't confide in Nicole what he planned to say to Colette when he called, though. Some things were best left confidential.

"Yeah?"

"You tell me what's going on with Gianna and a bank loan."

Nicole slid her salad plate to the side. "I don't know if I should tell you about that. If Gi wants you to know, she'll tell you."

"Oh, come on," he scoffed. "Whatever's going on isn't some great state secret. Half the customers that come into Villa Mare ask her about it."

She stayed silent for a minute while refolding her napkin over and over. At last, she sighed and picked up the martini glass again. She seemed surprised to find it empty. "Gianna wants to open a daycare center in town. She's got her eye on a property near Villa Mare—a doctor's office. Dr. Weber's retiring, and she'd like to convert his old examining rooms into classrooms."

Kyle shrugged. "So, what's so hard? She could probably make a pretty good return on her investment if she keeps costs down and tuition high."

A golden eyebrow arched as she tsked. "You don't understand her at all, do you? Gianna doesn't care about making a pretty good return—at least, not a monetary return. In fact, she wants to cater to families who can't afford to pay exorbitant tuition."

"Families like the Melendezes."

"Exactly." Nicole used her swizzle stick as a pointer aimed at his nose. "Her return on investment comes in the form of educating little minds to guarantee them a bright future. She firmly believes that the older generation has a responsibility to see the younger generation is prepared to take the reins when their time comes. The better prepared they are, the better the world will be for all of us. At least, that's how she sees it. Gi wants to help mold those young minds into great leaders. You ever see that bumper sticker that says, 'Be nice to your kids. They'll get to pick your nursing home'? It's kinda like that, but on a global scale. She's given herself a pretty ambitious dream that will take a sizeable amount of money, time, and effort."

Cupping a hand under his chin, he considered what Gianna faced. Lots of red tape, politics, and gambling. All things with which she had no experience. *He*, on the other hand, thrived on the chase, the challenge, and the small victories that resulted in winning the war over financial adversaries.

Maybe he should offer to help Gianna with this negotiation. "So, this daycare center is Gianna's Aegean stables."

Nicole did a double-take. "Huh?"

He sighed. "The phrase comes from Greek mythology. One of Hercules's great labors was to clean out the Aegean stables. They housed three thousand oxen for ten years with no one ever mucking out the stalls. Comparing something to the Aegean stables is like saying it's almost impossible."

"Uh-huh." Nicole cocked her head like a quizzical bird. "Is there a reason you need to rub your Ivy League education in my face?"

Something to reconsider: Nicole's thorny, righteous side got old fast.

"Touché," he replied with a mock salute.

"You just can't help yourself, can you?" With her swizzle stick baton, she waved off any apology he might have attempted. "Whatever. Now you know why I think she's got guts. Our Gianna's like Hercules, taking on the tasks no one else wants."

"So maybe she needs some help to succeed."

Nicole held up a hand. "Stay in your lane, bucko. The shopping spree and wedding date is enough from you. Another thing about Gianna you need to know. People can warm up to her fast. She's fun and witty and kind and generous. You know how I met her? We were in kindergarten. As I was leaving for the bus stop, Mom handed me my lunch and said when I got home, Daddy would be gone and wouldn't be coming back. That's how I found out my parents were getting divorced. At recess, I sat by myself under the slide on the playground. Gianna found me there and sat beside me. Never asked for details. She just knew I needed a friend, and she became that friend. After school that day, she took me home with her, brought me to Villa Mare. Her family became a sanctuary for me. Gi is, and has always been, deep down good. So, again, if you're not in this game for the long haul, don't get in any deeper. I would hate to have to kill you."

JOHN F. KENNEDY INTERNATIONAL Airport sat directly on Jamaica Bay in Brooklyn. The trip from Setquott Beach meant a ninety-minute drive for Gianna, but she looked forward to the long car ride. Enforced solitude allowed her time to think about where her life headed and what she could do to stop the downward spiral. As of yesterday, she no longer worked at Villa Mare. She couldn't live with the knowledge Mom and Dad supported her while her teaching degree went unused.

Thank goodness for Mrs. Melendez. She'd called earlier that morning to say CompTech had offered her a job. Beginning Monday, she'd require Gianna's services to watch her three little ones from seven in the morning until about five at night. Gianna was thrilled at her new employer's good fortune. Although the salary wasn't terrific for an entry-level position, the job would provide Mrs. Melendez with health insurance, a steady income, and the measure of pride her ex-husband's abandonment had stolen over a year ago.

Impotent anger made Gianna grip the steering wheel until her knuckles whitened. Why did men always run out when things got rough? Why did they think a better life waited just around the corner? A life apart from the women who supported and nurtured them, then found themselves discarded when their usefulness or good looks diminished? Or were women blinded by an all-consuming need to belong to someone? Anyone?

She nearly shouted her frustration, but bit her tongue. From an early age, females were taught they could have everything in life if they'd simply strive to acquire it all. And "everything" included a family. But despite what ardent feminists might proclaim to the contrary, a family, to most women, meant beginning with a husband. So the vicious cycle began. A boatload of single women fishing for Mr. Right in shark-infested waters, each hesitating to throw less-than-keeper-material back for fear of winding up alone.

God, what a depressing thought! Put on some music. You need something to take your mind off your morose opinions. She loosened her hold on the leather-covered wheel, flexed her fingers to get the blood circulating, and then flipped on the radio, scanning channels until she found the latest female empowerment pop tune to sing at the top of her lungs.

Nicole was right. She couldn't give up. She'd take a night job, work as a cashier in the local supermarket, if she had to. Whatever she had to do to get her childcare center up and running. She'd have to wait longer to achieve her dream, but she'd already waited ten years. What was another year or two? Sometimes in life, the harder things were to accomplish, the more you appreciated once you attained them. Her daycare center would be no exception.

Stuck in the usual traffic on the Belt Parkway, she glanced at the car in the center lane. In the back seat sat a young boy wearing a cowboy outfit. The thought struck her like a poisoned dart. Tomorrow was Halloween. At Madison Elementary, today would be the annual holiday celebration. The children would bring their costumes to school and change into them right after attendance was taken. Since the sun shone brightly today, the kindergarten classes would hold a parade outdoors. Four times around the bus circle near the front entrance while proud parents snapped photo after photo of their precious darlings dressed up as fairy princesses, monsters, or popular comic book heroes. What she wouldn't give to be there now!

The sigh that escaped her lips heaved frustration into the air around her, fogging up a small portion of the windshield. Still, she refused to give in to self-pity. Think positively.

When—not if, but *when*—her facility was established, she'd hold the very same type of celebration for her little ones. When she found the right building, one with a plot of land, she might even grow pumpkins, and let the children pick one for each class to decorate.

Another reason to want Dr. Weber's old office with the little garden and an arched gateway in the back. But, no. Best to stop thinking about Dr. Weber's place. She was unlikely to find the funds to lease the space before a stupid bagel shop or coffee franchise moved in. As if Setquott Beach needed another of those...

The boy in the car suddenly stuck out his tongue. God, all this time he must've thought she was staring at him! Screwing her face into a silly expression, she stuck out her tongue. His little body convulsed into such a fit of squirming giggles his car seat barely kept him restrained. The imagined sound of his laughter brought the first smile of her day.

Please stay sweet, she silently implored the impish face in the back seat. Don't grow up to be one of those men always seeking the new and improved version…

GIANNA WAS SUPPOSED to meet her parents outside of baggage claim. While various suitcases and packages revolved slowly around three active carousels, she scanned the throngs for a familiar face. One by one, hands and heads leaned over the conveyer belt to retrieve a piece of luggage, and then disappeared into the sea of nameless arrivals. Fifteen minutes passed. Still she saw no sign of Mom and Dad. Could she have the wrong flight information? She glanced at the scrap of paper in her hand and at the LCD display on the back wall. No. Right airline, right flight number, right arrival time. So where were they?

Maybe they missed the flight?

Ha! Not Mom, the self-proclaimed Queen of Punctuality. Because their flight left Rome at six a.m., Mom probably insisted she and Dad arrive at the airport no later than eleven the night before. A long-standing joke in the Randazzo family was to bring something to keep you occupied when you had an appointment. If she could, Mom would get you to your destination a full day ahead of schedule.

Thinking of her parents, she relaxed until a firm hand clamped down on her shoulder. "What's a pretty thing like you doing in a place like this?"

With a gasp she whirled to stare up into a pair of deep brown eyes. His bronzed face split into a proud grin, and every frazzled nerve crackling in her spine quieted. "Trolling for senior citizens to lure out to the boondocks with me."

"So how about a hug for your old man to show him how much you missed him?"

"I did miss you!" She flung her arms around his neck and squeezed with all her might. "Welcome home, Dad! Where's Mom?"

After retaliating with a hug tight enough to leave her breathless, her father stepped back and shrugged. "You know your mother. She made friends with another couple on the flight home. Now they're exchanging phone numbers and email addresses over there." He pointed to a row of hard plastic seats a few yards away.

Sure enough, there was her mother, sporting a fresh tan. And a new hairstyle. Amazing. Some brave hairdresser in Italy had risked life and limb to tame Mom's unruly black curls into a chin-length bob, giving her face a pixie-like appearance that perfectly matched her tiny stature. She wore a new outfit. A tailored white jacket and slacks—imagine, Mom in slacks—with a sapphire silk blouse. She looked like a completely different woman than the mother Gianna had known since birth.

As a matter of fact, the only familiar features she recognized were the slender hands. As she spoke to an orange-haired woman and bald man, Mom let her hands fly to emphasize.

Gianna guessed the couple to be in their mid-to-late-sixties. In contrast, Mom looked decades younger than her fifty-five years. Good genes, Mom replied whenever someone remarked upon her youthful appearance. All the Maldonado women have them, and despite her marriage to Dad, Mom was a Maldonado woman, through and through.

"C'mon." Dad sighed as he grabbed her elbow. "She knows you're here. You may as well get the torture over."

Queasiness always assailed Gianna when Mom interfered in her dating life, or lack thereof. Today would prove no exception. While nausea bulleted up her throat, she dug in her heels. "No. I can't."

"Of course you can. She's been bragging about you since Portofino. You can't cheat her of the opportunity to show off her bright, beautiful daughter."

"Her bright, beautiful, *single* daughter," she corrected. "I bet she'll mention the lack of grandchildren again."

"She'll mention the lack of grandchildren whether you're there or not. But if you start to get in over your head, I'll steer the conversation into safer waters before you drown. Deal?"

Good old Daddy, always on her side.

"Deal." She linked her arm through his. "Meanwhile, tell me all about the trip. Don't leave anything out. I want to know everything you saw, everything you did. Tell me about the prettiest place in the whole country, the best food, the nicest hotel accommodations—all of it!"

"We have the ride home to discuss the trip. And your mom will want to give her opinions on the subject anyway. Why don't you tell me about our newest employee instead? Kyle, was it?"

Unable to lie to him, she looked away before Dad's sharp gaze could notice. "Mmm-hmm. Kyle Hayden."

"Where'd you meet him?"

"At the restaurant," she replied.

"Oh? Did you post a help wanted sign in the window?"

Her focus remained on the blue uniform of a security guard standing nearby. Her father would kill her if he knew the truth. "No, I found him through sheer luck. He happened to show up looking for a job when we were in need of an employee."

"Divine providence, eh? Well, good. I'm looking forward to meeting him."

Her mother's screech of, "There she is!" saved Gianna from continuing their conversation. But at what cost? Taking a deep breath, she stepped into the lioness's den. "Gianna, sweetheart, how are you?"

"Hi, Mom." She embraced her mother with a slight hesitancy. Someone famous had once said mothers and daughters didn't get along because they competed for male affection. In Gianna's case, the distance came more from competing for dating independence. "Welcome home. How was the trip?"

"Later, Gi, later. First, I'd like you to meet Hal and Mavis Nestor. They're from Astoria. Hal, Mavis, this is my daughter, Gianna. The teacher."

Gianna smiled and shook hands with the couple. "Hello, nice to meet you."

"Pleasure," Hal said.

"So, Lucia tells us you're not married," Mavis greeted her.

Wow! Five seconds. A new Lucia Randazzo record!

"Hal and Mavis have a son," Mom hinted with the subtlety of a tractor trailer's air horn. "He's single, thirty, and manages a software company in Queens."

Could she possibly rewind the last few minutes and hide in the crowd around the baggage carousel? Maybe she could climb onto one of those conveyor belts and stow away on the plane. Take a flight to someplace safe, like Rome or Milan or the front lines of combat.

"I've given Mavis your telephone number so her Robbie can give you a call," her mother persisted. "Who knows? Maybe you two will hit it off."

"Mom," she whispered through gritted teeth, "please."

Mom's doe eyes widened in feigned innocence. "What? Would it hurt to meet him?"

"I'm not looking to meet anyone right now."

"But that's what makes this perfect! Haven't I always told you 'when you're not looking for your Prince Charming, he'll appear?' And," she added in a low whisper, "even if he isn't Prince Charming, he might have a friend who is."

Could the floorboards open up and swallow her whole? Please? "Yes, but—"

While the floorboards refused to cooperate, Dad took on the hero role. "Lucia, *cara*, we really should get going. We've a long drive ahead of us."

"Oh, all right. Mavis, I'll be in touch, and we'll set something up soon."

"Safe home, Lucia," Mavis replied.

Relief poured into Gianna's veins as her mother turned toward the airport's exit. "Nice to have met you," she managed to say to the Nestors as she followed her parents on trembling legs. She'd just dodged a bullet. But the barrage didn't end because the Nestors and their "single, thirty-year-old, software company-managing son, Robbie" were out of sight.

"Honestly, Gianna," her mother said as they walked to short term parking. "You could have been friendlier to the Nestors. What will they tell their son about you?"

"I really don't care what they tell their son, Mom. I'm capable of finding my own dates."

"Since when?"

She dropped a step behind her mother before rolling her eyes. The last thing she needed now was a, "Don't give me that look," lecture.

"Speaking of dates," Dad the Hero bravely stepped into the fray, "what happened with Frank's wedding? Are you going?"

The subject should have depressed her even more, but oddly, knowing she had Kyle to accompany her lightened her mood considerably. The heat returned to her cheeks full-force. "As a matter of fact, yes. I'm going with Kyle."

"Kyle?" Mom's interest piqued. A sculpted eyebrow arched in Gianna's direction, and when she spoke again, newfound hope tinged her voice with softness. "Our new employee, Kyle?"

"Yes, that's him."

"You know, Claudio says he's working out nicely. And if you're also dating him..." Mom stroked her chin. "Maybe you can find a man on your own after all..."

Yeah, sure. So long as you don't ask where.

Chapter Twelve

Gianna, with Nicole in tow, climbed out of the taxi in front of Gardener LeClair's mansard-style building on Fifth Avenue. Beautifully festooned windows flanked the main entrance. Behind a sheet of glass, mannequins dripped colorful gowns, scarves, and feathers from their slender forms. Peacocks in full regalia scattered around expensive Italian shoes in a rainforest background. A sci-fi motif, complete with a platinum robot wearing a diamond-encrusted bra and matching panties decorated another. Smaller windows revealed displays of delicate porcelain vases and carved figurines bedecked in red or black velvet.

Gianna took a shaky breath. A wisp of vapor escaped her lips, melding with the cool morning air to form a silver stream. Shivers gripped her shoulders, but from nervousness or cold, she couldn't guess.

A tall, whip-thin blonde stepped out of the store, ignoring the uniformed doormen standing sentry on either side. Calculating blue eyes focused on Gianna. An urge to dive back into the safety of the taxi overwhelmed her, but Nicole must have sensed her growing apprehension and clutched her elbow to keep her pinned to the pavement.

"Ms. Randazzo?" She recognized the twangy voice from the telephone call two weeks ago.

"Y-yes. I-I'm Gianna Randazzo."

"I thought so. I'm very pleased to meet you," the ice princess said, offering her hand. "I'm Lucinda Barrows. Welcome to Gardener's."

"Thank you." After shaking the outstretched hand, she gestured to Nicole. "I hope you don't mind. I brought a friend."

"Of course, I don't mind." Lucinda Barrows extended a hand toward Nicole. "I'm Lucinda Barrows. And you are?"

"Nicole Fleming." A toss of thick, golden hair communicated the not-so-subtle message, Back off. I don't need your help like this pathetic schlub does.

Lucinda Barrows must have caught the gist of Nicole's message because she gave a one-shoulder shrug, and then returned her attention to Gianna. "Well, Ms. Randazzo, Ms. Fleming, shall we go inside and begin our day?" Without waiting for a reply, Ms. Barrows swept into the building.

Gianna followed with Nicole at her side, two lost sheep in Eden. What the hell was she doing? She didn't belong in this place. Gardener's catered to the upper crust Central Park West crowd. Not to some Long Island pretender who wanted to show up a rival. Prices on the goods in this store went beyond exorbitant to border on ridiculous. Without the sweepstakes prize she'd received, she couldn't afford a soft drink in the restaurant here.

With her legs trembling, she barely made her way past the doormen.

Then a saleswoman stepped into her path, a crystal flacon in hand. "Care to try Golden Fields? A new signature fragrance by—"

"Not now, Angelique." Ms. Barrows waved off the saleswoman. "These ladies are with me." Ms. Barrows's squarish high heels click-clacked over the polished floor in direct rhythm to the beating of Gianna's heart. Rapid, puncturing sounds echoed in the relative quiet of both cavernous spaces.

"I swear to God, she's got the nose of an anteater," Nicole whispered.

Despite her growing apprehension, Gianna snickered. Bringing Nicole, something she'd hesitated to do, had actually been a smart move. Nicole's fun and familiar presence provided a buffer from Ms. Barrows's frosty façade.

"Where shall we start?" Ms. Barrows turned to ask. "Are you looking for an entire day-to-day collection? From the skin out? Shall we begin with lingerie?"

"What I really want," she said hesitantly, "is one stunning outfit. I have a wedding to attend this evening, and I want to..." *God, this sounds so stupid.* "I want to outshine the bride."

"The groom never bothered to tell Gianna he was two-timing her," Nicole added.

Gianna shot her friend an "I-can't-believe-you-told-her" look, but Nicole's return expression communicated, "What? It's the truth, isn't it?"

Where's a black hole when you need one?

A smile cracked through Ms. Barrows's frozen face, giving her a human mien. "Ah, I know exactly what you're saying. I had a similar situation a few years back. The heartless snake I was dating turned out to be married. I found out when his wife invited me to his surprise thirty-fifth birthday party. She found my name in his address book under 'Lou.' Thought I was a golfing buddy."

"Nice," Nicole remarked dryly.

"Mmm," Ms. Barrows replied. "I only wish I'd had the nerve to attend and watch the cretin squirm all night. So for you, Ms. Randazzo, who does have the nerve, we'll begin in the Artisan department on the fourth floor. After you've found the proper dress, we'll shop for foundation garments and accessories. Come along."

Nerve? Yeah, attempting to outshine the bride required a lot of nerve. As well as the maturity level of a preschooler. Seriously reconsidering her sanity, Gianna remained rooted to the floor.

One sharp elbow jab, and Nicole nudged her forward. "Stop looking like you're on your way to an execution. This is supposed to be fun. Remember?"

"Yeah, right. Fun." Instead of this shopping spree, she should've scheduled a CT scan. Over the last month, her brain had gone on the fritz. And today, she'd taken Nicole along for the ride. Guilt overwhelmed her, and she turned to her best friend. "You sure you don't want this prize?"

"No way. This is your day, Gi. Your day and your night. I'm only here to make sure you don't chicken out."

She quirked a brow. "Am I that obvious?"

"To me you are."

Suspicion crept up Gianna's spine. "You paid for all of this, didn't you? There is no sweepstakes or anniversary or anything."

Blue mascaraed lashes fluttered innocently against candy box cheeks. "Would you care either way?"

Would she? Well...sort of. "You know I can't pay you back."

"Who asked for payback?"

"No one, but—"

"Then stop arguing. Accept you've been given a fantastic gift, and leave it at that. Okay?"

Gaze pinned to her feet, Gianna sighed. "You'll never tell, will you?"

"Nope."

A little foot shuffle. "Then I guess I'll have to drop the subject."

"Yup."

"Come along, you two!" Ms. Barrows stood before the escalator, arms folded over her chest and the toes of one foot tapping impatiently against the tile floor. "We have a great deal to do. Let's not dilly-dally." At the woman's disapproving tone, visions of junior high school wafted through Gianna's memory. "Doesn't she remind you of our eighth grade math teacher, Mrs. Farris?"

"I was just thinking the same thing," Nicole replied with a snort. "Come on. Let's not give her a reason to keep us after school."

The fourth floor was a designer's wonderland. The moment Gianna stepped off the escalator, another woman appeared by her side.

But this time, Ms. Barrows did not wave her away. "Renee, Ms. Randazzo is looking for a dress for an evening wedding. Something chic, yet elegant." She tilted her head toward Gianna, enhancing the anteater look when a shadow fell across her sharp nose. "Where is the wedding to take place?"

"At the Crystal Palace in Sea Cove Harbor."

Ms. Barrows nodded, her brow etched in thought. "Something vivid then. That's to our advantage since, with your coloring, jewel tones work best. Sapphire, ruby, emerald."

"Her figure seems perfect for Karesse," the woman named Renee chimed in as she walked around Gianna in a perfect circle, eyeing her up and down.

"Yes, I believe you're right," Ms. Barrows said, appraising her in the same clinical manner. "We'll start with our Karesse line and move on from there. By the time we're finished, Ms. Randazzo, you'll outshine every bride from here to San Diego."

HOURS LATER, SUPPLE fingers soothed the tension from Gianna's neck and shoulders with skillful grace. A warm towel covered her bare body from waist to knees while grapefruit-scented oil soaked into her pores. God, this treatment was heavenly! No wonder women made regular appointments at spas and salons. The tension of the last few weeks—the anxiety about tonight, the frustration over the daycare center—all melted away as she gave herself over to Sonja's experienced hands.

"So you haven't seen Kyle in over a week?"

Nicole's question shook her from the sun-covered citrus grove where her mind played. Brow furrowed, she turned to Nicole who reclined on the adjoining table, receiving similar treatment. "No. Not since Mom and Dad came home. But we spoke on the phone yesterday. Why?"

"No reason," Nicole replied. "I'm just curious. You like him, don't you?"

"Of course I like him." She frowned. "I wouldn't be going with him tonight if I didn't like him."

"That's not what I mean, and you know it. I mean, you *like* him-like him. Don't try to deny it. Every time someone mentions his name your cheeks turn all pink." Nicole pointed at her face. "Just like that."

"I don't know what you're talking about."

"Bull."

Okay, so maybe her face got a little warm and she had trouble remembering her name when he was around. That didn't mean she liked him-liked him. For all she knew, she had some kind of allergic reaction to him, to his cologne, or his toothpaste.

Oh, who was she kidding? Still, barely able to admit her feelings to herself, she was hardly ready to admit anything to Nicole.

"You know what?" she said instead. "If you want to enjoy the rest of the massage my prize money is paying for, you'll change the subject. Otherwise I'll go back to Gardener's and ring up five hundred dollars' worth of shoes."

One pair ought to fill the bill. Hell, with the prices she'd seen, she'd be lucky to get one *shoe* for five hundred dollars.

"Okay," Nicole said on a sigh. "But I'm gonna say one more thing first. I like him, too, Gi."

"Good for you." Gianna feigned nonchalance, but inside, her stomach clenched.

How exactly did Nicole like him? Did she like him-like him? Or was Nicole simply offering her approval if Gianna decided to pursue him? Not, of course, that she would. Just because she liked him didn't mean she liked him-liked him.

"God, I wish I were going tonight." Nicole's wistful tone prickled her bare flesh. "You have to promise to tell me every detail first thing tomorrow morning. Before you tell anyone else."

The masseuse hit a tender spot in her neck, and she groaned. "I will, I promise."

"You'd better."

"I said I would. Now would you please drop the subject?" The words came out a little too terse, but Gianna wouldn't apologize. What did Nicole want anyway? A blood oath?

Nicole sucked a breath through her teeth. "Ooh, touchy, aren't we?"

"I'm not touchy."

"I understand. You're probably terrified. You haven't seen Frank or Rachel since the last day of school, and tonight, well, you're gonna have to confront them both. But no matter how blind Frank's been over the last few months, he's gonna have second thoughts when he spots you in that dress. He'll take one look at you and regret ever getting involved with Rachel."

Reminders of tonight sent butterflies scattering in Gianna's belly. Great. Now she had a pain in the neck from Sonja and an upset stomach, thanks to Nicole. With her luck, she'd take one look at Frank tonight and vomit all over his shiny tux.

Would that be a good thing or bad? Sonja's palms pressed into her spine from neck to the hollow of her back. A sudden heat traveled down her body and through her limbs. Not uncomfortable. More like a hot bath after a long day. Soothing and thoroughly ah-inspiring.

"All done," Sonja announced as she stepped away from the table.

"What time is Kyle picking you up?" Nicole's question splashed ice water in her face. "He *is* picking you up, isn't he? You're going to let him drive, right? God, there's nothing more embarrassing to a man than being in the passenger seat when a woman drives. Don't ask me why."

Propping her head on one hand prevented Nicole from seeing her eyes roll back. "I told him to be at the house by seven. The ceremony's at eight, reception immediately following in the same location. I had Dad drive my car today so I don't have to pick Kyle up. Satisfied? Did I miss anything?"

With her massage ended, Nicole rolled over, purring, "Even if you did, you won't have time to fix your boo-boo now."

"Gee, thanks. You sure know how to make a friend feel better."

"What can I say?" she replied with a giggle. "It's a gift."

"Well, I'd prefer you kept that particular gift to yourself from now on," Gianna grumbled over the butterflies wreaking havoc.

Chapter Thirteen

Any doubts Gianna had about her appearance disappeared the moment Kyle saw her. He stared, face drawn and mouth agape, for ten long seconds—she knew, she counted—then extended a hand as if touching a faraway constellation. The trip to Gardener's and all the ministrations had paid off.

Strapless gold brocade hugged her bosom and waist before cascading outwards with the help of a generous black tulle underskirt. Bare shoulders, dusted with gold powder, sparkled. Thanks to two hours in Jean de Viv's chair, her long hair now lay in thick ribbons of curls. Tiny golden stars pinned each tress to her head. Miniscule gemstones embedded in the center of each star, Jean had advised, would twinkle beneath the chandeliers inside the Crystal Palace, giving her a celestial appearance.

While she floated to where Kyle stood waiting, his gaze followed every move, never blinking, never turning away. Their hands made contact, and an electrical charge tingled from her fingertips to her wrist.

"I feel like a kid on prom night," she confessed.

"You look like a goddess." His voice was a husky whisper, thick and enveloping. "Any man who would willingly walk away from you is a fool."

New heat spiraled into her cheeks, and she waved a hand to cool the air. Her face had already been rouged enough. The last thing she needed was her own bloodstream adding additional color.

"You look good enough to grace the cover of a magazine," she said. If she felt like Cinderella on her way to the ball, Kyle definitely fit the role of Prince Charming in his black tuxedo, black tie, and white dress shirt. With this gorgeous man by her side, she could take on the world and come out on top. "Are you sure that's a rented tux?"

"*Borrowed*," he corrected with a grin that curled her toes. "Not rented."

God, would she ever get used to his smile? Or the way her heart pounded when he stood so close?

"Hard to believe." Did he hear the way her voice shook? "I mean, this tux could have been made just for you. You and your friend must be built to exactly the same proportions. Are you twins or something?"

He didn't reply, but folded her hand over his elbow instead. "Shall we go?"

"I'm..." The words stuck in her throat. She was nowhere near ready. Probably never be ready to play her part in this farce. Why couldn't they stay here, skip the wedding, try to make tonight into a real date and not some mock fix-up for appearance's sake? Go to the local diner for a burger and fries?

To buy a little extra time, she changed the subject. "You know, you haven't told me. How do you like working at Villa Mare with my parents?"

With an exaggerated groan, he grimaced. "You might have warned me your mother is the Grand Dame there."

Despite her teetering nerves, she giggled. "Everyone thinks Dad is the tough one because he's tall and burly when the truth is, he's a big pussycat. Now, Mom, on the other hand..." She sobered. "Daddy always says she looks soft and fluffy as a cloud, but cross her and you're in the middle of a hurricane."

His finger traced the inside of her palm in a slow, lazy fashion. The simple action sent skitters of electricity straight from her hand to the center of her heart. "You've got a lot of your mother in you, Gianna. Remember that tonight."

WHEN GIANNA AND KYLE walked into the Seashell Suite at the Crystal Palace, most of the guests already sat in a small alcove of the flower-bedecked room. Before the ceremony started, she and Kyle quickly sat in the back. Heads turned, and hands rose to hide hushed whispers. Discomfort wilted her until Kyle gave her hand a reassuring squeeze.

"Don't let 'em throw you," he whispered behind his smile. "Think of your Hurricane Mama. Show them your stormy side."

With his words bolstering her reserve, she sat up straight and completely at ease. "You're right. What do I care what they think? My presence here makes a statement. I survived the debacle they threw my way. And now, I'm stronger than ever."

The guests returned to their own conversations. All too soon, the groom and best man took their places at the front of the alcove before a large picture window festooned in arches of colorful autumn leaves. Piped-in music played "Here Comes the Bride" as Rachel, wrapped in a white sheath-style gown, her face hidden behind a fingertip-length veil, made her way to the altar with her father by her side.

"That's the famous Rachel?" Kyle asked, aghast. "She looks like a mummy in that get-up."

Gianna's lips quirked, but her amusement faded quickly. Frank's face alit with adoration at Rachel's approach, and self-pity stung like a thousand bees. Once again, Kyle's hand gave hers a squeeze. The pressure of his fingers filled her with a placidity she didn't know she owned. Having Kyle by her side lightened her gray mood to sunny yellow. Even when the couple spoke their vows, a moment she'd dreaded, his presence helped her to remain unruffled.

The ceremony ended, and the bride and groom walked down the aisle together, faces beaming with joy. As if on cue, the guests rose to form a receiving line at the back of the room. With Kyle behind her, she joined them. Since their seats had been in the rear, they found themselves in the front of the line. She couldn't have planned the moment better if she'd tried.

"Gianna?" The name erupted from Frank's mouth in a croak.

Rachel turned, a crocodile grin on her features. But her toothy satisfaction evaporated as her gaze skimmed Gianna from up-do to gold-dusted shoulders, all the way to the hem of the expensive designer dress. A deep frown and a slightly purple color blotched her normally flawless complexion. Gianna savored the moment as she would a sip of the world's finest Champagne. Without saying a word, she had rendered Rachel speechless—no small feat.

"Congratulations, Frank, Rachel," she said, leaning to place a kiss on each of their cheeks. She felt a bit like Judas, but tamped down her guilt with a quick press of golden-polished fingernails into palms. "I hope you'll be very happy together."

In that moment, she realized she meant what she said. These two deserved one another. And she was well rid of both of them.

"We're so glad you could attend our wedding, Gianna," Rachel purred. "We haven't seen you since you left Madison Elementary in June. The children wondered why you didn't return in September. I told them, of course, you had decided to leave teaching. I hope you don't mind."

Point, Rachel. Like a poisonous snake, she knew where to inflict the most damage. Well, Gianna refused to play the role of victim ever again. With Kyle beside her, she stood tall enough to look down on the smug face of the bride.

"Actually I do mind," she replied in a strong voice. "In the first place, I didn't ask you to speak to anyone on my behalf. And in the second place, your information lacks substance. I haven't left teaching."

"Oh?" Frank wrapped an arm around Rachel's waist, showing stalwart support for his wife. "You're working somewhere? Last I heard you'd gone back to the family pizzeria." He sneered the last two words, as if her family's lifetime business was worthy of derision.

An overwhelming urge to smack his face rose within her. What was this, tag-team insults? Terrific. No problem. She was armed and dangerous.

"That was only temporary. To help out while they were away. Joey and I sent them to Italy for their thirtieth anniversary. Don't you remember, Frank?" Her tone took on the sweetness of pure maple syrup. "You were with me when I made the arrangements with the travel agent."

Rachel's face changed from florid purple to beet-red. *Point, me.*

But she quickly recovered and volleyed back. "I assume you got the approvals for the daycare center you wanted to start? How exciting for you. When does the center open? And where on earth did you get that kind of cash?" She laughed, a sound full of malice and spite, and then placed her head on Frank's shoulder, suggesting ownership. "Don't tell me you won the lottery. Lucky Gianna. Just like those cats you rescue, always landing on your feet."

Pain seared her ribcage. Her daycare center. The mortal wound. The one dream she hadn't been able to make come true. Smelling blood in the water, Rachel had honed in for the kill. *Surrender. Admit defeat and move on.* "Actually, I—"

"*We* haven't completed the renovations yet," Kyle interrupted. "Isn't that right, darling?"

"Y-yes, of course," she managed, but she stared at Kyle's grinning face with wonder. How had he known?

"Forgive me," he said to Frank and Rachel, hand outstretched. "We haven't been properly introduced. Kyle Hayden. Congratulations on the occasion of your marriage."

"Thank you," Frank mumbled, confusion swinging from Kyle's face to Gianna's and back again. No doubt her own surprise mirrored back.

"Sweetheart," Kyle said to Gianna, his voice husky with promised sensuality. "We're holding up the line of well-wishers. Perhaps we should find our table."

Despite feeling adrift, she forced a carefree smile. "Yes, I think you're right, honey." His warm hand against the small of her back led her away from slack-jawed Frank and his equally stunned bride. Out of their earshot, she leaned closer to Kyle. "Thank you."

"That's what I'm here for, remember? To steer you through the rocky parts."

Knees knocking, she paused in the reception area beneath a rose-filled bower. "But how did you know about the daycare center?"

In an almost careless gesture, he shrugged. "Nicole told me."

"She did?" Gianna couldn't mask her surprise. When did he and Nicole have an opportunity to discuss her daycare? She scraped her memory for any specific conversation between them and came up empty. "What exactly did she tell you?"

"That Dr. Weber's old office had a perfect location and examining rooms that could be converted into classrooms fairly easily," he replied. "She also said you couldn't afford the place, but you were hoping to get some kind of grant from the state since the center would be for lower income families. But first you needed a bank loan to start construction."

The accuracy of his knowledge unnerved her, spilling her confidence onto the floor, leaving her a fragile shell. "Wh-when did Nicole tell you all this?"

"Last week. When you picked up your parents at the airport, Nicole treated me to lunch at the Inn on the Sound."

The Inn on the Sound, one of the most romantic restaurants on all of Long Island. Nicole sure could pick 'em. Something slithered into her belly, the green-eyed monster. "Funny. Nicole never mentioned your lunch date."

Neither had he, come to think of it, until now.

Kyle's expression remained impassive, and she gulped several breaths to remove the jealousy monster. She didn't own exclusive rights to him. They were friends, nothing more. And if he and Nicole hit it off, well, good. Nicole deserved some happiness in her love life, considering her mother's serial marriage record. Besides, Nicole and Kyle would make a perfect couple. Candy-box Nicole who never took anything seriously and oh, so proper Kyle who took everything too seriously. They'd balance each other out. Like Bethany said, opposites attract.

Still, she would have appreciated a heads-up regarding their romantic interests. Was this why Nicole had badgered her all day about whether Gianna liked him-liked him? Because she wanted Kyle for herself?

All Nicole had to do was say so and she'd back off. That was the first rule of BFFs: Best friends didn't bushwhack one another.

"You know, it wouldn't be difficult to do." Kyle's smooth voice broke into her troubled thoughts.

"Huh?" It? What it? Someone should throw her a life preserver before she drowned in confusion. "What's that?"

"If you want to fund a daycare center, all you have to do is hit up the right people for generous donations."

"Uh-huh." Acid laced her tongue, dripping from each word. "And who are these 'right people?' Mrs. Melendez, who can barely make ends meet on the pittance she earns every week? The ROMEOs who scrape by on Social Security and whatever IRA money they squirreled away? Or Bethany and her gaggle of friends who spend every spare dime they have on video games, pizza, and beer?"

"No, I mean wealthy people. Influential people."

"Yes, well, I don't know any wealthy people." Not even anyone attending this lavish affair. Regardless of what they flashed in glitz and glamour, no one here had the kind of money she needed. Or even knew anyone who did.

"I do."

"You?" Bitter laughter erupted.

He shrugged. "I still have contacts in my old world."

Oh, sure. Tell me another one. "You couldn't find a person to give you a place to live when you were about to become homeless. What makes you think you can get any of your so-called friends to pry open their wallets for a bunch of dirty-faced, snot-nosed brats on Long Island?"

"Because, unlike helping out an acquaintance, helping out a bunch of dirty-faced, snot-nosed brats on Long Island is tax deductible."

Her jaw fell. He had a point. Maybe she was being unfair. And maybe, just maybe, she was taking out her frustrations on the wrong man. But aside from a slight tightening around his mouth, Kyle gave no indication her comment fazed him. He must have known she was insulting him with the "snot-nosed brat" bit, yet he had the grace to take her verbal slap in stride. She stared at the floor, seeking a vortex to suck her into another dimension.

"I'm sorry," she mumbled at last. "I shouldn't have said that."

"Forget it. Besides, you're right. If someone approached me about a daycare center a few months ago, I'd say exactly what you expected. But I know better now."

"Oh? Why?"

His fingertips grazed the underside of her chin, and he tilted her head to meet his burning gaze. Trapped. His eyes held her as firmly as if cement encased her from the calves down. When his index finger drew a lazy line from her chin to her ear, her lips instinctively parted to draw his exhaled breath into her own mouth.

"Because an incredibly magnanimous woman showed me the error of my ways. And I want to pay back her generosity."

Screeeeech! In zero-point-two seconds flat, her interior engine went from revved to stone cold dead. He was so solicitous because he wanted to "pay her back?" Or worse, did Nicole have to convince him?

"I appreciate the offer," she said, jerking her chin from his grip. "But I have to take care of this on my own."

"Why?"

A chasm opened between them. In two backward steps, she widened the gap. "Because my problems are no one else's business."

He folded his arms over his chest and lowered his voice to a whisper more dangerous than a shout. "You know, Gianna, I've noticed something. You go out of your way to help everybody you know—hell, even people you don't know. But the minute someone tries to help you, or even makes the offer, you bolt in the opposite direction."

"I do not!"

"Yes, you do. I've seen you pull away from Mrs. Melendez, from Nicole, from Tony Garibaldi. Now me. Why don't you accept the fact you're not Superwoman and admit you might need a little help every once in a while?"

His words stung, and she sucked in a breath. "Because I don't need help. And even if I did, I doubt you'd know how to help me. Who set you up to be my caretaker? To make judgments on what I do with my life? You don't know anything about me."

"I know you're trying to do something noble. Is it stubborn pride that makes you turn down every offer of assistance?" His forehead pleated. "Or maybe you get some perverse satisfaction out of being the Queen of Beneficence. Maybe you think yourself above the rest of us mortals, like some Superwoman—too good to need the help of lowly creatures who aren't fit to be a part of your self-sacrificing existence."

Hurt stole the volume from her voice, but not the indignation. "How dare you! That's not true at all. How could you even say such a thing? I've never been anything but nice to you—"

"Why was that, anyway?" Stance resembling an attorney on cross-examination, he leaned closer. "And don't give me some crap about a stray cat. Why did I matter to you? Anyone else would have left me in the garbage. But not the perfect Gianna Randazzo. Not the Mother Teresa of Setquott Beach."

Each word pinged with the sharpness of a BB shot. "Is that what you think of me? I'm some frustrated martyr or something?"

"No." He sighed, sending the bad humors scattering with his expulsion of air.

The wave of some invisible magic wand relaxed his posture and smoothed the tight lines around his lips. In the blink of an eye, he transformed into the Kyle she'd brought with her, leaving the self-righteous, angry preacher behind.

"No," he repeated. "Look, I'm sorry. I didn't mean what I said. I think we're both uptight from that charming conversation with Frank and Rachel. Your business is your business, and I have no right to interfere, even if my intentions were pure. Am I forgiven?"

Soreness eased. Resentment deflated like air from a leaky balloon. "Of course, you're forgiven."

"Good." He squeezed her hand for a brief moment, and a fresh tingle skittered from her wrist to her shoulder. "Why don't you take a minute to get your bearings while I find out where we're seated for tonight's fiasco?"

When he turned away, her mind reran their conversation. Was he right? Oh, not about comparing her to Mother Teresa. Did she think of herself as Superwoman? Did stubborn pride keep her from asking for help? Maybe. But there was more to her reticence than pride.

After placing her faith in that weasel, Frank, and his perfect soulless mate, Rachel... After surviving their public betrayal... After facing the fact she'd been lied to for months... Why on earth would she ever trust anyone else again?

What was the old saying? Fool me once, shame on you. Fool me twice, shame on me. Well, this fool had learned *her* lesson the first time. There could never be a second time. She couldn't survive a fall like that again.

The episode at Madison Elementary taught her one valuable lesson: Rely on no one but yourself and you'll never be disappointed.

Her conscience simmered and stewed, but her gaze bored into Kyle's back as he bent to the lace-covered stand to study the small cards scattered over the surface. Still...

Eons of difference stood between the two men. Kyle had honor, integrity, and truthfulness on his side. Could she dare to place her trust in him? She'd rather not find out. Better to leave things as they were. She and Kyle were friends. In friendship, he couldn't break her heart. Besides, he was obviously attracted to Nicole.

The moment he turned, place card in hand, she pasted on a more serene expression. No way would she allow him to see how his bitterness affected her.

"We're at Table Eleven," he said, waving the folded cardboard as he came near. "Social Siberia. One step away from the street, no doubt."

Good. When she'd had enough of this circus, their proximity to the exit would make a quick getaway easy. Suddenly, she didn't feel like the victorious princess anymore. She felt like...

Like a doormat.

Chapter Fourteen

"How about a drink?" Kyle gripped her elbow and steered her toward their table. "A little Champagne maybe? Might help soothe your nerves a bit."

Wasn't his presence here supposed to do that? Once again, her mind tripped over questions. Why had he come with her tonight? Had Nicole promised some bedroom gymnastics to get him to agree to be seen in public with her? Was this his effort to pay her back? What was worse, his dating her out of pity or out of responsibility?

He stared until unease slithered down her spine. Maybe if she sent him on an errand, she'd gain a chance to sort through all the jumbled emotions bouncing around in her stomach. "Y-yes, thank you. That would be nice."

If he noticed her sudden change in attitude, he didn't mention it. He pulled a chair away from the table and gestured for her to sit. "Stay here. I'll be right back."

With a gentle squeeze of her shoulder, he disappeared into the glittering crowd. When a familiar couple approached the table, her disposition didn't improve. Mark and Adrienne Palmer. Adrienne was another kindergarten teacher at Madison Elementary. Apparently, Rachel had gone out of her way to stack the deck against her, right down to the seating arrangements.

"Gianna, hi!" Adrienne exclaimed as she lowered her very pregnant body into the nearest chair. "I haven't seen you in ages. How are you?"

"I'm fine," she replied automatically. "How are you?"

"Tired." Adrienne placed her hands on the mound of her black velvet-clad stomach. "And fat." She smiled.

"Not fat. You look beautiful, Adrienne."

"I agree," Mark interjected, leaning to kiss his wife's head.

Adrienne preened under his obvious affection, but kept her gaze on Gianna. "Thanks. But you're the one who looks beautiful, Gi. Where did you get that dress? It's absolutely stunning."

"It's just something I picked up at Gardener's."

Adrienne's eyes narrowed in envy. Gianna would have expected to feel some sense of satisfaction, maybe accomplishment. Instead, a vast emptiness left her hollow and...untethered, separate from everyone else in attendance at this masquerade. With a sigh she hoped would be mistaken for boredom, she turned to look out over the crowd.

Was this what her life had become? Sitting at a table making small talk with people she didn't like? Attending the wedding of a couple who'd made a fool of her? Waiting for the return of a man who only came out of sympathy?

Lord, she was pathetic. With a mixture of relief and anxiety she watched Kyle elbow his way through the crowd, two glasses in hand and an apologetic smile on his face.

"Sorry, but all they have is sparkling wine. Domestic, no less. I hope you can stomach this sludge." As he handed her a glass, he nodded to the Palmers. "Hello."

"Kyle Hayden," she introduced him in a flat tone, "Adrienne and Mark Palmer."

The three exchanged the usual pleasantries, but Gianna's focus remained on the crowds congratulating the bride and groom. She'd made a mistake coming here tonight. No matter how she looked and whom she had on her arm, she'd always be the booby prize in this little carnival sideshow. Gianna Randazzo, aka the one Frank ditched, the gracious loser.

What had made her think a fancy dress and a new hairstyle would change what these people thought? More importantly, why had she cared? After tonight, she'd never see any of them again. Except for Kyle. And she'd already resigned herself to dealing with her unrequited affection.

What a rude awakening. Despite her fears, despite her promises to never fall for a handsome face again, she'd already done so. Not that she'd ever let on. She'd remind herself his display of affection was a charade. Steel her heart to take his compliments, his attentiveness, and his thoughtfulness as part of an act orchestrated by Nicole.

Other couples filled in the empty seats at their table, two elderly neighbors of Rachel's parents, the principal of Madison Elementary and his wife, and a lesbian couple from Rachel's university days. While the remaining guests found their seats, a five-piece band played soft easy listening music.

Moments later, a guitar strummed, and the lead singer spoke into the microphone. "We'd like to invite Mr. and Mrs. Frank Capelli to the dance floor for their very first dance as man and wife. And for this special occasion, they've chosen the beautiful melody, 'You're My Love.'"

While the guests applauded, the couple rose and, hands laced, moved to the center of the room. They danced together, gazes locked in mutual adoration. Someone clinked a knife against a glass, and the noise became a symphony. Shouts of "Kiss her, kiss her!" filled the room until at last, Rachel grabbed Frank's collar and practically swallowed him whole.

Gag me.

Then, the singer announced, "We'd like to invite the bridal party to join them."

"So," Adrienne said to Kyle, "how did you two meet?"

Panic almost had Gianna bolting from the room, but she feigned acute interest in the couples on the dance floor and prayed Kyle would know what to say. Had he and Nicole discussed that subject? She thought they had, but couldn't clearly remember.

Before Kyle formed a reply, the bandleader interrupted with, "How about all you other couples in love? Let's see you out there now."

Kyle rose and pushed back his chair. "That's our cue, sweetheart." He turned to Adrienne. "Would you excuse us, please?"

"Of course," she replied with a nod and an indulgent smile. "Mark, would you care to dance?"

While Mark rose to assist his wife to her feet, Gianna took Kyle's hand and allowed him to lead her to the dance floor. Her legs trembled, and angry bees fought for space in her crowded belly. But the butterflies, the green-eyed monster, and all the other mythical creatures residing inside her disappeared the moment he took her in his arms. Then, she transformed into a thick liquid, pliant and completely dependent upon him to stay upright.

"Did I tell you how amazing you are?" he whispered.

She ignored the shivers his hot breath sent racing down her back and concentrated on her steps in the slow dance. "You said I looked like a goddess. That counts."

"No, it doesn't. You should be proud of yourself, Gianna. You showed a lot of guts, coming here and facing these people. I didn't realize how much until now."

"I couldn't have shown up alone. I'm so glad I had you." The heat in her face nearly overwhelmed her. "God, I'm sorry. That came out wrong."

"No, it didn't."

"Yes, it did. I realize you only did this as a favor to Nicole and—"

"Whoa, wait a second."

He stopped in mid-step, and she landed squarely on his toes. "Sorry," she mumbled.

Either her apology or her clumsiness spurred him into moving again. "Who said I did this as a favor to Nicole?"

"No one," she admitted. "I figured since you two are dating..."

"Me? Dating Nicole?" His laughter erupted. Gianna shrank about five feet in height. "Why on earth would you think I'm dating Nicole?"

"Well, you went to the Inn on the Sound together," she explained, the blush of embarrassment deepening to one of foolishness. "And since no one bothered to tell me, I assumed you were keeping the romance a secret until you were more sure of each other. I'm sorry if I blew it for you—"

"I can't speak for Nicole, but I didn't tell you because, in my world, a casual lunch isn't that big a deal. And that's all our afternoon was. One simple lunch." His thumb caressed her lower jaw in a slow, deliberate circle, and his eyes, those honest eyes, opened wider, as if inviting her into their realm. "Listen to me. I'm here tonight because I want to be here. Don't take this the wrong way, but I can barely tolerate being in the same room with Nicole for too long. I know she's your best friend, and I do like her. She just... exhausts me."

When his palm cupped her nape, she found a courage she never knew she had. Before the song ended or the sudden spurt of bravery disappeared, she dared, "Wh-what about me? Can you bear being in the same room with me? Or do I exhaust you too?"

His mouth descended upon hers in a connection more secure than words. The surrounding world faded. The music quieted. The guests evaporated in swirls of colorful mist. Doubt and fear flew miles away, far into space and time. Nothing existed but Kyle. His lips and tongue inside her, his warmed breath tasting slightly of sweet wine, his heart beating against her own, the citrus smell of his aftershave, his arms around her, his feet still moving to some unknown rhythm she no longer recognized. Nothing else mattered. Until she heard the applause.

Breaking away, gasping for breath, she whirled. The hazy daze left her in slow ticks of time. First, she remembered where she was, and then why. Still, the clapping grew louder, loud enough to drown out the thunderous heartbeat pounding in her ears. Another rush of heat flooded her face. But the crowd paid no attention to her. No one applauded the kiss she'd shared with Kyle. They applauded for the bride and groom standing nearby.

"Why don't we take a walk?" Kyle's gruff voice cut through the last of the fog. "I think we both need to clear our heads."

HOPING TO COOL HIS overheated flesh, Kyle pulled her toward the French doors leading to the exterior gardens. Cold night air wafted, and he escorted Gianna closer to an illuminated fountain in the center of the moonlit grounds. A fine spray of water descended upon his face, soothing lust and restoring logic. Attending this wedding was the biggest mistake of his life. Even worse than the error in judgment that had brought him to Villa Mare in the first place. What an idiot he was!

He thought he could play the lovesick swain without Gianna's nearness affecting him, but he'd been fooling himself. Tonight she resembled a golden trophy, the ultimate prize. Everything about her intoxicated him. The powdery floral scent of her skin enveloped him, drawing him closer, ever closer. The graceful length of her neck enticed him to taste that delicate column, to latch his lips upon her sweet flesh and drink from her pool. She folded into his embrace so easily, as if she were a part of him. Her rapid heartbeat echoed his racing pulse, promising a future they couldn't possibly share. Her innocent question regarding being in the same room became his undoing.

Didn't she realize how beautiful, how incredibly special she was? Damn those Bambi eyes of hers! They batted and fluttered and made his lips thirsty to kiss her every single time. Like the sirens of legend, Gianna lured him into shallow waters, enticing him with eternal happiness, but delivering a much more somber destiny. And like those doomed sailors, he'd follow her to his own end.

When they kissed, she fused to him with such ferocity, he'd rather die than part from her. With a casual sweep, he cast a quick glance inside at the bride and groom on the dance floor. What fools! Especially Frank.

Comparing Gianna to Rachel was like comparing Da Vinci's Mona Lisa to Dogs Playing Poker. Where Gianna had warm, brown eyes full of laughter and generosity, Rachel's incited visions of the North Sea in the middle of February. A warm, giving heart versus a cold, bitter stone. In every possible category, Gianna Randazzo came out the winner over Rachel Capelli. Hands down.

Oddly enough, he didn't compare the golden Gianna beside him now to Rachel. No, he compared the Gianna he saw every day since the very first time he set eyes on her. The one who wore her hair in a high ponytail, who covered her lush curves with a white canvas apron, and who needed no artificial enhancements to give her face a glow. The one with a sprinkle of freckles dancing over the bridge of her nose. The one with a smile that lit the night sky like fireworks. The one who made little children laugh and grown men burn. The one with a heart as deep and wide as the ocean.

Oh, he had to give credit to Lucinda. She'd gone way over the budget Rory had set, but the end result was too spectacular to hold a grudge. Gianna looked like a goddess, just as he'd described her earlier. But he far preferred her without the glitter and glamour. To a man who discovered her after a long, tumultuous journey, she represented a clear spring deep in the mountains, pure and cleansing, unspoiled.

Yet whether dressed to the teeth in formalwear or leading a parade with a foil hat on her head, she touched a secret part of him he never knew existed. And he would never be the same again. His mind tripped over the earlier episode when he'd accused her of martyrdom. Why? The answer burned his conscience: to take back the offer he'd made to help her raise the funds for her daycare center. He couldn't commit to the time and energy such a project would require. He couldn't promise her anything beyond the next two weeks. Caught up in the moment, entranced by her vulnerability, he'd volunteered his services without considering the repercussions.

Gianna had only one flaw he couldn't ignore; her boundless generosity brought out the zealous protector in him. Even now, he wanted to keep her tucked inside his embrace, safe from the barbs and sharp looks of the other guests at this fiasco. Safe from the cynical few who would take advantage of her vulnerability and naïveté. Including himself. Hadn't Nicole warned him this would happen? God, he was an idiot!

In their few hours together tonight, she'd managed to weaken his resolve in ways no other woman ever had. He found himself changing from the role of appreciative escort to champion to victim of his own fantasies.

If this evening didn't come to a close soon, he'd have one last role to play, that of a dead duck. Because somehow, if he allowed her the opportunity, she'd trap him in her heart and never let him go. And as much as he'd love to indulge his longings, any relationship they began would end badly. They were too different, extreme ends of the same spectrum.

"You okay?" Gianna asked, derailing the train of his thoughts.

"Of course," he said.

"I'm sorry to put you through all this. I can't imagine you're enjoying yourself."

Despite his jumbled emotions, he forced an air of nonchalance. "Don't worry about me. How are *you* doing?"

She smiled, and he had to fight the urge to toss her over his shoulder and carry her out of this place. Something about her brought out the Neanderthal in him.

"Better now," she said. "Thanks to you. At least the hard part's over."

If only he could be so certain...

THE COUP DE GRACE CAME in the ladies' room when Gianna sat before one of the gilt mirrors, touching up her makeup. The door hissed open, and Adrienne entered to sit beside her. An uncomfortable silence filled the room. While making a great fuss about reapplying her mascara, Gianna stole a glance at Adrienne, currently involved in the same pretense.

"Gi," Adrienne began hesitantly. "Can I tell you something? Just between us?"

She tucked the mascara into her gold beaded purse. "Sure."

Adrienne swiveled in the velvet chair to face her. "When Rachel told me she'd invited you to the wedding, I thought it was the meanest thing I'd ever heard. But to see you happy with that gorgeous man, well, I pity Rachel now. Kyle is everything Frank isn't. He's witty, charming, and so devoted to you. Anyone can see you've moved up in the world. Poor Rachel! Looks like she turned out to be the loser after all."

Before Gianna could form a reply, Adrienne's eyes widened, and her mouth opened in a wide O.

Rachel stood in the doorway between the stalls and the powder room area, her face a mask of outrage. "Thanks a lot, Adrienne! I thought you were my friend."

"Oh, get off your soapbox, Rachel." Adrienne waved a hand. "You only invited Gianna so you could make her feel badly about losing Frank. Well, take a good look. Does she look like she's suffering? I don't think so. I think she looks more radiant now than I've ever seen her. And I'm glad. She deserves to be happy."

With a stamp of her satin-shod foot and an exaggerated "Oh!" Rachel stormed out of the ladies' room.

"I know we've never been close, Gi," Adrienne said when the door closed. "But take some free advice from someone who's been in your shoes. Hang on to Kyle. He's perfect."

She smiled. Yeah, he was perfect. A thousand images flitted through her imagination. Kyle as she'd first met him, humble yet proud. The way he tossed a pizza, hands twirling beneath the stretchy dough. Those same hands caressing Crystal's chubby cheek. His kisses, which left her breathless and boneless. Oh, he was definitely perfect. And God help her, she wanted to hang onto him. As long as possible.

The rest of the night passed in a sparkling blur of wine and kisses. Kyle played the adoring suitor to the hilt. They danced every slow dance together and even a few of the faster ones. Throughout the remaining hours, Adrienne Palmer's advice echoed in Gianna's head. And when she and Kyle left the reception a short time after Gianna caught the bouquet, she was ready to take the free advice to heart. She used the car ride home to gain a little courage, replaying the events of the evening in slow motion, running her tongue over her lips to feel the tingle still dancing there. When he took the exit ramp off the Expressway, she made her move.

"Kyle?"

"Mmm?"

"How about we go back to your place?"

"What for?" His gaze skimmed her quickly, without a hint of interest, before refocusing on the road.

Were all men obtuse about a woman's subtle signals? Well, she'd have to be more direct. Leaning over the console, she placed a hand on his thigh and squeezed. "Because I'm not ready to say goodnight to you yet."

He veered to the right with a screech of tires and a sharp turn of the wheel, and she tumbled into his lap. Throwing the car in park, he righted her and placed her hands in her own lap. "Gianna, listen to me. I'm flattered. Really. But—"

"But I'm not your type," she finished with a sigh. To ward off his look of pity, she crumpled into a tight ball against the passenger door and stared out the window at the shadows of pine trees.

"That's not what I wanted to say." He touched her shoulder.

She jerked away, slamming her elbow against the door, but the pain in her heart overrode other sensations. "I'm sorry."

"No, I'm sorry. The truth is I like you too much to accept your offer. You're a little drunk, extra vulnerable, and too damned tempting for your own good. I'm not going to take advantage of your current state. That would make me a snake. And I'm no snake."

Shame stole her ability to speak. Staring at the ragged shadows on the other side of her window, she concentrated on finding a means of escape. If she could find a boulder on the side of the road right now, she'd crawl beneath it and hide.

"I'll take you home now," he mumbled. Again, she nodded, and the car lurched forward onto the paved road.

Chapter Fifteen

Gianna woke the next morning with a headache that would bring an elephant to its knees. But the hot needles of pain behind her eyes didn't burn as much as the stinging humiliation of the memories of last evening's finale. She'd thrown herself at Kyle. He'd turned her down. A bubble of acid rose in her throat, and she swallowed with a grimace.

Oh, God. How would she ever face him again? What had gotten into her last night anyway? Sparkling wine. And vanity. Two things she'd had only limited experience with in the past. And this morning, she was paying the price for indulging both.

Pulling the blankets over her head, she huddled into a cocoon of darkness. With any luck at all, she could stay here until next spring and emerge as a beautiful butterfly. Okay, so that wasn't about to happen. Maybe she could sleep until the night's drama faded like a bad dream.

But even that wish dashed on the rocks she had for brains when the phone beside her bed jangled. The noise struck her last surviving nerve ending, fraying beyond repair. Worse, she knew who sat on the other end of the ringing box.

Nicole.

Oh, God, not now. She was definitely not ready. Her overtaxed brain still hadn't processed all the information from last night, and now she'd be expected to run the play by play with armchair quarterback Nicole.

What should she do? Ignore her best friend's call? Pretend she wasn't home? No. Nicole would keep trying until she got through. Better to face the fire and move on. With a sigh of defeat, she snaked an arm out from the blankets and fumbled for the receiver.

"Hello?"

"I tried your cell, and you must still have your ringer off. Spill, sweetie." The chipper, eager voice short-circuited Gianna's brain. Sparks flew behind her eyes. "Every last drop. Don't hold anything back. Start where he picked you up, and don't stop 'til you get to this moment right here and now."

"Nicole," she muttered, "can I get back to you later?"

"Why?" Her voice dropped to a whisper. "Is he there?"

"No."

"Then you can't get back to me later." Loud again. "I want details, and I want 'em now!"

"I have to pee," she replied in a sickly sweet tone.

"I'll hold," Nicole said, using the same inflection.

With a groan of exasperation, she slammed the phone on her nightstand, rolled out of bed, and headed for the bathroom across the hall. Before returning to her bedroom, she swallowed two aspirin with a handful of water. She'd need all the help she could get to deal with Nicole's third degree. The pills stuck in her throat before dissolving, leaving a bitter aftertaste.

Big whoop. Last night's memories had the same acrid flavor. When Gianna picked up the receiver again, Nicole wasted no time in getting to the point.

"Well? C'mon! The suspense is killing me. Tell me what happened."

"There's not much to tell."

"Bull. Quit holding out on me. How did it go last night? What did Frank do when he saw you with Kyle? What did Rachel do? And what did you and Kyle do afterwards?"

Oh, God, strike me dead here and now. Please.

But apparently, God wasn't taking requests this morning.

"Wh-what makes you think Kyle and I did anything afterwards?"

"Hell-o? Gi, it's Nicole. Don't play dumb. The guy's gorgeous, and he obviously likes you—"

She couldn't stop the snort that flew out of her nose. "Oh, yeah, right. Obviously."

"What do you mean? Something happened between you two, didn't it? C'mon, you can tell me. What happened?"

"Nothing happened." *And thanks so much for reminding me.*

"Bull."

"No bull. Nothing happened. Ab-so-lute-ly nothing."

"Aha." She could almost hear the hamster wheel turning in Nicole's head. *Squeak, squeak, squeak.* "And you wanted something to happen, didn't you?"

No way did she plan to divulge the details of her humiliation. "Can we drop the subject?"

"No. Now tell me what happened."

"I caaaan't," she whined like a three-year-old, stamping her feet on the carpeted floor and burying her head in the pillow. "It's too embarrassing."

"More embarrassing than the time we gave each other home perms? More embarrassing than the night we followed Jason home from the amusement park and wound up driving into his garage door when my foot slipped off the brake and I panicked and hit the gas? More embarrassing than setting the kitchen on fire in Home Ec class? More embarrassing than when you fell off the top bleacher during the homecoming game?"

Flames licked her cheeks. "More embarrassing than all those things."

"Oh, well in that case, you *have* to tell me."

Gianna groaned.

"Now, now, come on, sweetie," Nicole replied in a mock-shaky voice. "Tell Auntie Nicole all about it."

With a deep breath for fortitude, she began her confession. *Bless me, Nicole, for I have sinned...*

"We were driving home from the wedding..."

"Yeah?"

"And I asked if we could go back to his place. I told him I wasn't ready to say goodnight yet." God, just saying the words aloud sent nausea bulleting to her stomach.

"And?"

One more deep breath. "And he turned me down. Said I was drunk and vulnerable and he didn't want to take advantage of me."

"Oh my God, that is *so* sweet!" Nicole lapsed into an old school-age rhyme. "Gianna and Kyle sitting in a tree, K-I-S-S-I-N-G—"

"Nicole, are you listening? I said he turned me down."

She stopped singing long enough to say, "I know. Didn't I tell you he liked you?"

"If he likes me so much, why am I alone right now?"

"Because you *were* drunk, you *were* vulnerable, and he didn't want to take advantage of you."

"Huh?" Maybe her brain needed rebooting, but Nicole's explanation did not compute.

"Don't you know anything, Gi? The fact he turned you down says he wants to make certain you're sure of your feelings before he jumps your bones. That's the most romantic thing I've ever heard. So, what are you going to do now?"

"What do you mean?"

"The ball's in your court, baby. Kyle probably thought the alcohol did the talking last night. So now you have to talk to him when you're sober, and tell him how you feel. Dare to take a risk. Put yourself out there and grab your happiness."

"Oh, no." She shook her head until something loose rolled around in her brain. Goody. Maybe she'd have a stroke, and she wouldn't have to continue this inane conversation. "Forget it. I can't go through that humiliation again."

"What humiliation? Trust me. Talk to him today. If you tell him how you really feel when you're not drunk and vulnerable, I guarantee you'll get different results."

"How do you know?" A long pause followed her question and for a moment, she thought maybe the line had disconnected.

"Did I tell you Kyle and I had lunch together last week?"

No, and it might have been nice to know before I made a fool of myself last night. "Kyle mentioned something."

"Well, I doubt he 'mentioned' all he did was talk about you. Quite frankly, I doubt he even noticed, but it's true. Every sentence out of his mouth began with 'Gianna says this,' and 'Gianna does that.'"

"You're making that up."

"God's honest truth. I swear." She clucked her tongue. "Be real. When have I ever told a story about being alone with a guy where I wasn't the sole object of his attention?"

True. Nicole's main interest was always Nicole.

"So what if he did talk about me? What does that prove?"

"Jeez. Who knew my best friend was so dense about men? Don't be a coward. Talk to him, face to face. I'll bet if you tell him what you're feeling, you'll discover he feels the same way about you."

Could she? Did she dare? *Oh, God.* "I'll think about it, okay?"

"No, that's not good enough. What's with you? I've never known you to be so shy before. Are you hesitating because he's broke?"

Gianna sat up with a jolt, sending painful starbursts into her head. "Hey, thanks. Now you think I'm a gold digger."

"Well?"

"Of course not. You know me better than that."

"So then, what? If you really like him, you have to talk to him. Now. Today. What's holding you back?"

What *was* holding her back? Fear? Sort of. But more than fear. Maybe dread was a better word. Dread she'd make another awful mistake. Like she did with Frank. Some sixth sense warned her to scuttle back to her Cinderella world, forget about the ball and the handsome prince, that real life wasn't a fairy tale.

But she didn't dare tell her best friend. Nicole with her "flit and don't commit" mentality could never understand.

"I can't go there now," she said. "I don't have my car. He drove last night. It's probably parked outside Villa Mare."

"Perfect! Now you have an excuse to see him. I'll be over in twenty minutes to pick you up. Be ready."

Without waiting for the refusal she must have known Gianna would attempt, Nicole hung up.

THIS IS THE STUPIDEST thing I've ever done in my life.

Gianna sat in Nicole's car outside Villa Mare, trying to breathe. Her brain hummed with a thousand recriminations. Softly.

In her current state of hangover, even her conscience knew better than to yell. Her knees shook so badly they slammed against the glove compartment in a staccato rhythm.

"You keep that up, we'll be able to get you a gig at Club Heebie Jeebies," Nicole said.

"Ha, ha, very funny."

"No joke, babe. They've got open talent night on Fridays. Couldn't you just picture the scene?" As if unrolling a banner, Nicole swept her hand over the dashboard. "'Gianna Randazzo and her Fabulous Drumming Thighbones.' You could be the next rock legend."

"Could you try to be a little supportive here?"

"You don't need support." Nicole leaned across Gianna's trembling lap to push open the passenger door. "You need to get your butt out of my car and go talk to Kyle. Now!"

"Some best friend you are." She flashed a look meant to wither corn on the stalk and climbed out of the car. "I'll remember this."

"Yeah, yeah," the unflappable Nicole replied with a grin. "Just make sure I get to be maid of honor at the wedding. Now stop being a jellyfish and get going."

The door slammed closed. Panic gripped Gianna. The nearer she came to the front entrance of Villa Mare, the louder her heartbeat pounded in her ears. Her mouth filled with sawdust as she struggled to come up with something clever to say. Maybe a joke to break the ice. Unfortunately, no witty repartee came to mind—only knock-knock jokes—and she dismissed that idea before her feet hit the sidewalk. Maybe just a light, humorous attitude would suffice.

A funny thing happened to me on the way to the wedding last night, Kyle. I came to realize how much I care for you.

Forget it. She'd be better off with a knock-knock joke.

Knock, knock.

Who's there?

Olive.

Olive who?

Olive you.

Last year, Samantha Mayer got a kiss and a wedding out of Nicholas Lanford when she told him that joke during snack time. Samantha, wearing the white Barbie gown and veil from the dress-up trunk, walked through the hallway with her two best friends serving as bridesmaids. The "groom" stood in the classroom with a stuffed SpongeBob as best man and the rest of the class as guests.

Oh, to be five years old again. Why did life become so difficult when a person reached adulthood?

With a sigh, she stepped onto the curb and wrestled with the idea of walking straight past the pizzeria. Yup, past the pizzeria, the nail salon, the Chinese restaurant, and the liquor store, past the back parking lot, past the copse of pine trees and into the pond. If she kept going from there, well, she wouldn't have to worry about saying something stupid to Kyle, would she? The idea was so tempting.

Not the bit about drowning. But definitely the part about walking by.

No confrontation, no confession, no chance for Kyle to laugh in her face or give her a look of disgust. Or worst of all, confide he was already married, engaged, involved, whatever. She couldn't take another rejection.

So sue me. I am a jellyfish. Transparent and spineless. And this jellyfish just might ooze her tentacles to the water and forget about sharing her feelings with anyone.

Fate conspired against her. Dad, wiping down the booth in front of the window, spotted her and tapped on the glass to gain her attention. He gestured for her to come inside, and then unlocked the front door.

"So my Sleeping Beauty's awake, eh?" He kissed her cheek. "Can I get you something to drink? Espresso or Sambuca?"

"Sambuca? At ten o'clock in the morning, Dad?"

He fixed her with his dark eyes and wagged a finger. "Hair of the dog, sweetheart."

She shook her head slowly, not wanting to wake the hairy dog sleeping in her skull. Something told her Fido would be a bit cranky if she did.

"No Sambuca. Espresso sounds good. Nicole dragged me from the house before I could grab a cup of coffee."

"You sit." He pointed to the booth he'd wiped down. "I'll get your espresso."

While he headed into the dining room, she slid across the orange bench and folded her hands on the tabletop. Morning sunshine streamed through the window, burning her retinas. Blinded, she fumbled out of the booth and headed for one as far away from the glass as possible.

When her father returned with the tiny cup and saucer, he looked from the booth near the window to the place where she sat now. "That bad, eh?"

She nodded as she picked up the thick lemon peel and stirred it in the aromatic black liquid. After returning the peel to the saucer, she lifted the cup to her lips. A little like battery acid in her empty stomach, but no denying the instantaneous jolt the pure caffeine gave her.

"So how was the wedding last night?"

Over the rim of her cup, she tried to look blasé. "Good."

"That's not what Kyle said." He slid into the booth across from her.

Clink! The cup fell back on the saucer. Oh, God. Kyle had already talked to Mom and Dad.

"Wh-what did he say?"

Her father leaned across the table to push a wisp of hair off her forehead. "He said you turned that place on its ear last night. And you were the prettiest girl there and made sure everyone knew."

"Was that all he said?" God, she hoped so!

"No, there was one more thing." Heart pounding in her throat, she waited for her father to berate her trashy behavior. "He also said throughout the entire night, you were the epitome of grace, elegance, and class—a true princess."

Relief spilled into her stomach like liquid antacid. "I think he exaggerated a bit, Dad."

"And I think you probably underestimate your effect on people. You've always known how to shine."

As much as her father's compliment soothed her bruised ego, she didn't wish to pursue this subject. Not while she continued to avoid the real reason for her early morning arrival. "How's everything going here?"

"Pretty good. That purple-headed girl—Bethany? She applied for a job yesterday. Wants to work here nights and weekends. What do you think?"

Draining the last of the espresso from the cup, she shrugged. "She's here all the time anyway. She might as well get paid for the privilege. And she seems responsible enough. She's not a troublemaker, that's for sure. She'd definitely be able to handle the ROMEOs and their nonsense. I'd say go for it. Claudio probably won't like your employing her though."

"Claudio's retiring at the end of the month," he confided. "That's why I'm thinking of hiring Bethany."

Her eyes blinked in rapid succession. "Claudio? Retiring?"

"He's sixty-two, sweetheart. He wants to stop working while he's still young enough to do something with his days. Even if he just hangs around with the ROMEOs."

"But," she argued, "you're the same age."

"And your mother's always trying to get me to slow down, too. You know that."

"But you never do."

Dad beamed brighter than the morning sunshine streaming through the storefront window. "I've been fortunate. I love the restaurant business. I've never considered leaving Villa Mare. You have that same passion for teaching. Even after all you suffered with Frank and Rachel, could you turn your back on the little ones?" Giving her hand a quick, comforting squeeze, he answered for her. "No, you couldn't. And that's why your mother and I are thinking about selling the business."

"Wait. What?" First Claudio's retirement, now Dad selling Villa Mare? What was happening? Was she still asleep? Still dreaming? None of this made sense in any other way.

The squeeze transformed into a series of pats on her wrist. "I've made up my mind, Gianna. Your mother and I have talked about this at great length. You and your brother have your own dreams to pursue. Villa Mare was *my* dream. Well, mine and your mom's. If I sell now, we can retire and enjoy our lives, and who knows?" He waggled silver brows in her direction. "Maybe, one day, fairly soon, we'll have grandchildren to bounce on our knee, eh?"

Whoa. Not ready, not ready, not ready.

She still had trouble dealing with her feelings for Kyle, especially considering they didn't know each other very long. She'd been with Frank for three years and look how badly that had turned out!

"Daddy, I—"

He held up a hand. "No rush, *cara*. You focus on planning your career first. In the meantime, some of the money from the sale of Villa Mare could go into an investment or two." He nudged her with a jab of his finger in her cheek. "Do you think there's a super-talented teacher who needs some seed money to start her daycare center? I bet we could help her out."

Her jaw dropped as realization struck. "Oh, Dad, no. I can't ask you to do that. I'm not a little kid anymore. You shouldn't have to risk your future to finance my life. Besides, I've been thinking. I'm going to take a second job. I'll start small, but I can make this work. I know I can."

"Ah, Gianna, sweetheart, what better way for us to show how much we love you and how proud we are of you than to give you the opportunity to follow your dream?"

No point in continuing to argue. Only one person could talk Carlo Randazzo out of doing something: Lucia Randazzo. She'd have to speak to her mother. "Where is Mom anyway?"

His silver head jerked toward the storage room. "In the back with Kyle. She's teaching him how to tally the receipts." Leaning closer, he winked and whispered, "If you tell her I said so, she'll deny it. But I think your mother has a crush on Kyle."

Yeah, well, there's a lot of that going around.

"Do you think she'd mind if I borrowed him for a while?"

Rising, Dad picked up the empty cup and saucer. "It better be a short while. I'd bet my argyle socks your mother's got a dozen tasks her Kyle has to do before the lunch crowd arrives."

"'*Her* Kyle?'"

"Yup," he replied, tossing a sly grin over his shoulder. "I told you she's sweet on him."

Almost as if summoned by their conversation, Gianna's mother stepped out of the back room with Kyle behind her. The minute Gianna saw him, her heart ascended into her throat, and the espresso re-percolated in her stomach.

"Who's sweet on whom, Carlo?" her mother asked.

"You on Tony Bennett, *cara*," Dad replied smoothly.

"Mmmm." Mom's smile grew dreamy. "He can leave his slippers under my bed anytime."

Gianna lowered her head to the table, partly to hide her amusement at her parents' nonsense, but also to shield her telltale face from Kyle's scrutiny.

"Good morning, Gianna." Her mother leaned to kiss the top of her head. "What brings you here so early?"

Her gaze drilled into the orange Formica. "Kyle, actually."

"Oh?" The rise in his tone reflected open curiosity.

Gianna took the time to count to ten and recoup reserves. If she didn't do this now, she'd never find the nerve again. Feigning a casual attitude far from the anxiety skittering like marbles in her veins, she turned her focus to him. "Yes. If you have a few minutes, maybe we could take a walk?"

Kyle's face registered nothing. "Actually, I should stay here. Lucia, didn't you want me to run those receipts one more time?"

Her mother giggled. In twenty-nine years, Gianna had never heard her mother giggle before. Dad was right; Mom had a crush. Big time.

"The receipts can wait, *tesoro*. Go with Gianna."

Tesoro? Even her brother, Joey, only heard that term of endearment once a year. On his birthday.

Still wearing a blank expression, Kyle reshifted his attention to Gianna. "Sure. Why not?"

Why not? She could think of a thousand reasons why not, chief among them the fact she was about to make a first-class fool out of herself. But she bit her tongue.

"Great! Let's go."

Chapter Sixteen

Contrary to his cool pretense, Kyle knew exactly why Gianna wanted him to "take a walk" with her. When she crossed the parking lot and headed for a side street running perpendicular to the strip mall, his brain cells squirmed. Dammit, why now? He only had thirteen days left.

Thirteen days and this farce would be over. Thirteen days and he'd go home. Thirteen days and he'd get his life back, keeping Aurora in the process. Thirteen days and he'd be free. Thirteen days and he'd leave this place, forgetting everyone and everything he'd come in contact with over the last two months.

As if debating his silent argument, the autumn wind rustled. A flurry of leaves whirled on a familiar powdery scent. No, the wind reminded him, that last statement wasn't entirely true. He'd never forget Gianna.

How could he? The scent of her skin, the sound of her voice, the innocence sparkling in her eyes. Her gentle, unobtrusive manner, her generous spirit...

"Have you seen the beach here yet?" she asked, staring at him over her shoulder.

He shook his head, and she smiled. A chill crept into his bones. If only the expression of joy on her face could last. She deserved nothing less than to be happy for the rest of her life. Without Gianna finding him, he never would have survived the last month. And yet, without Gianna, he wouldn't have to face this excruciating moment.

"Setquott Beach is one of the only beaches on Long Island where the sun actually sets in the water," she said. "Legend says Native American tribes celebrated marriages at dusk on this shore. The union of earth, sky, and water in one fine line represented the joining of families. The shifting tides indicated the give and take needed by the wedding couple, and the sinking sun symbolized the ending of unmarried lives and the beginning of their future together as one."

Well, she'd left no doubt where this conversation was headed. But he said nothing as they walked on, content to let silence build up as long as possible.

When they finally reached the shoreline, he had to admit the view was as breathtaking as at some of the finest beaches in Europe. At mid-morning height, the sun glinted off blue-gray water in shimmering diamonds. Rocks, vivid hues of red, gray, pink, and every shade of cream imaginable, crunched under his shoes. An echoic honk sounded as a V of Canadian geese, wings spread across the white-streaked sky, flew overhead. Salt air, always discernible in the town itself, now infused every breath he took, stinging his nostrils with a sharp tang, leaving an indelible flavor on his tongue.

"Isn't the view magnificent?" She linked an arm through his. "I've been coming here since I was a little girl, and the beauty never ceases to call to me. I think the Native Americans were right. This is the perfect place for two people to begin a relationship. Don't you think so?"

To slice through the thick tension building in his gut, he forced a cheery voice. "How are you feeling this morning?"

"Better, thanks to several aspirins and Dad's espresso," she replied. This time her gaze remained fixed straight ahead. "I guess I had a little too much to drink last night."

"It happens."

"Not to me." She picked up a handful of stones, and plucked a smooth pink one from the pile to skip across the water. "I've never done that before. I guess having to face Frank and Rachel..." She stopped, staring at him with wide, shining eyes. Trusting puppy dog eyes. "Did I tell you how grateful I was for your company last night?"

Had she intentionally chosen the heart-shaped stone to toss into the sea? Pins and needles prickled his flesh. "About a thousand times."

A charming rush of color bloomed in her cheeks, raising a moral dilemma in his conscience. She wanted something permanent. And he couldn't give her that. In the end, he'd be forced to leave her behind. His world was miles from hers. He was a bird, she was a fish. Neither could survive in the other's environment.

"Kyle, I know you think I was too drunk last night to know what I wanted, but the truth is I like you very much."

"Gianna, I—"

She quickly pushed a fingertip against his lips. The contact sent a flame straight to his mouth, making him burn to kiss her once again.

"No, let me finish. I have to get this out while I still have the nerve. Last night, when I said I wasn't ready to say goodnight, I meant what I said. I didn't ask to come home with you because I drank too much Champagne or because I was high on some power trip. Last night I realized how much you mean to me. I think...I think I may be falling for you." Her hands settled on his shoulders, and she tilted her head, poised for a kiss. "And I was sort of hoping you felt the same way about me."

His lungs constricted, making breathing impossible. With reluctance, he removed her hands and stepped back. "No, Gianna. I mean, I do like you. But I can't do this."

"Why not?" Her face blanched, the roses disappearing beneath her skin, leaving chalk circles.

Her hand covered her mouth, but the words spilled through, nonetheless. "Oh, God, you're married."

"No."

"But there *is* someone else."

"No."

"Then why?"

How to put this delicately and yet leave no room for argument? Yeah, right. Might as well ask how does one kick a kitten and make it come back for more? He'd have to settle for the truth or a reasonable facsimile thereof. Not a lie, per se, just not the entire truth.

"I can't promise you a future."

To his amazement, she laughed. "Is that all? Oh, Kyle, I don't care about your finances. My parents had nothing when they fell in love. They married, and then struggled together to open Villa Mare. They lived in the same apartment you're living in now. They didn't see a profit for two years." She plucked another stone from her fist to send dancing across the water, this one snow white—like her soul. "But if you asked them, they'd say their hard work and sacrifice was worth the hardship. There's no reason we can't do the same. Mom's always trying to talk Dad into retiring. They obviously trust you, and I know running a pizzeria might not be what you planned for your life, but it's an honest living and—"

Stuffing his hands into his jacket pockets, he stared at the high cliffs where a few sprawling homes with walls of windows facing the Sound lay scattered in the scrub pines. Among them, he found the pretty Spanish-style hacienda Nicole's agency had on the market. Nice views, solid-looking house. Might make a good investment. Vacation home or rental.

"Kyle?"

His mind turned from real estate business to the business at hand. He frowned. "I think you're oversimplifying things."

"No, I'm not." Another stone plopped into the water. "Sometimes, the future is what you make it. Last night you accused me of not accepting help because of stubborn pride. Don't let your stubborn pride override the future for us."

Dammit, how could he make her stop?

"There *is* no future for us," he insisted at last. "I'm sorry if you believed differently, Gianna, but I won't make promises I can't keep."

The remaining stones fell to the beach with a scatter of clacks. "Oh."

The acknowledgement, so simple and yet so profound, had the effect of dynamite bringing down a ten-story high rise. Gianna's shoulders sank, and the hopeful expression she'd worn moments before transformed to one of shame. Her gaze dropped to the multi-colored stones as if weighted down by them.

He knelt to look up at her, fighting a wince as the sharp edges of the rocks cut into his pants. The last thing he wanted was for her to confuse his grimace as distaste. There were enough misunderstandings flying around at the moment.

"Gianna, please, look at me." But she didn't. He was forced to press on while she continued to stare at the ground. "In another place and time, I'd be thrilled you find me even remotely worthy of your affection. But I'm not—"

Her hand rose in front of his face. "Don't." The word came out strangled. "Don't you dare say you're not good enough for me. I've heard the line before. I'm sorry if I put you in an uncomfortable position, but I think I'd better go now. I'll see you around, okay?"

Without waiting for an answer, she took off, practically running across the beach. Although his first instinct was to race after her, he hesitated. What would be the point? He'd always known their relationship would end this way. If he caught up to her, what would he say? No matter how much he cared, he couldn't change their differences. Better to hurt her feelings now, when their relationship was still platonic, than to become romantically involved and have her wind up hating him. For both their sakes.

He should have backed out of the whole wedding charade. At the very least, he should have made her understand his pretense last night was simply that. He scooped a handful of the pretty stones and, rising again, flung them into the Long Island Sound.

SOAKED IN FLOP SWEAT and blinded by tears, Gianna stumbled to Villa Mare. She couldn't go into the restaurant, couldn't face small talk with her parents. And spilling her guts to Nicole was completely out of the question. Given a choice, she'd climb into her car, drive home, crawl into bed, and forget she ever woke up this morning.

Darn it, her car! With everything that had gone wrong in the last half-hour, she'd forgotten to ask Kyle for her keys. Which meant she'd have to face him and his pity again. Good God, what else could go wrong?

"Excuse me," a deep, cultured voice said from behind her.

She whirled and came face to face with a distinguished, black-haired gentleman in a camel-colored cashmere topcoat. "Yes?"

"I'm looking for Kyle Hayden. Do you know where he might be?" He jerked his head toward Villa Mare's window. "The couple inside said he'd gone for a walk. Have you seen him?"

Unfortunately, yes.

"He should be back any moment," she managed to croak. And somehow, she thought as she strode past the man, I'll have to find a way to regain my dignity before I get my car keys from him. She'd only taken two steps when he gripped her arm, stopping her.

"Are you all right, my dear? You seem upset."

The unfortunate part of living in a small town, everyone knew everyone else's business.

"I'm fine." She might have attempted a smile, but her muscles refused to cooperate. "I've just had a bit of bad news today."

I fell in love with the wrong man. Again.

"Ah, I'm dreadfully sorry about that."

Not as sorry as I am.

She stared at his face, trying to discern something familiar in his patrician features. Nothing came to mind. "Forgive me, but have we met before?"

"No, but if I had to guess, I'd say you were Gianna Randazzo."

"H-how do you know that?"

His expression turned smug, and he rocked on his heels. "Well, now, from the moment I first saw your name, I had a picture in my head of what you'd look like. You're a little taller than I anticipated, but in every other way, you're a dead ringer for my mental image. I'm Rory Abernathy."

He held out a hand and she shook it, automatically replying, "Gianna Randazzo."

"Yes, I know," he said with a smile. "I believe we already established that."

Okay, so maybe the recriminations buzzing in her head affected her ability to carry on an intelligent conversation. But her curiosity remained firm. "May I ask where you saw my name?"

"On the copy of the paycheck Kyle sent me."

Kyle? Her gaze automatically strayed toward the road leading to the beach. Before she could form another question, Kyle stepped around the corner.

His eyes opened wide, and his mouth dropped. "Rory? What the hell are you doing here?"

Mr. Abernathy turned. "I see you still have those gracious manners, Kyle. I would have expected you to learn a little humility from this experience."

"Yeah, well, come back in two weeks." A dark glower lent his features a grizzly bear look. "Perhaps, by then I won't be such a disappointment to you."

"You don't have two weeks. That's why I'm here."

A frigid breeze fluttered across Gianna's shoulder blades. She should leave. Whatever was about to occur, the prickly hairs on her neck warned her she should walk away. She'd known a downfall was headed her way before she left her bedroom at Nicole's insistence this morning.

But her feet refused to cooperate, and her ears burned to learn the identity of this Rory character and his reason for being here.

"What do you mean I don't have two weeks?" Kyle demanded. "Today is Day Forty-seven. I know. I've been counting since this whole damned thing started. I have thirteen days left." Cold, calculating and humorless, his smile did nothing to warm Gianna. "Or are you and David ready to admit defeat?"

"David and I aren't admitting anything. But your sister's little stunt left us with no alternative. So we told her about the wager and—"

"Wager?" The conversation whirled in dizzying speeds, and Gianna could no longer keep up without an explanation—or SparkNotes. "What wager?"

Rory's interested expression flew from her to Kyle and back again. "You really don't know, do you?"

To ward off the chills, she folded her arms over her chest. "Know what?"

With a look of pity, Rory stroked his chin. "I'll be damned."

The tiger's eye ring on one finger glinted in the sunlight, nearly blinding her, and she framed her face with the back of her hand. "What don't I know?"

"I have to give you credit, Kyle. I told David we shouldn't have paid the penalty because I thought you were pulling the wool over our eyes. Turns out, you were pulling the wool over hers."

She cast a glance at Kyle, but he dropped his gaze to the sidewalk. As if she rode a high-speed roller coaster, her belly flipped and twisted. "Kyle? What's he talking about?"

"She really doesn't know, does she?"

"I believe we already established that," she snapped, turning his words against him.

Rory shook his head. "Forgive me, but I simply can't believe this. The whole scenario is too extraordinary."

"Shut the hell up, Rory," Kyle growled. "This isn't the time or place for this conversation."

Her throat tightened, choking her airway. "Kyle?" she rasped. When he refused to look at her, the roller coaster's restraint wrapped around her ribs, squeezing, accelerating her heartbeat until her entire body pulsed and throbbed. "Kyle, please? Tell me what's going on."

"Not here. Why don't we go inside and—"

Despite her growing dread, a flicker of courage sparked. "No. I'm not moving until you tell me what's happening. Who is this, and what's he talking about?"

"Not here. Please," he murmured, his gaze fixed on the curb.

In all the time she'd known him, she'd never seen him so uncomfortable, not even on that first night by the dumpster. Whatever he hid would wreck her trust. She sensed that much. Still, she needed to know.

"All right, Mr. Abernathy. Since Kyle suddenly seems incapable of speech, why don't you tell me what he's hiding?"

Mr. Abernathy looked no more secure than Kyle, but she continued to glare until he sighed. "What Kyle is trying not to tell you is, this was all a set-up."

A silent scream rose inside her, but she tamped it enough to ask, "What was a set-up?"

One swift glance at Kyle—an apology, maybe—and Rory Abernathy clasped his hands behind his back. "A few months ago, three of us were sitting in the lodge of the Legacy Club. Kyle had sipped a little too much brandy that night and actually bragged to David and me that if he were to lose every dime he owned, the people in his life would stick by him because that's the kind of loyalty he inspired. David and I called him on the boast. Told him to prove it. We made a wager right then and there."

The roller coaster took a steep dip, flipping her heart into freefall. "A wager?"

Adam's apple bobbing as he swallowed, Rory nodded. "Over the next few days, we went through his books and creatively hid all his assets from his friends and family. Then Kyle had to approach everyone he knew, explain his financial situation and ask for assistance. Just as David and I expected, every door slammed in his face. So our friend here was forced to pay a penalty."

She didn't want to hear the rest, but couldn't stop her mouth from overriding her brain. "What kind of penalty?"

"If Kyle couldn't find anyone to help him, we would take him to a small town where no one knew him. Wearing nothing but the oldest clothes in his closet and carrying only his driver's license and Social Security card, he had to get back on his feet within sixty days. He could not use his money, name, or family connections to help him in any way."

Understanding dawned, and questions she'd had for so long were answered. "You were the friend with the tuxedo. And you arranged for the Gardener's shopping spree, too."

"Payment for Kyle's success in finding a job and a place to live," he replied with a solemn nod.

A thousand emotions tumbled inside her. Horror, humiliation, indignation, and anger all clamored to reach her surface.

"You were playing a game? A sick game between spoiled rich boys?" The urge to slap Kyle's face overwhelmed her. "How could you do this? I thought you were in trouble. I thought you needed someone. You used me!" To keep from assaulting Kyle, she slapped her forehead with the flat of her hand. "My God, Bethany's right. I *am* a doormat. A big, stupid doormat with 'Welcome' painted across my forehead in bold red letters. I can't believe how stupid I was. I thought you were noble, and decent, and honest. I actually thought I was in love with you."

Rory chuckled. "Still a heartbreaker, eh, Kyle?"

Gianna's gaze flew to this new enemy, wishing for power to hurl lightning bolts. Like a chastised child, Rory shuffled his feet, and she turned her anger back on the true source. "I hope you gained something important by making a fool of me. I'd hate to think I lost my trust, my *dignity*, over a few dollars."

Kyle didn't look her in the eye, much less attempt any sort of explanation or defense. What could he say?

"Important?" Rory replied. "Yeah, I guess you could say he gained something important. He gets to keep Aurora."

"I see. Well, I hope you and *Aurora*..." She practically spat the name. "...will be very happy together." She held out her hand, palm up. "Now if you'll just give me the keys to my car and to the apartment upstairs, you can be on your way back to your precious Aurora."

At last, he spoke. "Gianna, I—"

"You're too late. Don't say anything. Just give me the keys. And get out of here. Go home. Go home to your wealth and your empty values and your club and your childish games."

He finally slapped the keys into her open palm. "Would you give me a chance to say something first?"

Her fingers curled around the keys, tightening the hold on her emotions. "There is absolutely nothing you can say except goodbye."

Despite the pain corkscrewing her heart to shreds, she managed to turn on her heel and get to her car under her own power. She started the engine and drove out of the parking lot, too blinded by blinking back tears to speed the way she wanted to. Once she returned to the house, she flew up to her bedroom. The golden dress dangled from a hanger on the front of her closet door. She pulled the gown down, gathered up the hairpins, shoes, and costume jewelry she'd been so excited to wear last night. With everything amassed into a glittering pile on her bed, she grabbed a plastic bag and shoved the collection inside. The house phone rang, but she ignored the noise. She had no desire to talk to anyone. Nothing anybody might say could appease her now: no sweet apology from Kyle (not that he would dare!), no crazy (and wrong!) explanations about how love works from Nicole, no offers from her parents to invest in her future (how crazy was that?!).

The ringing stopped with no one leaving a message. Good. A breath later, the ringing began anew. With the bag of clothing in her hand, she pulled the door closed on the jangling phone. She tossed the bag on the passenger seat, got behind the wheel again, and pulled out of the driveway.

Once she reached her destination, she took the bag inside and dropped it on a counter near the entrance. "Hi," she said to the woman on the other side. "I've got some stuff to donate." Reaching into her purse, she pulled out two twenty dollar bills. "The dress was only worn for a few hours, and normally, I'd send it to the dry cleaners before bringing it here." Her voice cracked, and she swallowed the scream rising in her throat. "But I can't stand to look at..." Her vocal cords strained, and she placed the money beside the bag. "This should cover the cost. Thanks."

Before the woman could react, she grabbed her purse and fled the thrift store.

Goodbye, Cinderella. Hello, Gianna Randazzo, Woman With a Purpose. Men need not apply.

Chapter Seventeen

"Honestly, Kyle, what on earth were you thinking?" Colette Hayden Townsend riveted a stare colder than a queen about to order his execution. "Do you have any idea how worried I was?"

Kyle stood in the center of her parlor while she sat in judgment with that stupid dog on her lap. How did she manage to use just the right tone and expression to make him feel two feet tall?

"You weren't too concerned when I came to your door that day."

"I thought you squandered a fortune on horseracing and baubles for your ice princess. Papa always worried you'd wind up begging in the streets. Which is why he made you wait until you were thirty to receive the bulk of his estate. He'd hoped by that venerable age, you'd have discovered what was important in life."

Since he didn't dare argue, he let his toes scrape the poppies in her antique carpet. "So he was off by six years."

"Six years and an idiotic escapade that might have killed you if you hadn't been fortunate enough to meet Gianna Randazzo."

The sound of her name evoked visions of the last time he'd seen her. Eyes bright with outrage and, a moment later, the long curve of her back when she'd walked away. By now he should be used to that view. First Lana, then Gianna. Even their names sounded similar. But the parallels ended in those last two letters. Lana, the superficial socialite, didn't have a scintilla of Gianna's style, generosity, or capacity for love. If he'd been worthy of her, Gianna would have stayed with him. She'd given him her heart, and he'd trashed that priceless gift. He'd pushed her away. She hadn't deserved any of what he'd put her through.

"Do you realize if you had died out there," Colette's disapproving tone brought him back to his trial by sister. "I would have never known what happened?"

Kyle shrugged and resisted the urge to look away from her steady gaze. Older by ten years, Colette always found a way to emphasize his escapades into high crimes and misdemeanors so that every conversation became an interrogation made up of a list of every mistake he'd ever committed. And Chaucer, poised on her lap, must have picked up his mistress's habit of glaring. Bad enough to have his sister look at him with such disapproval, but to suffer the disdain of the best-dressed Yorkshire terrier in New York was more than he could handle.

"Would you have cared if I had died out there?"

Her mouth tightened, leaving spidery lines around her lips. "I'm not Lana, you fool. I'm your sister. A relationship I don't like to admit publicly, but there it is."

"You admitted it publicly on NNC." Ha. Victories, minor or otherwise, were rare against Colette.

"Because wastrel or not, you're still my baby brother and I love you." Dabbing beneath her eyes with a silk handkerchief, she sniffed. "I was devastated when you disappeared. And then to find out it was all a lark? You went *beyond* the boundaries of common sense with this little exploit."

"I know." He clasped his hands behind his back and ducked his head, the posture of the penitent. So much for victory.

She slammed her hand on the settee's upholstered arm. "And why did you put us all through this charade? For some noble cause?" Without waiting for a reply, she rambled on. "Of course not. You indulged your escapade for Aurora! Imagine! Sacrificing a noble young woman's decency and generosity for an overpriced charger!"

Each word sliced his conscience with razor-sharp accuracy. Although defending his actions seemed futile, his pride needed some support. "I didn't expect I'd lose. I thought you and Lana would stand by me." He pointed an accusing finger. "You slammed your door in my face. And Lana—I barely got the words, 'I'm broke,' out of my mouth before she started packing."

Colette clucked her tongue. "I can't speak for Lana. Lana's actions speak for themselves. She never cared for anything except your wealth and pedigree." Chaucer growled in agreement. "Quiet, boy!"

For a minute, Kyle thought she meant him. Then the dog relaxed into a stance worthy of the lions outside the New York Public Library, front paws outstretched. His resentment returned, icy in its intensity. "And what was *your* excuse, Colette?"

She rewarded the dog's obedience with a series of pats before replying. "If you'd waited another day rather than taking off with Rory and David to pay your penalty, you would have known I intended to help you all along."

"Okay, so the wager was stupid. I admit I was impulsive, obnoxious, and hard-hearted." The words were bitter on his tongue, but the truth often tasted harsh. "Are you happy now?"

The smile spreading across her face suggested she was extremely happy now. "Well, if you've learned something valuable from all this, I'll consider my fears and inconveniences worthwhile. Living like a pauper was an eye-opening experience, hmmm?"

His gaze dropped to the poppies at his feet again. "In more ways than you could possibly know."

"I may have to try such an experiment on my Harry. The boy's been expelled—again. If he doesn't straighten up and fly right soon, he'll follow in your misguided footsteps." Her eyes rolled to the tops of their sockets. "Heaven forbid. Perhaps your Miss Randazzo should open a school to teach foolish rich boys proper behavior, and gratitude for all they've been given in life."

"I doubt she wants anything more to do with foolish rich boys, Colette."

She sniffed her derision. "Can you blame her? You abused that gentle lady badly."

A new emotion, shame, washed over him. "I'm well aware of that."

"She deserved better." Colette poured a cup of tea from the sterling service on the table and sipped.

"I'm well aware of that also." And he desperately needed to atone for all the pain he'd caused her. "I screwed up, Lettie. I screwed up so badly. And I don't know if she could ever forgive me."

"Kyle, only someone who loves you unconditionally and knows there's good buried deep inside of you could forgive what you did."

As if his admissions somehow softened her rock-hard exterior, she gestured for him to sit on the settee beside her, nudging Chaucer to move to the floor. A first. He actually received preference over her dog.

"So," she summed up, handing him a cup of tea. "What do you propose to do about all this?"

"That depends."

A finely shaped brow arched on her flawless face. "On what?"

"On how much help you're willing to give me now."

Colette leaned against the settee, one hand pressed to her forehead in a posture of shock. "The cynical, egotistical Kyle William Montgomery Hayden III asking for help? Now I know you've learned something."

KYLE SAT IN THE BUTTER-soft leather chair and stared at the Manhattan skyline outside. In the distance, the shining spire of the Chrysler Building glistened in shades of orange, red, and gold beneath the fire of the setting sun. But he barely noticed.

All other views paled in comparison to the memory of Gianna's face, the hurt shimmering in her eyes. Like the tolling of a funeral bell, her angry words echoed in his brain, and his conscience gave him no respite.

"Are you listening to me?" David's gravelly voice sifted through the quicksand of Kyle's self-recriminations.

He nodded and, in an attempt to concentrate on David's legal advice, turned from the window.

"The project will need at least a hundred grand to start operations. Now, the way I see it, your best bet is to set this up under a new corporation, wholly owned by you and..."

The sun flashed on a Waterford paperweight, a cut crystal globe, sitting atop his desk. How much did that little dust collector cost? He'd bet whatever the amount, it could have covered a child's daycare expenses for three or four months.

As it did a thousand times a day, his gaze moved to Crystal's crude stick figure drawing. He'd discovered it folded up and tucked into his billfold after his return home. He'd totally forgotten it existed until that moment. Now, it hung incongruously beside framed diplomas, various plaques, and meritorious service awards, a stark reminder of what was truly valuable in life.

Meritorious service. Ha! What a joke. What was so meritorious about writing a check to a charitable organization? Or showing up at some inane dinner party for a thousand bucks a plate?

His meritorious service couldn't compare to Gianna's. She worked in the trenches every day while he remained safely tucked in his ivory tower, content to believe he was doing all he could to make the world a better place. And somehow believing he was better than the less fortunate because of an accident of birth. Until a woman of incomparable values showed him how shallow his life really was.

The memory of her lighthearted giggle tickled his spine and slowed his heartbeat. What was she doing these days? Could she ever forgive him?

Doubtful. He couldn't forgive himself. And what about the kids? Did Gianna still take care of Crystal and her brothers? Did they realize how lucky they were to spend time with her?

They knew. They were children, not fools. Not like him and Frank, two idiots who had held a treasure in their hands and let it slip through their fingers like fine grains of sand.

Yet, what about the Crystals who didn't have a Gianna in their lives? Who cared for them? How did parents without live-in nannies or ample money at their disposal find affordable quality daycare for their kids? And searching the other side of the coin, how did a daycare center show a profit without charging clients an arm and a leg for their services? He'd done his research these last few weeks, had learned an encyclopedia of information on the dearth of decent childcare available to working parents, had discovered how atrocious salaries were for teachers—even the best teachers, like Gianna.

What had she told Mrs. Melendez?

"I don't look after children to become wealthy." Well, he'd vouch for that. Then again, with her friends and family, those people who genuinely loved her, she was far wealthier than any man or woman he knew.

How could you let her go? Without an explanation? Without an apology? You promised a dozen people you wouldn't break her heart. Claudio, Nicole, Carlo and Lucia, the ROMEOs, even Bethany knew she was falling for you and tried to warn you. But you kept right on with the deceit, thinking so long as you didn't admit to loving her, she wouldn't feel the pain when you left. Nice going, moron.

"Kyle?" David, sitting across the desk, stared at him, waiting.

Waiting for what? Damn! His mind had wandered again.

"She must be some woman to have you so distracted you can't concentrate on business," the attorney said with a wide grin.

"I wasn't distracted," he lied. "I heard every word."

"Uh-huh." He rose from his chair in front of the desk, tossed the manila folder into his briefcase, and snapped the case closed. "I'll tell you what. Why don't you leave the legal details to me? I'll have everything in order before the day is out. Who's heading the fundraising end of this project?"

"Colette."

David whistled through his teeth. "Good choice. Your sister could pry a pearl from a greedy oyster. If *she* ever lost her fortune, she could have a successful future in the strong-arm industry."

For the first time in over a week, Kyle laughed. "I'll be sure to tell her you said so."

David's normally pale complexion turned ashen. "God, no! I never want to wind up on Colette's bad side again. I don't think I could survive another confrontation with her. You should have seen her when we told her about the wager. If she could spit flaming arrows from her eyes, we would have been sizzling nuggets on her carpet."

Yeah, he knew the feeling all too well. "So no one will turn her down when she asks for a generous donation."

David walked to the door, and then paused. "You know, you might not want to admit this, but your experience on Long Island changed you. I think I'm beginning to like this new Kyle Hayden."

"Thanks." Although he appreciated David's comment, only one person's opinion mattered now. Would Gianna like the new Kyle Hayden?

RIIIIIIIPPPPP!

While removing the carpets from the apartment above the restaurant, Gianna listened with half an ear to Nicole's well-meaning but useless advice.

"You gotta slow down, Gi," she said from her perch on the old rattan couch. "So Kyle wasn't Prince Charming. You can't burn yourself out to keep from remembering him."

"Remembering him?" Gianna had to fight the urge to shake some sense into her best friend, but her frustration erupted in a bitter laugh. "Not a day goes by that I don't remember him. There's no way I could *stop* remembering him. You should've seen me that morning. There I was on Setquott Beach, telling him about the old legends. How the shoreline at sunset was the perfect place to begin a relationship. Like a total love-besotted idiot, pouring out my heart to him. And all the while he was planning on returning to his money, his Central Park West penthouse, and some debutante named *Aurora*."

Fingers curled around a metal bracket, she yanked, pulling the carpet tacks out of scarred linoleum and wishing she could reach into her skull and yank out her memories with the same ferocity. Morning, noon, and night, that scene on the beach haunted her—especially at night, when her imagination would go into overdrive, envisioning new and different endings. Sometimes, he took her in his arms and told her he loved her, too. Sometimes, Aurora appeared behind her, her arms held wide, and Kyle walked past Gianna to stroll away with his ice blond princess. No matter how the dream ended, she always woke up alone, humiliated, and determined to never let herself play the romantic fool again.

"I know it was awful, Gi, but—"

The brackets fell to the floor with a clatter. "Awful? Is that what you think? Wrong-o, reindeer! Try excruciating. Do you have any idea how stupid I felt? How stupid I still feel every time I think about that day?"

Nicole cringed and sucked in a breath. "I'm really sorry."

With a sigh, she sank onto the floor and regarded Nicole's downcast expression. "What happened with Kyle isn't your fault."

"More my fault than yours. I'm the one who told you he was crazy about you." She slapped her hands on the cushions. "I don't understand. The signs were all there. I would have bet everything I own that he was falling for you."

"Then you'd have lost." She didn't add, "Just like me," but the thought danced in her mind.

To erase the memories—at least while she was awake—she got up from the floor, stretched her aching muscles, and checked the other side of the room where Mr. Whiskers slept, recovering. Antibiotics would get his feline rhino-pneumonitis under control, but the greater indignity was that he'd been neutered during his trip to the vet. Another day or two, and she'd be able to release him from his cone of shame. In the meantime, he made his anger known in angry meows whenever he was awake.

Satisfied he slept peacefully, she returned her attention to the faded, old carpet. Anything to keep her mind busy. "You know what?" she said as she pulled at the next strip. "We've spent way too much time on the topic of Kyle in the last two weeks. Let's not talk about him anymore. He's gone, and he's never coming back."

Riiiiipppp! Another taupe fragment sent decades' worth of dust aloft in the sunbeams.

Waving the motes away from her coffee, Nicole frowned. "Keep using all your energy to forget about Kyle and you'll burn out."

God, the woman was clairvoyant. Didn't characters in sci-fi movies have a brain barrier that kept outsiders from reading their minds? How soon would that technology be available?

"I'm not burning out. And Kyle has nothing to do with my sudden burst of energy." At Nicole's dubious look, she amended her statement. "Well... technically he doesn't. But of course, if he hadn't gone home, I wouldn't have the apartment available. All in all, his departure was the best thing that could've happened to me."

In lemon-sucking style, Nicole's lips scrunched. "Bull."

"No bull." Okay, maybe a little bull, but Nicole didn't have to know everything. "This place isn't as great as Dr. Weber's old office, but it will suit my needs temporarily. Best of all, my parents won't have to pillage their retirement funds, and I'll still get a head start on the daycare center. So, good riddance to Kyle Hayden."

"Good riddance, my foot. You haven't cracked a smile since he left. We're all worried about you."

"Well, stop worrying. I'll be fine." She forced a smile, but couldn't amass the energy to reflect happiness. "See?"

"Mmm, yeah," Nicole replied. "What's the latest on the money front?"

"Mrs. Melendez is going to put in a good word for me at CompTech. I have an interview with their personnel director on Monday. With luck, they'll hire me to work the night shift. Every dime of that salary will pay costs for getting the center up and running." Her tone shadowed with disappointment. "It'll be on a smaller scale than I originally wanted. I'll have to take only a few kids to start, but who knows?" She forced light into her words. "In time, I might be able to get a larger space and increase enrollment."

"Can't you get the funds any faster?"

"Mom and Dad still insist on lending me the money, but I don't feel right about them financing my future." *Now or never, Gi.* "Kyle had once mentioned asking for donations. I don't know how, but I'm thinking about trying a few fundraisers—bake sales, car washes. That sort of stuff." She swallowed the lump in her throat and plowed ahead before she lost her nerve. "W-would you be willing to help?"

"Do you need to ask?" Nicole retorted. "Yes, I'd help. Half the town would help if you let them know you need it."

Gee, that was easier than she thought. Maybe Kyle had been right about something after all. Maybe all she had to do was ask for help, and help would appear. Then again, maybe not. Sighing in the hope of exhaling her bad mood, she dropped the carpet segment out the window to land inside the dumpster one story below.

For a brief moment, she saw Kyle's image, blurry but familiar, leaning against the garbage receptacle's wall. Blinking back tears, she turned away.

"So that's good news, right?" Nicole's smile looked almost as forced as hers.

Uh-oh. Something was up. "Okay, spill." She folded her arms over her chest, protecting her heart. "What bad news do you have for me?"

"Nothing."

"Uh-huh, right." Hard to tell which one of them was the worse liar. Although, come to think of it, Nicole had managed to dance around the truth when it came to that Gardener's outing. "Whatever you're hiding, just tell me. I'm a big girl. I won't fall to pieces."

"Dr. Weber's office went off the 'available' list yesterday."

The last brick in the wall Gianna constructed to keep herself supported collapsed. "Who leased it?"

"A company out of Westchester called Kigeeah, or something. I don't know much about the deal yet."

"Why not? I thought it was your property."

Nicole sat up higher, tucked her feet under her bottom. "It's my listing, but the contract has a lot of legalese. Bruce felt I'd be in over my head, so he gave it to Ryan. I'll still get a nice chunk of the commission, though."

But no credit. "I think that's the suckiest thing I've ever heard."

"No sense complaining, right?"

Gianna shook her head. "Why shouldn't you complain? You did the prep work, got the listing from Dr. Weber, took the photos, placed the ads. Now Bruce will send in the big guns to take the credit for your hard work."

Blue eyes widened as she stood. "It isn't like that. I'm happy to turn the sale over to Ryan. He's got a law degree, remember? Trust me, a deal this complicated, I'd only screw up some minor but mega-important detail."

"Personally, I think you're the one getting screwed."

When Nicole attempted to hug her, she shrugged off the softness. Poor Nicole stood alone in the spotlight of the setting sun, hurt registering on her face.

"Don't become a hardnose because of what happened with Kyle. Not everyone in the world is out to screw everyone else."

"Prove it."

She sucked in a sharp breath. "Jeez, Gi. If I thought you'd hurt this badly afterward, I never would have encouraged your feelings for Kyle. I'm not sure I like this side of you."

"Well, get used to it. Gianna the Doormat no longer exists. I'm tired of being stepped on and walked all over. From now on, I'm looking out for Number One."

As if punctuating her declaration, Mr. Whiskers chose that moment to wake up and growl.

GIANNA SPENT THE NIGHT working on the apartment, drinking an endless supply of coffee to keep her focused.

By Sunday morning, she'd scrubbed the floors and walls and removed all the old furniture except for the kitchen table and one chair. She sat there now, sketching plans to create classrooms with toddler-proof windows, doors, and cabinets, transforming a one-bedroom apartment into a cheery school for youngsters.

Sunny colors, she thought. Shelves with books, games, and toys. Maybe tack blackboards to the lower sections of the walls for chalk drawings. She could see the finished project in her mind. Yes. This would work. All she needed was more time, and a little more coffee. Empty travel mug in hand, she padded into the kitchen when the telephone's ring stopped her in her tracks. She set the mug beside the coffeemaker and picked up the receiver.

"Hello?"

A vaguely familiar voice spoke from the receiver. "Ms. Randazzo?"

"Yes." Who was this? For a moment, her heart skipped. Kyle? But, no. The voice held no accent, no conceited air.

"Wow," the man said. "You're a hard lady to reach. This is Ryan McKnight at Setquott Realty."

A frisson of discomfort slinked up her spine. *Oh, Nicole, don't tell me you set me up with one of your coworkers.* "Yes, Ryan, of course. How are you?"

"Fine, just fine, thanks. I was wondering if you could stop by the office this afternoon, if you have some time."

No wonder the man hadn't had a date since his divorce four years earlier. She'd always suspected his eternally rumpled appearance and appalling habit of picking his teeth with a matchbook were the culprits. Maybe his lack of social grace played a factor, too.

Just wait until she got her hands on Nicole. Concerned friend or not, she had no right to sic this bulldog on her.

"Um, Ryan? Could I get back to you later? I'm kind of in the middle of something..."

"Well, we really need you to sign the lease papers as soon as possible," Ryan replied.

With a screech fit for a car going from sixty to zero in two seconds, her mind forgot about an excuse to turn down Ryan gently.

"Lease papers? What lease papers?"

"For the building at 135 Main Street."

The moisture in her mouth evaporated, leaving her tongue too thick and dry to form a sound. 135 Main Street. Dr. Weber's old building.

"Hello? Gianna? Are you there?"

Yes, but... no. This was a mistake. A dream. *Wake up, honey! Snap out of the fantasy!*

"Are you sure you're looking for me?"

"You're Gianna Randazzo, right?"

"Yes." At least she was five minutes ago.

"Then you're who I'm looking for. So whaddya say? Do you have time to sign the paperwork today?"

"I-I guess so." This had to be a mistake. And one she should straighten out as soon as possible. "I'll be down in about a half-hour. Is that all right with you?"

"That'll be great. I'll see you then. Goodbye."

"Goodbye." Even after she heard the click on his end, she held the receiver. The ear-splitting *buzz-buzz-buzz* of the telephone reminded her to place it back on the hook.

As if the noise had awakened her, she quit puzzling over questions and headed into the bathroom to shower and change. Whatever the reasoning behind this conundrum, the only way to learn the truth was to drive to the realty office and find out.

THE CELL PHONE IN KYLE'S shirt pocket vibrated against his chest, and he quickly answered. "Hello?"

"She's on her way. She'll be here in about a half-hour."

Excitement made him buoyant. "Excellent. Thanks, Ryan."

"No problem, Mr. Hayden. You want me to tell her where you are when she shows up?"

"No, have her sign the lease first. Once she figures out what's happening, she'll know where to find me."

"Whatever you say."

Disconnecting the call, Kyle smiled at the older couple standing with anxious faces and twisting hands. "She's on her way."

With a squeal of delight, Lucia Randazzo flung her arms around his neck. "Go get my girl, *tesoro*! Make her happy."

Showing only indulgence at his wife's exuberance, Carlo grasped Kyle's hand. "I'd wish you luck, my boy, but if Gianna really loves you, you've already got paradise."

"Thanks," he said before grabbing an old threadbare jacket from the coat rack in the corner.

Thirty more minutes, Gianna. Just thirty minutes until you get the surprise of a lifetime.

Chapter Eighteen

Gianna entered Setquott Realty's office, prepared to hear the phone call was a horrible error. They'd read the wrong file, mistaking her for the real lessee of the property at 135 Main Street.

Only one man sat at his desk near the front door.

"Gianna!" Wearing his usual rumpled suit and coffee-stained tie, Ryan McKnight rose with an outstretched hand. "Nice to see you again. How are you?"

"Fine," she replied, shaking his hand. "So, what's up?"

He laughed. "Fifteen years in the real estate game, and that's the first time anyone's ever said that. Come over to my desk and we'll see 'what's up.'"

While she sat across from his desk, he walked to a file cabinet and withdrew a manila folder from the top drawer.

"Most of the preliminary stuff has already been completed by your partner." He dropped the folder on the desk and returned to his seat. "But since you'll be the manager-in-residence on the property, it's imperative we have your signature on the lease agreement. Nicole told me you wanted to open a daycare center there. You've made a great choice."

She nodded to feign interest in Ryan's chatter, but her eyes concentrated on the upside-down file, hoping he'd flip it open so she might find a clue about the identity of her "partner." At long last, he took a breath and pulled out a long, thick sheaf of papers attached with a fat binder clip.

"Okay," he said, unclipping the pages. "Here it is." He placed the lease agreement before her and pointed at the pertinent sections with the tip of his pen. "This says you are Gianna Randazzo of The KyGia Foundation—"

"Of what?"

He looked up, his basset hound eyes round. "The KyGia Foundation. That *is* the name of the organization, isn't it? Don't tell me Lydia spelled the name wrong, and no one caught the error. We'll have to rewrite the whole contract."

Nicole's remarks from last night replayed in her mind. "A company out of Westchester called Kigeeah..."

Invisible fingers snapped before her eyes until everything became crystal clear. *Not* Kigeeah.

KyGia. Gia, for the first three letters of her first name. And Ky could only stand for one other person: Kyle.

With hope burning a trail from her heart to her mind, she scanned the bottom of the page, seeking the signature line. In bold black ink, with a flourish so reflective of the man she knew and loved, the name, "Kyle William Montgomery Hayden III" flashed like a beacon on a foggy night at sea.

Slamming her palms on the table, she jumped out of the chair. "Where is he?"

The real estate agent smiled and pointed to the line beneath Kyle's signature. "Sign here first."

Fingers trembling from happiness and excitement, she scrawled her name across the dotted line.

Nodding, Ryan placed his notary seal beside her signature, and then slid the documents into the folder. "He said you'd know where he was."

And suddenly, she did.

She circled the desk to wrap Ryan in an enthusiastic bear hug. "Thank you."

"You're welcome," he eked.

While her heartbeat echoed Kyle's name, she flew from the office and out to the parking lot. He had to be there. He just had to be there. She raced across the street, dodging a car that came around the corner too fast, and ran past the stores in the strip mall. Around the bend at the end of the row. To the heavy green dumpster where he stood, surrounded by at least a hundred pots of mums in gold, dark red, and purple. He clutched another large bouquet in his hands—roses this time—and wore a grin as wide and welcoming as the open sky. He opened his arms, and she collided into him, crinkling the cellophane that wrapped the roses. While he held her in his embrace, she rained kisses on his cheeks.

"I take it you're pleased," he murmured. She nodded, too afraid she'd awaken from the dream if she uttered a sound. "Aren't you going to say anything?"

When she shook her head and kept kissing him, he laughed. His finger brushed across her chin, whisper-soft and full of... dare she think... love?

"Okay, that's fine by me. This'll probably be the first and last time I get to speak anyway."

The low rumble of his voice told her this was no fantasy. He truly was here, and he'd truly given her this magnificent gift. "Before you start thinking I'm buying your affection, hear me out. All the money used to fund this project was donated to The KyGia Foundation, a charitable organization dedicated to educating this country's future generations. I did not put one dime into the leasing of the building. All I did was get some very wealthy people together in one big room. My sister put the squeeze on them, and a few friends handled the messy details of incorporating us into a not-for-profit organization. You'll need to sign another contract to make the whole she-bang legit, but the signatures are only a formality at this point."

"But—"

"The building itself is in very good hands. Nicole, Tony Garibaldi, the ROMEOs, and a few others will take care of getting the site up to code in time for the state inspection. All you have to do is hire your staff and see to the day-to-day running of the place. You can do that, can't you?"

"Yes." Inside her head, a chorus of children echoed her answer.

"Good. Now, I have just one more thing to add. I love you, Gianna. What better way to show you than to give you the opportunity to follow your dream?"

Her heart nearly flew from her chest. Love.

He'd said, "I love you, Gianna."

Had she heard him correctly? Did he really mean the words? What about the debutante with the crazy name? The woman he earned by winning his wager?

"I thought you loved Aurora."

"Ah," he said with a wistful smile. "Aurora. Sad, but true. You'll never have legs as fine as Aurora's, but I'm willing to make some sacrifices in the name of love."

Fear, nervousness, joy, they all vanished, and she shoved him against the dumpster. "Ooh, you miserable—"

His raucous laughter interrupted the rest of her tirade, and she glared with razor sharpness.

"What's so funny?"

"Aurora is a racehorse, sweetheart. Aurora Borealis, fast as a streak of light across the sky."

"A racehorse?"

"Mmm-hmm. And so there's no jealousy, I surrendered his ownership to David and Rory the day after I left here."

"But you won the bet."

"No, I didn't. I didn't succeed on my own. I had *you*. And I don't ever want to live without you again. To that end, I sold my place on Central Park West and bought that Spanish hacienda sitting on the bluffs of Setquott Beach. Paid way too much for the place, but Nicole can be a very persuasive saleswoman. I figure we can settle down there and raise our own future generation. That is, if you're willing to marry a spoiled rich boy who didn't appreciate the treasure he'd been offered until almost too late."

He gathered her close, and the misery of the last few weeks melted away, leaving her as limp as a wrung-out dishrag.

"Tell me I'm not too late."

His hot breath tickled her ear. Heart dancing, she listened to his words, committing them to memory.

"Please. Tell me you love me. Tell me you'll spend the rest of your life with me. Will you marry me, Gianna?"

God, could a person die from happiness?

"Yes!" She flung her arms around his neck and drew his lips down to hers.

Her world ignited in a fiery kiss, broken only when a smattering of applause erupted. With stars still flashing behind her eyes, she stepped out of Kyle's embrace to see a crowd of people standing outside Villa Mare's back door. Her parents, Claudio, Nicole, Tony Garibaldi, the Melendez family, all the ROMEOs, Ryan McKnight, and Rory Abernathy cheered.

As she looked around at the fairy godparents who had lent a hand to make this moment happen, Gianna suddenly knew what Cinderella learned when she found her Prince Charming. Fairy tales could come true.

She and Kyle were living proof.

Dear Reader,

Thanks so much for reading THAT'S AMORÉ! I originally wrote this story about fifteen years ago. At the time, I was a sports mom, running from karate class to football and baseball fields for my kids, and pizza was a weekly meal when time was short and I still had to deal with dinner, homework, and bedtime rituals. One night, I happened to be wearing a t-shirt emblazoned with the logo of my local romance writers group when I ran into Via Pizza & Pasta, Etc. in Setauket (the real Setqoutt Beach). One of the guys behind the counter remarked on it, I told him about my writing, and he said to me, "You know, no one's ever set a romance in a pizzeria." I promised I would. A year or two later, when the book was published as A LITTLE SLICE OF HEAVEN, the staff was so thrilled they hosted a signing for me there and kept bookmarks and postcards with the book's details on all the tables.

The world was a different place back then than what faces us today. When I reacquired the publishing rights to my pizzeria romance last year, I knew there would be a few things I'd want to change, things my editors made me leave on the cutting room floor or insisted had to be included against my better judgment, but I had no idea how many aspects I'd have to delete or alter, due to the changes the world has undergone in that time!

Maybe I'm naïve or a bit of an ostrich, but I'm not ready to incorporate the new normal of social distancing and face masks into my stories—yet. This doesn't mean I refuse to acknowledge the pandemic and its effects on all of us. And there may come a time when, in order to ground my story in some semblance of reality, I'll have to tackle those issues. But for now, I'll keep writing the world I wish to see for my characters. It is fiction, after all, and at least, in my books, I have the luxury of being in control, a fact that delights my domineering heart.

Whether you read the original version or this version, or both, I hope you enjoyed walking the streets of Setquott Beach with Gianna and Kyle.

If you did enjoy it, I'd like to ask a favor. Please consider writing a review on your favorite retail site. We independent authors need reviews in order to compete with bigger names and bigger houses with bigger budgets for advertising. Like other small businesses, I rely on word of mouth to find new readers. Your voice helps. And yes, I do read my reviews. Good or bad, I appreciate whenever a reader takes the time to share their thoughts about my work.

You can contact me at gina@ginaardito.com or through my website, https://ginaardito.com. And yes, I answer my emails, too. I don't have an assistant, so it's always me behind the name.

Want to be among the first to know about new books and have input into story lines and cover art? Sign up for my monthly newsletter[1]! You can also follow me on BookBub[2], Facebook[3], Twitter[4], and Instagram[5].

And of course, be sure to check out my backlist for other stories that will make you fall in love...with your laugh!

Until next time, stay safe, share love, and be well!

Fondly,
Gina

---

1. *https://landing.mailerlite.com/webforms/landing/w7a0f0*
2. *https://www.bookbub.com/authors/gina-ardito*
3. *https://www.facebook.com/GinaArditoAuthor/*
4. *https://twitter.com/GinaArdito*
5. *https://www.instagram.com/ginaardito/*

BOOKS BY GINA ARDITO

THE SETQUOTT BEACH SERIES

That's Amore!
A Run for the Money
The Bonds of Matri-money

THE NOBODY SERIES

Nobody's Darling
Nobody's Business
Nobody's Perfect

THE AFTERLIFE SERIES

Eternally Yours
In Your Dreams
Waiting in the Wings

THE CALENDAR GIRLS HOLIDAY NOVELLAS

Charming for Mother's Day
Fortune for St. Patrick's Day
Detour for New Year's Day

THE CALENDAR GIRLS SERIES

Duet in September
Reunion in October
Homecoming in November
Memories in December

OSPREY COVE PETS SERIES
Even Now
Twilight Time

Chasing Adonis
Duping Cupid
A Love to Keep Me Warm
Lightning in a Bottle
Echoes of Love
Play Action Pass

ANTHOLOGIES
Kaleidoscope Hearts 2
Kaleidoscope Hearts 3
Caught Under the Mistletoe

About the Author

Gina Ardito is the award-winning author of more than twenty-five romances in contemporary, historical, and paranormal sub-genres. In 2012, she launched her freelance editing business, Excellence in Editing, and now has a stable of award-winning clients, as well.

She's hosted workshops around the world for writing conferences, author organization chapter meetings, and library events. To her everlasting shame, despite all her accomplishments, she'll never be more famous than her dog, who starred in commercials for 2015's Puppy Bowl.

Read more at https://ginaardito.com/.